Published by BSA Publishing 2017 who assert the right that no part of this publication may be reproduced, stored in a retrieval system or transmitted by any means without the prior permission of the publishers.

ISBN 978-1-9997640-1-2

BOOKS IN THE DCS PALMER SERIES (SO FAR)

BOOK 1 FUTURE RICHES
BOOK 2 THE FELT TIP MURDERS
BOOK 3 A KILLER IS CALLING
BOOK 4 POETIC JUSTICE
BOOK 5 LOOT
BOOK 6 I'M WITH THE BAND

All are available individually as e-books online or in double case paperbacks online or from your favourite book shop.

THE PALMER CASES BACKGROUND

Justin Palmer started off on the beat as a London policeman in the 1970s and is now Detective Chief Superintendent Palmer, running the Metropolitan Police Force's Serial Murder Squad from New Scotland Yard. Not one to pull punches, or give a hoot for political correctness if it hinders his inquiries, Palmer has gone as far as he will go in the Met and knows it. Master of the one-line put down and a slave to his sciatica, he can be as nasty or as nice as he likes.

The mid 1990's was a time of re-awakening for Palmer, as the Information Technology revolution turned forensic science, communication and information-gathering skills upside down. Realising the value of this revolution to crime solving, Palmer co-opted Detective Sergeant Gheeta Singh onto his team from the Yard's Cyber Crime unit. DS Singh has a degree in IT and was given the go ahead to update Palmer's department with all the computer hard- and software she wanted; most of these she wrote herself, while some are, shall we say, of a grey area when it comes to privacy laws, data protection and accessing certain databases. Together with their small team of officers, and one civilian computer clerk called Claire (nicknamed 'JCB' by the team because she keeps on digging), they take on the serial killers of the UK.

On the personal front, Palmer has been married to his 'princess', or Mrs P as she is known to everybody, for nearly thirty years. The romance blossomed after the young Detective Constable Palmer arrested most of her family, a bunch of South London petty criminals, in the 1960's. They have three children and eight grandchildren, a nice house in the London suburb of Dulwich, and a faithful dog called Daisy.

Gheeta Singh lives alone in a fourth floor Barbican apartment. Her parents arrived on these shores as a refugee family fleeing from Idi Amin's Uganda. Since then her father and brothers have built up a very successful computer parts supply company, in which it was assumed Gheeta would take an active role on graduating from University. She had other ideas on this, and also on the arranged marriage her mother and aunts still try to coerce her into. Gheeta has two loves, police work and technology, and thanks to Palmer she has her dream job.

The old copper's nose and gut feeling of Palmer, combined with the modern IT skills of DS Singh, makes them an unlikely but successful team. All their cases involve a serial killer, and twist and turn through red herrings and hidden clues, keeping the reader in suspense until the very end.

CASE 1   FUTURE RICHES

Chapter 1

'He was a real sweetie you know, a real gentleman. It was such a shock to us all. Especially after poor Lisa's murder too.

The petite office secretary in her tight pencil skirt was almost running along the corridor in her efforts to keep up with the long strides of the lank six foot frame of Superintendent Justin Palmer. His second in command Detective Sergeant Gheeta Singh was doing better, as she had the advantage of the Met's standard issue WPC trousers.

'A real gentleman he was. Not many of them in this business I can tell you.' The secretary loaded the word 'them'.

'One less now isn't there.'

Palmer was in a droll mood. He hadn't much time for arty types, least of all the 'luvvy' television industry brigade, and they'd been all he'd met so far today. But he supposed that was to be expected if you're investigating serial murders in the world of television; and he was right in the middle of that false world as he strode down the corridor of Midlands Television in Birmingham, to look at the office where the late lamented head of Light Entertainment, one Tony Fox, had met his bloody end.

The day had not started well for Palmer; not well at all. Five days of overdue leave had been cut to two with the demise of Mr Fox being passed from Regional Crime Squad to Serial Murder Squad, Fox being the second executive of Midland Television to be murdered in their offices. Palmer had been halfway through painting the stairs at home when the call to duty came through. He wasn't too upset, as one thing Palmer loathed was DIY.

Mrs Palmer, on the other hand, was not best pleased at being left with a half-done job and no stair carpet down, especially with her Gardening Club scheduled to be holding their next meeting at the Palmer house. But then being a copper's wife for twenty-eight years, she knew that to plan ahead further than twenty-four hours was asking for trouble, especially if hubby was the head of the Serial Murder Squad at Scotland Yard.

'Here we are sir,' the secretary panted breathlessly, using a key to open a frosted glass door into a rather plush office. 'This was Mr Fox's office. Shall I leave you to it? Lisa's office is three doors down. Nothing's been touched since your colleagues were here.'

'Colleagues, who's that then?'

Palmer had walked in, and was taking in the office layout.

'Regional Crime Squad sir,' Sergeant Singh reminded him. 'It was their case.'

'Oh yes, that lot.'

He walked over to the window, which offered a panoramic view of Birmingham. Singh gave a short cough to attract his attention, and cast her eyes toward the secretary. Palmer smiled at her.

'Yes, you can leave us to it thank you. Oh, and leave the keys to both offices with the Sergeant if you would.'

She gave Singh the keys and stopped by the door.

'If you want anything, just dial 9 on the phone.'

She indicated a black phone on the desk, both of which were covered in the forensic team's silver fingerprint graphite dust. Singh ushered her out of the door.

'I'm sure we'll be okay for a while, thank you.'

She shut the door after the departing secretary and locked it before casting her eyes over the office.

'Nice office guv.' It was 'guv' on a one-to-one basis, or 'sir' if others were present, 'And very expensive furniture.'

The office was fitting for the head of a very important department in one of the country's major independent television companies: spacious and minimally furnished, with a large executive mahogany desk, behind which a black leather swivel chair could be swung round for the occupant to gaze through the wall-to-wall window looking out over the bustling concrete jungle of Birmingham twelve floors below; a sumptuous leather sofa; two equally sumptuous chairs and a large glass cabinet completed the furnishings. The glass cabinet proudly displayed various awards and certificates gained by the department. A deep pile carpet seemed pristine except for a worn path from door to desk, and the leather inlay on the desk was also showing signs of wear, mostly from biro doodlings.

Palmer was still gazing out of the window.

'Stupid really; you work hard for years and finally get the big office on the management floor in a prestigious building like this, and then you have to look out on that load of garbage.'

He nodded towards the city spread beneath them.

'Birmingham?'

'Could be Birmingham, or Leeds, or Coventry; all look the same really. I'd rather look out over rolling hills or an ocean than NCP car parks and building sites. Are we sure Mr Fox didn't top himself when he saw this view?'

A sarcastic smile flickered at the corners of his mouth.

'And I have to make do with a twenty-foot square box of an office at the Yard, full of ex-MOD filing cabinets, metal desks that fall apart or stab you in the leg at every opportunity, and wooden chairs that are so hard they give you corns on your backside. Yet these arty types who do nothing for humanity get this luxury.'

He waved his hands at the office in exasperation.

'Excuse me,' Gheeta said, faking indignation. '*We* have to make do with a twenty-foot square box, guv; *we*.'

Every now and again she gave Palmer a gentle reminder that they shared an office, and that she was his number two.

He smiled and nodded.

'Correct Sergeant, we. Right then, let's get to work.' He took off the old Prince of Wales check jacket that had become his trademark at the Yard, and rubbed his hands together in anticipation of the investigation ahead. Palmer liked the start of a case; he likened it to the hunt getting ready to go after the fox, or aniseed trail, or whatever they used nowadays. He was an old fashioned copper, and the thrill of the chase and the unknown twists and turns to come were grist to his mill. Or, as he'd once said to Mrs P, *'It's what floats my boat'*, which she had totally misunderstood and quietly popped into their bank the next day and checked the account, looking for a large expenditure on a cabin cruiser or similar.

'Right then,' Sergeant Singh sank into an armchair, took her laptop from her shoulder bag and opened it. 'Let's see what we've got so far shall we?'

A graduate of computer skills and programming at university, Gheeta Singh had taken the road into the force against the pull of the mega money offered to her by the international software companies at university job fairs. She honestly felt that using her skills to attain a moral ending was preferable, and more mentally stimulating and fulfilling than programming Death Battle 8 for the Play Station; and she'd been right. Palmer had noticed her skills early on when she started at the Yard in the computer room, and had fast tracked her into his unit. They had immediately hit it off, and from not knowing his motherboard from his mother-in-law, Palmer had embraced the fast growing technical and computer era, realising how important and time saving it could be to his work load. He'd given Gheeta her head, and channelled hard won upgrade funds into her hardware and software requirements.

And it was paying dividends. With Gheeta's bespoke programmes loaded and updated regularly into the bank of computers she had built in the unit's team room, all and every bit of information he asked for was there on screen at the touch of a button; with programmes that were able to take on the mundane and time-consuming checking and shifting of facts, statements and records in seconds, tasks that had previously used up many team hours.

'For such a big company, Midland Television isn't very security conscious guv. I'm using their Wi-Fi and bandwidth without the need of a password.'

Palmer tut-tutted. Truth be known, in the modern technical world he had grasped what Wi-Fi was; but *bandwidth*? Gheeta carried on.

'The local CID report has Tony Fox found face down on the floor behind the desk, laying with his feet to the right. One large bruise to the temple, and several deep wounds in the back of the head and neck. Probable cause being an irregularly-shaped blunt instrument, struck with force.'

She stood and placed the laptop on the desk in front of him.

'Photo of the scene, guv.'

Palmer bent over the screen.

'The furniture is all where it should be, no signs of a struggle.'

Gheeta nodded.

'SOCO couldn't get anything from the body or the scene that couldn't be accounted for as normal. Post mortem pics.'

She hit a key.

'Big bloke, wasn't he?'

Palmer nodded.

'He looks to be more than capable of defending himself, if he was aware of an attack coming. Seeing that he didn't, he probably knew the killer.'

Gheeta clicked again and read off the screen.

'Just turned fifty, wife and two adult children, both with their own families; local man, been with the company twenty-six years; worked his way up from being an assistant floor manager. No previous.'

Palmer had moved to the display cabinet and opened it. He pulled out the awards one by one and read them.

'I've never heard of any of these programmes.'

He put them back, turned and paced out the distance from the desk to the door. '*Steptoe and Son, Charlie*

Drake, The Two Ronnies; they made me laugh. What programmes make you laugh, Sergeant?'

'Don't watch much telly guv. I read mostly.'

'Tony Hancock…'

Palmer smiled at the memory.

'Don't know him guv, what's he written?'

'Hasn't written anything, poor chap's dead now. He had a top comedy show in the seventies.
"Ha…Ha…Hancock's Half Hour."'

He did a poor impression of Tony Hancock.

'Is that funny, guv?'

'It was a very funny show actually,' Palmer said, slightly embarrassed.

'I'll stick to my books, guv.'

He was on his knees behind the desk now, checking for any secret keys taped underneath.

'Mrs P likes to read… usually when I want to go to sleep… likes to read in bed, she does… anything to do with gangsters and the mafia… she should have married Elliot Ness.'

'Who, guv?'

'Elliot Ness, he was in *The Untouchables*… big TV series.'

Gheeta shrugged ignorance.

'Never mind.'

Palmer straightened up, wincing at the stab of pain in his right thigh.

'Bloody sciatica, catches me every time.' He sank into a soft chair. 'So, somebody gave Mr. Fox an almighty bang on the face, sending him to the floor, and then finished him off with a few more to the back of his neck and head. When was this?'

'June 12th.'

'A month ago. Everybody interviewed by local force and no leads, eh?'

'Not a thing guv, zilch. He was apparently well liked by everybody.'

'Not everybody Sergeant, somebody disliked him enough to kill him. He upset some bugger in a big way.

What we have got to do is find out what triggered that dislike. What had Tony Fox done to his killer to push him or her over the edge, eh? Get a team in here to go through all his papers. I know Regional will have done it already but I want all the names, facts, dates, in fact everything fed onto your systems. I want records of his meetings too; use that secretary girl, check through the minutes of his meetings, if there are any; check what he vetoed, any shows he cancelled and the people involved. This business is full of 'jobs for the boys', so check any contracts his department had with people and companies. Could be somebody thought they had a big contract coming and it didn't materialise. That might at least show up a motive, and at present we haven't got one. Is there anything worthwhile in the Regional report?'

'No, clean as a whistle. Loads of fingerprints but that's expected. The secretary says he was a very busy man, and normally there'd be production meetings and panic meetings and general mayhem in this office. Seems it was more a focal point of the entertainment department in total than a private office. Apparently he liked it that way, sort of open house.'

'Bit like mine.' Palmer smiled. 'Right then, that's Mr. Fox done and dusted for the time being. So, what have we got on this Lisa James person?'

Gheeta scrolled down a few pages on the laptop.

'Lisa James, producer of game shows. Found dead in her office March 18th, three months before Fox was killed. Cause of death, heavy head wound."

'Well, that's one similarity. Anything else?'

'Nothing has come to light yet, guv. She worked under Fox, and had been at Midland six years. She had an office three doors down the corridor.'

'Very handy. Right, let's have a look at it then.'

Gheeta closed the laptop, stood up, walked to the office door and unlocked it.

'Ahem…'

Palmer coughed to get her attention; he was stuck. He'd sunk into the luxury grip of the soft chair, and it wasn't about to let him go. No amount of his rocking back and forth could get him out. He held out a hand.

'A little help if you would be so kind, Sergeant.'

'Certainly guv, you know you can rely on me to get you out of tight situations.'

Her tongue was firmly in her cheek as she pulled him up. He winced.

'Don't mock the afflicted.' It was his best Frankie Howerd impression. 'He was very funny too.'

'Who was?'

'Frankie Howerd.'

'Never heard of him, what was he in?'

'Never mind.'

He gathered his jacket and made for the door.

'Come on, let's see what Lisa James's office has to offer.'

Chapter 2

'She wasn't very old was she?'

In Lisa James's office Palmer was looking at a picture of the lady, very obviously taken at some sort of awards ceremony. She was seated at a large table, laughing at the camera, whilst those around her were pulling silly faces.

Her office was much smaller than Tony Fox's, and obviously a 'work' office; untidy, with files and folders strewn in a random way on shelves and over a large table, many with post-it notes stuck everywhere in profusion. Three rickety chairs completed the room.

'Thirty-eight, single, media graduate. She did three years at Scottish TV in Inverness before coming here to work.' Gheeta scrolled down her laptop screen. 'Family live in Edinburgh, she rented a serviced flat in Solihull. Oh dear.'

She gave Palmer an old-fashioned look.

'Numerous boyfriends.'

'Oh great, that's very helpful. Numerous suspects then.' Palmer sighed.

'No steady boyfriend as far as her parents are aware.'

'Even better, eh?'

Palmer tested a chair before sitting down on it.

'Same again then, Sergeant. Put a team on her: background, meetings, contracts, associates. Just like Mr. Fox she's upset somebody, possibly the same person. Hassle that secretary, or Lisa James's secretary, or PA if she had one; get all the info, and bung it through to Claire to run it through our systems. Hopefully we'll find something in common with the Fox murder.'

Claire was the civilian computer operations manager that Gheeta had persuaded finance department to release funding for. Using Gheeta's software programmes, Claire would input all the information known about victims and crimes, and the computer would compare, sort and search for similarities. Same names known to each victim, car numbers, club membership, associates, friends, in fact anything similar at all; if Tony Fox and Lisa James bought their petrol at the same garage it would find out by Credit Card comparison. Both the victim's lives would be stripped bare inside a computer server and compared. Palmer was hoping it would churn out similarities for the squad to look into. His fear was that in this case it would churn out too many similarities, seeing that both victims worked so closely in the same industry.

He folded his arms and sat back in the chair.

'I think this is going to be a hard one to crack, Sergeant. Imagine how many people in the business these two must have known between them.'

'You think the killer is somebody in the business, guv?'

'Got to be; it has to be someone who didn't seem out of place wandering in here. It's what happened in between that's going to be important.'

'In between, guv?'

'Yes, that's got to be relevant; Lisa James gets killed in March, and then we have a three month gap before Tony Fox gets whacked in June. So what happened during those three months, eh? Something did, because our murderer would have done 'em both at the same time if he or she had a grudge with both of them, so we can assume that his or her beef with Mr. Fox came up in the three months after he or she killed Lisa James.'

'Or we've got two different murderers, with two different reasons?'

'No, regional boys would have solved one of them if not both if that was the case. No, it's the same bugger alright, and he's a clever so and so.'

'And a vicious so and so too.'

Gheeta was looking at the crime scene photos.

'Yes, that too.'

He rose from the chair, this time, thankfully, without assistance.

'Come on, we can't do anything more here. Better warn that secretary girl that our team is about to descend on her.'

He donned his jacket and they left the room, locking the door after them. They had started off down the wide shiny corridor when a rather short, portly middle-aged lady with a short fringe, who seemed to be all flapping skirt and blouse, thundered up behind them, puffing like a steam train on an incline.

'Excuse me!' she panted, trying to catch her breath. 'You two should be in make-up by now! All extras should have been through it half an hour ago!'

She reached out and fingered Palmer's beloved Prince of Wales jacket, and tugged at the shoulders.

'Oh no, no that will never do. Back to wardrobe with you my dear, and get one that doesn't look like a charity shop reject. Off you go, quickly now!'

Chapter 3

Palmer was in his usual recumbent position in their small office at New Scotland Yard; feet up on the edge of his desk, and his chair leant back against the plain faded wall where years of banging against it had begun to gouge out a groove. Gheeta was at her desk, which was at right angles to Palmer's. She was inputting material into her main computer terminal.

Palmer tossed the papers he was reading onto his desk, and brought his chair down onto the lino floor with a loud crack.

'Going nowhere with that!' he said, rubbing his tired eyes. 'I've spent two days going through all the witness statements from Regional, all their interviews, all the scene of crime and forensic reports, and nothing; bloody zilch. I cannot believe that our two victims, who worked in such a bitchy and back-biting industry, were such nice people!'

He picked up the files and threw them down again in exasperation.

'Everybody liked them. Not a bad word anywhere. You'd think they were Mother Theresa and Gandhi! These statements from their work colleagues are as bloody fictional as the programmes they make.'

He stood and paced to the window looking out over Victoria Street below.

'Golden Sunrise.'

Gheeta was a bit bemused, and checked her watch.

'Not at one-fifteen on a Thursday afternoon it's not.'

'What's not?'

'It's not a golden sunrise at one-fifteen in the afternoon, guv. You've either gone barmy, or Armageddon's coming.'

Palmer chuckled and went back to his chair.

'No, it's the colour Mrs P wants the landing painted, Golden Sunrise. Bloody silly name, eh? Yellow, that's what it is, yellow; so why don't they call it yellow? She has to have something on the walls that will show up her cut flowers in their vases. I was halfway done with Burnt Sienna ,that's beige to you and me, when she changed her mind. Sounds like a posh pudding at a posh restaurant, doesn't it? Burnt Sienna, stupid name; and then she changed her mind to Golden Sunrise.'

He leant his chair back against the wall, and the groove deposited a further small amount of plaster onto the lino below.

'I can't find a tin of it anywhere, I've been to all the local DIY stores – mind you, she'll have changed her mind again by the time I get home. And getting home might be sometime away for us, judging by the progress we're making on this damn case. Better cancel the milk and papers at home, Sergeant.'

Gheeta carried on inputting.

'Already have, guv. The teams are sending in data by the bucket load. Our two victims had lots of mutual acquaintances and business associates. Too many really, but that's to be expected as they were closer than we thought.'

Palmer smelled a scandal.

'In what way closer?'

'Not the way you think, guv. Lisa James was a senior producer in Fox's department, so he had responsibility for all her programmes as well as his other projects. So they both dealt with lots of the same people; directors, writers, designers and the rest; there's tons of them.'

'No scandal? No extra maritals?'

Palmer felt cheated.

'No, both seem to be squeaky clean so far. But there is one thing that could be relevant. Fox was killed just a month after their annual Budget Review, which apparently is when future projects get cut to pay for the previous year's projects that went over their budgets or flopped.'

'Really?' Palmer thought aloud. 'So if somebody had a project keyed up ready to go that was suddenly dropped, they might be a bit miffed. Get Claire to work on that; look at any projects that got dropped recently. Could have something there; everybody in that industry works on a freelance basis, so if you were expecting a nice little earner and it got dropped you could be very angry. Especially if you earmarked the money for something else, eh?'

Gheeta nodded.

'Or your nice little earner had been going along for a couple of series and was suddenly dropped; then you could be very angry, if your lifestyle was going to suffer and your finances would be hit. If that was dropped on you out of the blue, some people might overreact in the heat of the moment.'

Palmer looked at the crime scene photos on his desk.

'Big chap, Fox. Whoever gave him that clout on the temple must have put some force into it, so it couldn't have been done from the front of the desk, with Fox standing behind it. It's too wide a distance, the blow would hardly reach. No, the killer must have been behind the desk with Fox –which suggests Fox knew him or her well. Must be somebody Fox thought of as a mate, as staff would stay the other side of the desk. The killer was round with Fox, maybe sitting on the corner of the desk… very informal, old mates… Tell you what Sergeant, pull out the five names that go back the longest in business relationships with Fox. Let's have a good gander at them, eh?"

Chapter 4

Tommy Vaughan closed his dressing room door behind him with a bang, and flopped exhausted onto the tatty sofa bed. He looked around the old end-of-pier dressing room, with its peeling paint and damp patches. If it were an antique it would be called distressed.

He sighed loudly. He'd been resident star of the Bournemouth summer season end-of- pier show for nine years on the trot, and knew every inch of that room; every knot in the wooden walls was like an old friend. Now, at nearly seventy years of age, he wondered whether it wasn't time to bid those old friends farewell. Summer Season was still fun, just, but a recliner on a nice Spanish beach would suit him better. The arthritic pangs and stiffness of oncoming old age were making their presence felt a little more each year.

He sighed again, took a drink from his mineral water bottle, and lay down to get his breath back. It was good that gin looked like water, and nobody had sussed that he had the same 'mineral water' bottle all season. Just time to relax for a couple of minutes, and then put back on the big false smile and scrawl his name on crumpled programmes thrust at him by elderly fans as he left the stage door.

Yes, his ego liked Summer Season; his body didn't. He hated the two shows a day, the matinee to kids who were more interested in running up and down the aisles, and shouting loudly to each other across the auditorium, than in what was happening on stage. For all that it seemed a bit like home, and it was where he'd started out at the bottom of the bill all those years ago on his comedy career. He still remembered doing the seasons at the dying Holiday Camps in the seventies, even then only half full as the other half jetted off to Spain for the same money and definite sunshine, courtesy of Laker Airways. Then he'd taken a job as warm up man in the BBC studios and soon was getting more laughs than the shows name artist. In a few short years he was number one; a TV series, sell-out tours, guest appearances, advertising contracts, and big money.

He smiled to himself; nothing lasts forever, least of all in the entertainment business. Peering into the big lit mirror that seemed to fill one wall, he had to admit to himself that the cracks were appearing; not only in the mirror's silver backing, but also in his face. Three face lifts, hair implants, a nip and tuck here and there and botox injections had kept him looking, on the outside at least, pretty good. And that was what the fans wanted; they wanted you the same year after year, decade after decade.

A sharp knock at the door startled him. Probably a fan who had sneaked past the stage door. Oh well, best be civil. Nothing the tabloids liked more than an upset fan telling them how rude you'd been.

'Come in it's open.'

He sat up straight, pulled in his stomach, and clicked on the false smile that showed his brilliant white false teeth.

Palmer poked his head round the door.

'Mr. Vaughan?'

'That's me.'

'Palmer and Sergeant Singh entered, closing the door behind them.

'I'm Detective Chief Superintendent Palmer,' he said, showing his warrant card. 'This is Detective Sergeant Singh, Scotland Yard.'

Vaughan was bit taken aback as he shook the offered hand.

'I think your agent, Rebecca Bannerman, arranged for us to come and have a chat with you, sir?'

'Oh yes, yes of course.' Vaughan said, his memory jogged. 'About Tony, wasn't it? Yes, sorry, it takes me a little time to come back to reality after doing a show. Do sit down, please.'

He indicated the sofa bed, but both Palmer and Singh opted for chairs which looked to have less wildlife in them than the sofa bed.

'Sorry I can't offer you a drink; been teetotal all my life. I'll get coffees organised in a few minutes, or tea if you prefer? I tend to hide in here until the punters with their cameras and autograph books have dispersed. Shouldn't really, but…'

He shrugged. Gheeta clicked on her recorder, in the hope Vaughan might drop a few names that she could match on the computers; but the only thing he dropped was his backside onto the sofa bed.

'Poor old Tony. Known him for years, lovely fellow; we go – went back a long long way.'

Palmer thought the affection sounded genuine enough; but he'd been fooled before, and took nothing at face value.

'How long is long, Mr Vaughan? Or better still, perhaps you could take us through your dealings with Mr. Fox, from the start of your business relationship with him?'

Vaughan went a bit white.

'Oh my God, I'm a suspect aren't I.'

It was statement not a question. Palmer smiled.

'Well, I suppose the honest answer is yes sir, you are. But everybody is at present, so don't feel too bad. You see, we have a problem; we don't seem to be hitting on any lines of enquiry that are bearing fruit, so, as you appear to be the oldest friend of his in the business, we hoped, and still hope, that your recollections might just put us a bit farther forward than we are.'

Vaughan visibly relaxed.

'Well, we hadn't seen too much of each other lately, which was a shame. But people were very jealous at the beginning you know; oh yes, very jealous. He had a great impact on my career, did Tony, and vice versa; you see…'

He settled back, like an old raconteur about to expound the meaning of life.

'I was doing the club circuits in the sixties, stand-up routines: three clubs a night and about twenty circuits, mainly Working Men's Clubs. First spot was nine-thirty, then onto the next one for eleven, and finally a late spot about one in the morning; sixty quid a time, which was very good money for those days. Three spots a night at weekends, and another four or five spots during the week, plus a bit of radio if you were lucky; Workers Playtime and the like. Remember that, do you?'

'I do,' Palmer said, and smiled at the recollection.

'I don't,' Sergeant Singh shrugged.

'You're far too young Sergeant,' Vaughan laughed. 'But the beauty of it was that a good forty minute act could last you six months as you worked the circuits. No television shows where the whole of Britain saw your act and it was dead in the water. So you never used your act if you did get on the telly; if I was lucky enough to get a telly spot they'd usually ask for about four minutes, so I'd get something written specially for it. Great times, you know, and great people.

'Anyway, I'm getting misty-eyed, and off the subject of poor Tony. He'd just been made up from floor manager at the Beeb to associate producer on a variety show; he was in a club checking out a juggling act when he caught my act and liked it. He saw the potential of comics cracking gags, and he knew they wouldn't do their act; so he put a dozen of us in front of an audience telling gags, and then edited it into a quick fire show, bam, bam, bam! It was a huge success. Four series followed: twelve shows a series, plus Christmas specials. For some reason the public liked me a lot; Tony signed me up and produced my own series which went out Saturday peak time. I went from sixty quid club spots to ridiculous amounts of money, because we pulled in twenty million viewers. Then the fledgling independent television companies wanted me and Tony, as they could charge millions to advertisers on the back of that number of viewers. Being the support act on the Tooting Grand Panto every year gave way to a three-month top of the bill Panto season at the Palladium!

'And all because dear old Tony took a chance on a comic he saw at a club. I paid him back; I insisted he produced all my television work. If you wanted Tommy Vaughan, you got Tony Fox as well, or no deal. The money offers got bigger and bigger, and we eventually went to ITV. Like two peas in a pod we were.'

'And socially, outside of work?' Palmer asked.

'No, never mixed the two. Never saw each other outside of work. Right from the start our relationship was purely business and work. Better that way. It worked for us.'

Palmer nodded.

'He did do other work though?'

'Oh, of course he did. By now he was executive producer at Midland, and juggling loads of shows in his department. But he always produced mine himself; from the initial meetings, getting writers and set designers, right through the rehearsals and recordings to the editing suite he took charge. He was as confident of me as I was of him.'

Palmer thought this was developing into an autobiography, which was not what he wanted, and decided to steer it in the direction he wanted to explore.

'How about enemies, he must have made a few?'

Vaughan laughed.

'Lots, but not really enemies; most were just jealous of his success. I had the same. Some comics said I was getting the shows because Tony was my mate. Producers who had made flops said it was because top artists only wanted to work for Tony. All bullshit, Chief Superintendent; pure bullshit. You find these artist and producer relationships throughout this industry. Did you know that just two artist management agencies provide over eighty percent of the beeb comedy output today? It's the way things get done. It's who you know, not what you know. And it stands to reason, if you've got a winning formula you don't destroy it.'

'What about your contracts? Did you get together on those too?'

'Absolutely not,' Vaughan was adamant. 'I'm not financially astute, Chief Superintendent. If I was I wouldn't still be working at my age, would I? No, I always had an agent do all that stuff; contracts, expenses, anything financial. All I had to do was sign the contract, and to be honest I don't think I ever even read one. Then I'd turn up, learn the words and do it, hassle free. Tony and I were strictly producer and star. You know, I never even met Tony's wife in all the years we worked together. I went to her funeral of course, but not back to the house after. Too personal, not business.'

Palmer nodded.

'When did you last see him then?'

'Month before he got killed. Rotten meeting it was too.'

Palmer's eyebrows raised.

'Oh? Rotten in what way?'

'Not rotten enough to make me want to kill him, Superintendent.'

'*Chief* Superintendent.'

'Sorry, *Chief* Superintendent. Well, it was basically to end my relationship with Midland Television. I'd been with them and Tony since they started, although they weren't called Midland Television back then – I can't recall what they were called. Anyway, there have been so many mergers and takeovers in the media industry, so God knows who really owns them now; probably a Japanese computer giant in an offshore tax haven, eh? That seems to be the way of things these days. You see it's all changed, and not for the better. For the past five years I've been hosting God awful game shows on their satellite channels. Two series a year, twelve shows a series; mind numbing work I can tell you, churning out two shows a day, and a series in the can inside a month. Easy money for me, and cheap to make for them: same set each show, no writers or artists to pay, and an audience bussed in from the local care home.'

Gheeta was shocked at this.

'Really? The local care home?'

'No, not really; just seems like it most of the time. The floor managers like an older audience, as they clap and cheer when they are told to. It's all false, you know. I go on before we start for real and tell them a couple of rude gags, which they genuinely laugh at, and that laughter is recorded and spliced into the show in the editing suite afterwards. The only new thing each show are the questions, and they nick them from various reference books. Easy money, eh?'

'Well it sounds simple, but I'm sure it isn't. I don't think I could do it.' Palmer said, trying to instil an amount of self-esteem into Vaughan.

'Oh you could, Chief Superintendent. You have an idiot board, or as they now call them, an auto cue. It's all written down for you to read off. If you can read, you can host a game show on telly. Anyway, we are getting away from Tony and the meeting. He'd called me in with my agent, and in his usual gentlemanly way softly dropped the bombshell that the network had cut the budgets again, and no new shows were going to be made as the dividends to shareholders had to be raised, and to achieve this they were going to run more repeats and buy in more cheap 'fly on the wall' stuff.'

Gheeta hadn't heard the expression before.

'Fly on the wall?'

Vaughan grinned at her.

'You take a handheld camera, with a sound microphone, and follow the staff of a hotel, department store, call centre or similar for a week. Then cut it and move bits around, and you've a very boring and very cheap programme or two; and, for some reason, they are also very popular. Reality TV; the bottom of the barrel has been reached.'

Palmer shifted in his chair, noticing his leg had gone to sleep. He rubbed his thigh.

'Anybody else been dropped that you know of?'

'Quite a few shows I think. It was a severe cut in Tony's budget, we could tell that he wasn't happy about it.'

He stood up.

'Let me organise some coffee, I'm absolutely parched myself. I usually relax with a cup about this time.'

'Of course,' Palmer apologised. 'I'd forgotten you'd just finished your show. Would you prefer to meet later?'

Vaughan wouldn't hear of it., 'No, no; not often I get company, other than the late middle aged to elderly blue rinse brigade, who saw me in a club forty years ago and wonder if I remember them!'

He laughed and winked at Gheeta.

'I always say I do! Milk and sugar?'

He stood and made his way to the door. Palmer rubbed his leg again.

'White, no sugar please.'

Gheeta relaxed and clicked off her recorder.

'Same, with one sugar please.'

She wondered if she could ask for biscuits, but decided not to. All the basic body requirements, like food, drink and sleep seemed to vacate Palmer's mind when he got into a case; he'd probably not given a thought to them. They'd been driven all the way from London without a stop, and come straight to the pier. She was sure her stomach was about to rumble loudly and embarrass her.

'I won't be two minutes.'

Vaughan opened the door, and was half way out when he obviously saw somebody he knew. Whoever it was, they were out of sight of Palmer and Gheeta.

'Hello?' Vaughan sounded surprised. 'I didn't know you were coming down today. Why didn't you let me know? Lovely to see you, I hope you've got the stuff? I'm actually in the middle of an interview with the police about Tony's death; I'm going along to the café for coffees. Come on, we'll chat on the way, and I'll phone the hotel and book you in.'

With that the door closed, and his cheery voice could be heard disappearing into the distance.

And that was the last time they saw him alive. After twenty minutes, Palmer went to search for him and the coffees. The staff in the café hadn't seen him, and nor had anybody else. He wasn't back at his hotel either, and by the evening Palmer had a full-scale hunt going on, plus a very bad feeling inside.

Tommy Vaughan's body, complete with multiple stab wounds to the back of his neck, was washed up onto the beach under the pier on the next morning's tide.

'I feel very responsible you know.'

Palmer stood inside the cordoned-off police area under the pier, looking down at Tommy Vaughan's grey face and prone body.

'Very responsible indeed.'

'Dead before he hit the water.'

The pathologist who had been called to the scene rose from his knees, and brushed the wet sand off his trouser legs.

'Very quick; first stab severed the spinal cord at the base of the neck, and he went out like a light. Probably didn't even know anything about it.'

Palmer thrust his hands deep into his pockets.

'That doesn't make me feel any better.'

Gheeta joined them from a little further up the beach, where she had been making mobile calls.

'Well, that should narrow down the suspects, sir,' she said as she closed her phone. 'The team are checking the whereabouts of all the names on our files to see who was where yesterday afternoon.'

'Mmm, be nice if one of them was in Bournemouth wouldn't it, eh?' Palmer said, although he didn't hold much hope for a match. 'We know a murderer was here, and we know he or she was on the pier.'

He stepped back a pace or two out from under the pier to get the entrance in his sight.

'Sergeant, check if there's a CCTV at the entrance of the pier, or any outside the shops and hotels around it that might cover it. If you find any, seize the discs.'

Gheeta nodded.

'And the railway station arrivals? They are bound to have CCTV cameras there, sir.'

'Good idea, grab those discs too.'

Gheeta was gone, ducking under the crime scene tape and pushing through a gathering crowd of nosy holidaymakers, most of whom thought it was a TV show being made and were trying to put actors' names to Palmer and the pathologist.

Resisting the urge to sign various pieces of paper thrust her way for an autograph, Gheeta made for the pier's entrance kiosks; with a bit of luck, she'd find the café open and be able to grab a sandwich. They'd been booked into a hotel last night at Palmer's insistence, and when she'd come down for breakfast the full English arrived at their table at the same time as Tommy Vaughan's body arrived on the beach. So the full English went back, and Gheeta and Palmer went to the beach. So far, this trip to Bournemouth wouldn't rank as a gastronomic success for the Sergeant.

'Funny isn't it,' the pathologist broke into Palmer's thoughts. 'I remember his television shows from way back. Bloody good they were too, I used to sit and chuckle at him. Now, here I am all these years later, and I must say it's not the way I'd really like to meet him.'

He nodded, and sighed in a resigned manner.

'His final curtain call.'

This wasn't doing Palmer's guilt complex any good at all. He called over the local officer in charge and handed the crime scene over to him, before making his way after Gheeta.

'Oi! Is you famous, mister? What you bin in then?' enquired a red-faced, obese slob of a woman, in between slurps of a double cornet ninety-nine. 'I knows yer face from some fink.'

Palmer thought this totally justified his lack of confidence in identity parades.

Chapter 5

On the fourth floor at New Scotland Yard, the Serial Murder Squad's team room, which had once been a small canteen, was opposite Palmer's office, which had once been its stock room.

Claire had set up the main computer server and all the add-ons across several old canteen tables, set away from the one and only large window to avoid reflections on the screens. She was busy sorting and collating the information Palmer's team were sending in via their mobiles and laptops, while around her at various desks several team officers were inputting their notes into terminals and downloading to the main server directly. Somewhere inside this server Gheeta's bespoke software programmes were silently at work: sifting, looking, comparing, and listing.

Gheeta had had Claire transferred from the Yard's Admin Pool, where she had been collating the mundane day-to-day report processing of traffic violations and witness statements from interview tapes; all very interesting, but as a young, newly married twenty-one year old, she wanted a bit more out of life, and had been taking Computer Studies courses at evening school and via the web. Gheeta learnt of this over lunch in the new ground floor canteen, and had Palmer pull a few strings to have Claire relocated within the Serial Murder Squad team on a permanent basis.

'Lots of matches so far Sir.'

Claire had caught a glimpse of Palmer and the Sergeant's reflections in the window as they came into the room behind her.

'But don't get too excited,' she qualified the statement. 'A television company's head of entertainment, a producer and a national comedy star are bound to have lots of common acquaintances.'

Palmer looked down over her shoulder at the screen.

'At least we aren't drawing blanks. Anything unusual stand out?'

'No, not yet; but it's early days, sir.'

He sauntered off, chatting encouragingly to the officers as he circled the room, like a predator waiting for its victim to show itself.

Gheeta sat next to Claire and began to input their Vaughan interview from her laptop recording, typing it in as she listened. She stopped and replayed a segment a couple of times, listening intently before removing her headphones and turning to where Palmer was.

'Sir, I think we might have a very important sentence in here.'

Palmer moved across to her side.

'Go on.'

'It's what Tommy Vaughan said to the person he saw outside the dressing room door. Have a listen.'

She pressed play, and Vaughan's surprised voice could be heard: 'Hello. I didn't know you were coming down today. Why didn't you let me know? Lovely to see you, I hope you've got the stuff?'

Gheeta turned off the recording.

'"Stuff"? "I hope you've got the stuff?"' she said, repeating Vaughan's words.

Palmer drew up a chair and sat down.

'Drugs? You think Tommy Vaughan was on something then?'

Gheeta shrugged.

'Why not? He could have got hooked earlier in his life. Let's face it he's in – was in the entertainment industry, which is not known for abstention, is it?'

Claire was tapping furiously away at her terminal.

'Nothing about drugs in any of his press cuttings…' More tapping. 'Nothing coming up on cross referencing to suggest involvement with others known as users… no prosecutions or warnings either.'

Palmer nodded.

'I would have thought the only things he'd have been on would be statins and aspirin. Has the pathologist's post mortem report come through yet? If he was taking something it would show up during the PM.'

Gheeta shook her head.

'No, they can take a while. I'll email for a preliminary report.'

'Mmmm.' Palmer wasn't convinced. 'So what was the "stuff" he was talking about then?' Gheeta knew as Palmer did, this *stuff* could unravel the case.

'Drink?'

'No, he was teetotal.'

Palmer rested his head in his hands for a moment.

'Got to be something that's pertinent to him.'

'Jokes,' Claire said, putting her penny's worth in.

'Jokes?'

Palmer wanted clarification.

'Yes, I bet it was new jokes for his show. Summer Season comics like to have a few topical jokes, one-liners about politicians or celebrities in the news; up to the minute stuff, their audience appreciates it.'

Claire raised her eyebrows, waiting for praise. None was forthcoming. Gheeta continued the thread.

'So, who would usually bring him new material for his act?'

'A writer,' Palmer said. He turned to Claire. 'Who was his writer?'

'Or writers,' Gheeta added.

'Hang on…'

Claire busied herself at the keyboard, inputting the key words 'writer' and 'jokes'.

'Nothing coming up, nobody listed.'

Palmer was getting agitated.

'His agent would know. The Bannerman woman, where does she work?'

'I've got that here somewhere,' Claire said, tapping frantically. 'Here we are, Rebecca Bannerman, Bannerman Artist Management, 1st floor, 172 Knightsbridge. She's made a statement.'

Palmer almost jumped off his chair and made for the door.

'Come along Sergeant, we are going visiting. Well done ladies, well done indeed.'

Gheeta grabbed her laptop and stood up, giving a large extended bow towards Claire, who returned the gesture from her seat, licked the tip of her index finger and wrote the figure '1' in the air. Praise, however faint, from Palmer was a rarity.

Chapter 6

'These old buildings are like a maze aren't they, eh? A ruddy maze,' Palmer said, as they stood in the poky, poorly lit entrance to 172 Knightsbridge; a few doors down from Harrods but a million miles away in comparison. It was run-down, grubby, with a dirty floor, dimly lit, and obviously hadn't seen a coat of paint for a number of years.

Gheeta smiled.

'You could put in a quote to do this place over with a coat of Golden Sunrise once you've finished your landing at home, guv. Golden Sunrise would perk it up no end.'

Palmer grunted. The thought of Mrs P's face if the damn landing at home wasn't finished before the Garden Club meeting was not a pleasant one. They looked up at the peeling paintwork on the tenants' name board; half the names were illegible through age.

Gheeta pointed to it.

'Bannerman Artists, 4th floor.'

Palmer looked at the old metal cage lift with its sliding iron latticework doors, and decided not to risk it.

'I think I'll take the stairs, I don't fancy getting trapped in that thing. I hate to think the last time Health and Safety paid this place a visit. Come on, if nothing else the stairs up four floors will be good for the heart.'

They started off up the creaking, uncarpeted stairs that twisted upwards beside the lift shaft, their footsteps breaking the silence as they left the noisy traffic sounds of the foyer behind them. It was hard to imagine a star of Tommy Vaughan's stature having an agent in this building.

'This is like a lot of things in life,' Palmer said, panting, to his Sergeant a few steps behind him. 'Sounds great doesn't it, a Knightsbridge address…'

He took a few gulps of air.

'Not so great when you actually get to see it. Like a false alibi really.'

'Fur coat and no knickers, eh guv?'

'Really Sergeant!' he said, feigning shock; then: 'Fourth floor at last, hoorah.'

He leant against the lift door, getting his breath back as they scanned another distressed-looking tenants' board which had a few crossings out, a couple of additions, and rampant woodworm. It told them that the Bannerman Agency was Room 23, along the corridor to the right. They found it; the notice on the door invited them to 'Enter', so they did.

The difference between the communal parts of the building and the inside of the Bannerman Agency suite was a surprise. The size of the suite was such that Palmer reckoned it must take up the whole of the front of the fourth floor, with panoramic windows affording a bird's eye view of Knightsbridge. It was open plan, and lit by banks of fluorescent tubes set into the false ceiling; a separate office behind a frosted glass partition sat at one end, which Palmer took to be the boss's enclave. The place was a hive of activity, with lots of people of all ages working behind two rows of busy desks; most had a phone held to their ear, and a flickering computer screen in front of them.

It's amazing what effect the appearance of a police uniform has on people; as soon as Gheeta took a step inside and into view, the heads turned, the noise notched down a couple of decibels, and several minds no doubt thought: *'Shit, I knew I should have paid that parking fine!'*

Access to the main floor was barred by a waist-high room divider that ferried visitors to a reception desk, in front of which were two low chairs and a round glass table with copies of *The Stage* newspaper piled on top of it.

'Rebecca Bannerman please.'

Palmer smiled falsely at the lady receptionist behind the desk, who was obviously a senior figure of authority in this office; late fifties, grey straight hair, dark power suit, and thick rimmed Buddy Holly spectacles that she peered over in a very disdaining way. She replied to Palmer's false smile with an even falser one.

'Do you have an appointment?'

The unsaid words were, *'you aren't getting past me without one.'*

Palmer tried to top her false smile with one that was rapidly turning into a sneer, as he pushed his warrant card into her view.

'I don't think we need one, do you?'

She read the card.

'One moment please.'

She lifted a phone handset and pressed a button on its base; then she explained to whoever took the call that a certain Detective Chief Superintendent Palmer was paying them an unexpected visit, without an appointment. She listened to the reply, and then replaced the handset.

'Would you follow me, Chief Superintendent?'

She opened a swing door in the divider, and led them through the rows of desks to the office at the far end, with every pair of eyes following them. The receptionist tapped politely on the door and opened it for them.

'Miss Bannerman will see you now.'

Palmer raised another false smile, removed his trilby and entered Rebecca Bannerman's office, followed by Gheeta.

She was mid-forties, and the jewellery on her fingers, wrist and neck shouted money; trim figure, blonde swathe of hair that looked as though the she'd just walked in from the hairdressers but in reality was a solid mass of hard set mousse; a designer two piece, with the top cut too low for her age; and manicured nails and shiny lip gloss which she'd topped up while watching Palmer and Gheeta coming through the main office via the one-way mirror on her office wall. The word 'elegant' came into Palmer's mind; the word 'Barbie' came into Gheeta's.

Bannerman was sat behind a very large, well-polished modern mahogany boardroom table, working at a computer which she flicked off as they entered. She stood up and offered her hand to both. Introductions over, she motioned them to a long button back antique sofa and sat opposite in an equally expensive antique leather chair. Her eyes moved to a picture of a beaming Tommy Vaughan amongst the many framed photos of current stars of stage and screen that adorned the walls, like a gallery of wanted posters without the sideways shots.

'I suppose this must be about poor old Tommy?' Palmer nodded.

'Just a few questions, if you wouldn't mind.'

'Of course not. Can I get you both something to drink?' she asked half-heartedly.

Palmer had got her taped. She obviously didn't want them there; tongues would wag, eyebrows be raised; not good for business when a client gets murdered. But he wanted a drink after four flights of those damn stairs.

'Coffee please; white, no sugar. Thank you.'

Bannerman looked enquiringly at Gheeta.

'Sergeant?'

'Tea please; white, no sugar. Any chance of a biscuit?'

It was a cheeky request; the battle lines were drawn. Bannerman pressed the intercom.

'Margaret, could we have a coffee and a tea, both white no sugar please – oh, and biscuits if you have any. Thank you dear!'

She didn't wait for a reply before clicking off the intercom. Her cold eyes turned to Palmer.

'Now then Superintendent, how can I help?'

'Chief Superintendent actually. We'd like some background information please, Mrs – Miss Bannerman?'

He's fishing, thought Gheeta. She'd seen him throw out the double answer line many times; a single answer usually came back, and it did this time.

'Miss, actually. But please, call me Rebecca.'

The patronising smile flashed across to Palmer.

'Thank you…Rebecca.' His killer smile flashed back at her. 'Mr.Vaughan was in a business where it's not unusual to have many friends and acquaintances, hangers on and the like; and we obviously need to compare

Vaughan's social circle with that of Tony Fox and Lisa James.'

She was visibly taken aback.

'They are connected? All three deaths are connected? Oh my God!'

'Well, that is our belief at present, yes,' Palmer said, wondering why she was so surprised. 'So it's important we uncover any links between them. Or more to the point, any person known to all three who had enough of a grudge against them to murder three times. So, as Tommy's agent - '

'And Tony's,' she interrupted him.

'Tony Fox's agent. You were his agent too?'

'Yes.'

No wonder she was worried; one of your clients being murdered is bad enough, but two was definitely not good for business. Or maybe even three.

'Lisa James?'

'No, not one of our clients.'

'I didn't know producers had agents.'

'Everybody in the entertainment world has an agent, Superintendent – sorry, *Chief* Superintendent; everybody. We handle the careers of several producers and directors, writers, designers, make-up artists. It's a different ball game to handling actors and performers like Tommy, totally different. With the stars we handle everything for them on a day to day basis, practically organising their life. With the producers and directors we get the television and film companies coming to us, looking for a suitable person for an upcoming project. You can't have a serious drama producer taking on a comedy sketch show, or vice versa, so we sort out the suitable candidates and pitch them up to the client. If one of ours gets the contract, we then negotiate the money and expenses, and that's it.'

They were interrupted by the tea and coffee arriving, together with a small plate of digestives that Gheeta made a bee-line for. As a 'ground bean' man himself, Palmer made an effort not to grimace as he sipped the supermarket instant coffee. One thing certain to get him out of bed the morning after a late night was the distinctive aroma of a freshly brewing pot of Brazilian roasted wafting up from the kitchen.; a ploy Mrs P had often used to get him mobile on a Sunday morning, when the lawn needed cutting or the hedge trimming.

'I have given a statement to your people already, you know,' Miss Bannerman continued, obviously trying to end the meeting as quickly as possible.

'Indeed you have, and thank you for that.'

Palmer had read it on Gheeta's laptop in the car on the way over; she might as well have said 'I knew Mr. Vaughan, he was a nice man' and ended it there, because that's about all she said in a three page statement that offered nothing new. Palmer put down his cup and took on a more serious air.

'Yes, indeed you have; but, you see, once it became part of a serial murder case it becomes far more complicated and my department takes over; and, unfortunately, we start again from the beginning. This, as you'll appreciate, means retracing steps. At present we have three victims we believe were linked in some way to the killer, or killers. Now, knowing both Mr. Vaughan and Mr. Fox as you did, I was hoping you might be able to provide some insight into their world of celebrity culture. A world I know nothing about.'

He gave her a smile and his little boy lost shrug,

'So, any input would be greatly appreciated.'

Out came the killer smile, the little boy lost look that Gheeta knew so well. She gave Bannerman about ten seconds to melt; it took three.

'Of course, Superintendent. Anything I can do to help I will of course be only too pleased.'

She used the intercom to get the receptionist to hold her calls, and no interruptions. She settled back in the chair, slowly crossing a pair of long shapely legs for maximum effect that was totally lost on Palmer, but not on Gheeta, who was quickly growing to dislike Miss Rebecca Bannerman intensely. Bannerman folded her arms; even

Palmer knew that folding of the arms was basic body language of building a wall.

'I'm all yours, superintendent.'

Gheeta forced herself not to comment, and switched on her recorder.

'Right,' Palmer said, as he stroked his chin, 'enemies first then. Who didn't like Tommy?'

'Oh, lots of people; fellow pros who he wouldn't have on his shows, old girlfriends, any amount of hangers-on who thought he'd ignored them. Some of his fans would write every day you know, expecting a reply too.'

Gheeta hoped that Palmer wouldn't want all that mail read through and held her breath. Thankfully, he didn't ask for it, and she relaxed again.

'Is there anybody you can think of who didn't like him enough to kill him?'

'Heavens no, Chief Superintendent; it's a very catty business and people get trampled on or passed over all the time, but not to the extent of wanting to murder anybody. Good Heavens, no!'

'On the day he was killed in Bournemouth we know he had a visitor, somebody who knew him well. That somebody is the person we now need to find urgently, and the only clue is that there was a business connection of some sort because we heard Tommy ask whether the visitor had brought him the *stuff*.'

'Stuff?'

'Yes, *stuff*; that was the word Tommy used. Now, we know from the post mortem that Tommy didn't take drugs or legal highs or anything like that, and it's been suggested that by *stuff* he could have been talking about new material for his act. Is that possible?'

'Gags, you mean? Well, yes that's possible. He liked to keep the act fresh with topical jokes.'

'So who would take those down to him?'

'Writers; but he used quite a few. Most comics do.'

'Any regulars? Did he have any favourites?'

'Well, he had three under contract. He paid them a retainer; not a lot but it meant he got first refusal on any material they wrote, and could call on them for specials.'

'Specials?'

'One-offs, after dinner speeches, Variety Club dinners, that kind of thing. I'll give you their names and addresses before you leave. But I can't imagine any of them being a murderer; killing Tommy would cut off their income stream. Except for Angela.'

'Angela?'

'Angela Hartman. She was his main writer, been with Tommy since day one really. In fact, Tony Fox introduced them. She was the script editor on all Tommy's shows, wrote most of it and edited the other writer's contributions. Rumour had it that he'd looked after her in his will.'

Gheeta wanted clarification.

'Did you say Angela?'

'Yes.'

'Isn't that unusual, a female comedy writer?'

'No, there's lots of them; check the credits on the TV sketch shows.'

Palmer wanted to back track.

'Hang on a minute, just now you said you couldn't imagine any of his writers being a murderer except this Angela woman. Why her?'

Bannerman sighed.

'I wasn't being that serious, but they had an almighty row about six months ago, about money. You see, Tommy had his own writers and paid them himself, which is unusual as most shows contract the writers and the TV company pays them. But Tommy always used his own writers and negotiated the money with them directly, and the contract always gave him sole rights to the material.'

Palmer nodded.

'I presume he paid less than the TV companies? He seems to have been a very astute man.'

'Oh yes, a lot less. But he had the whip hand. There are always a lot more writers around than there is work for them, and that includes the best ones. So if you hooked up with a star who had regular shows, you took what was offered. Regular income, however small, is better than no income.'

'And this Angela Hartman didn't like that, eh?'

'Been simmering for years; she was forever complaining, but Tommy's contracts were always take it or leave it. But she always took it in the end. The real explosion was when the network repeated an early series of Tommy's on a new station via satellite. If Angela had had a contract with a TV company she would have got a repeat fee, but with Tommy's contract she got nothing. She took him to task because he got his own repeat fee, plus he got the writers repeat fees because he always turned up at the studio with his script all written and paid for; so he got the writers fee anyway, as well as his performers fee. And as he had sole rights to her material, and she had no repeat fee clause in the contract, he had no legal reason to pay her, or any of the other writers, a penny for repeats. And he didn't.'

Gheeta was intrigued.

'What sort of money are we talking about here?'

Bannerman thought for a second or two.

'Around twenty thousand for a series.'

Both Palmer and Gheeta exhaled loudly.

'Blimey,' said Palmer. 'I know a lot of villains who would kill for less!'

Miss Bannerman shook her head.

'I really can't believe Angela would do such a thing. She's a strong-willed lady, and a bit head strong, but she would never do anything like that. And in any case, where's the tie in with Tony Fox and Lisa James's deaths? I doubt she knew either of them'

'Might not be one,' Palmer said, shifting his position as his damn sciatica jabbed his thigh. 'But if there is we will find it. I have a favour to ask, if you wouldn't mind.'

'Of course not, fire away – if I can help I will.'

'Thank you. The Sergeant here will send you copies of the CCTV discs taken at Bournemouth railway station on the day of Tommy's murder; it shows the station exit and the entrance to the pier. Would you mind viewing them and seeing if you recognise anybody? It's a long shot, but you never know.'

'Of course I will, send them over.'

Gheeta fished out a contact card from her bag and gave it to Miss Bannerman.

'And should you think of anything else that might be useful, please phone me on that direct number. Everything is treated in the strictest confidence of course.'

They stood to go. Palmer shook his leg.

'Damn sciatica, old age creeping up. Thank you for your time Miss Bannerman, and the refreshments. We won't impose on you any longer.'

'Please, it's Rebecca.'

The big smile again.

'Rebecca,' Palmer said, as he shook her hand. 'Right then Sergeant; things to do, people to see.'

They left her office, as Gheeta and Rebecca Bannerman exchanged cold, false smiles. They swivelled through the office desks and the divider gate, where the receptionist also gave them a false smile. Palmer stopped and admired the photos of the agency's more high-profile clients.

'You've got some big hitters here haven't you, eh?'

The receptionist pushed her glasses down into place from their perch on top of her hair and joined him.

'Oh yes, Miss Bannerman is well respected in the business. She turns a lot away, you know. Some very big names included.'

'Well, when I write my memoirs I'll know who to come to then, won't I.'

Gheeta couldn't resist.

'Don't think they do 'kiss and tell', sir.'

Palmer ignored this as he put his hat on.

'Thank you for the coffee.'

He resisted the urge to give the receptionist the name of a good Kenyan bean, opened the door for Gheeta, and they left.

'Well, what a patronising bimbo that Bannerman woman is.'

'Mutton dressed as lamb my mum says, guv.'

Behind them a voice said: 'You forgot these.'

They turned to find Miss Bannerman standing in the doorway, holding out a piece of paper towards them.

'The names of Tommy's writers, and their addresses.'

She had obviously heard their comments, as her cold expression would have frozen the sun. Gheeta accepted the paper, avoiding eye contact, and Bannerman turned back into the office, slamming the door with such force the whole building shook.

Rebecca Bannerman stood at her office window looking down onto busy Knightsbridge, watching Palmer and Sergeant Singh negotiate through the gridlocked rush hour traffic to their waiting car. She watched as it pulled out into the flow and moved slowly out of view.

She stood for a minute or two, her face expressionless, her mind weighing up the pros and cons of the situation, before she turned and sat back in her large chair, her well-manicured fingernails strumming on the desk. Things were getting a bit too warm for comfort. Blast Tommy bloody Vaughan!

She lit a cigarette, inhaled deeply, and turned her computer on.

Chapter 7

Palmer couldn't sleep. He'd paced up and down his office trying to pull the strings of the case together, but nothing was falling into place; and he'd finally got a patrol car to drop him off at home in Dulwich well past midnight.

The slices of boiled bacon and the accompanying pease pudding that Mrs P had left beside the microwave went untouched. His faithful hound Daisy, an English Springer, had noticed this, and was trying to figure out a way to nudge the plate off the kitchen top onto the floor, without it breaking or making a noise after her master had gone to bed. Palmer sat and made a fuss of her for a few minutes, managed half a cup of milk which was his bedtime habit and, with as little noise as possible crept upstairs. Washing and donning his pyjamas, which Mrs P always left over the banisters on the landing so he didn't wake her up hopping about on one leg putting them on in the bedroom, he slipped into the large, comfy, double king-size bed beside her and closed his eyes.

He couldn't sleep. His mind was whirring. *Where oh where was the link? A television producer, a television executive and a television star; all dead, but why? No apparent motive, except maybe an angry writer. But then why would the angry writer kill the executive and producer? It didn't add up. What was the stuff Tommy Vaughan had hoped for? Rebecca Bannerman was a link with Vaughan and Fox, but not James; Lisa James seemed to be the odd one out. Fox and Vaughan were bedfellows from a long way back – was there another, as yet, unfound bedfellow in the early days, who got pushed out of the bed and was taking revenge?*

But that still left Lisa James outside the circle. Did she find out something that she shouldn't have found out? Had she seen something she shouldn't have seen? And where does the tin of Golden Sunrise come into it?

Golden Sunrise?? What the hell am I thinking about – going barmy...

Tired… Hungry too… Wish I'd had that boiled ham, and Burnt Sienna for afters… God I'm tired now…
Burnt Sienna… mmm, tasty…

Chapter 8

Gheeta was very much the live-wire when Palmer walked into the office the next day. He'd slept late, and felt better for it.

'Eureka!'

Gheeta hardly let him hang his hat on the stand and sit down at his desk before slapping a print-out from her computer in front of him.

'What's this then, overtime claim?'

'Not big enough for that, guv – it's the first inkling of a possible motive. I took the liberty of downloading the Companies House business registration and financial records of Bannerman Entertainments and Artist Management Ltd, thought it might be worth having a peek at. It's very interesting too, guv.'

Palmer stared blankly at the paper. The columns of figures meant absolutely nothing to him. 'Okay hotshot, cut to the good bit then.'

'Tommy Vaughan owns, or should I say owned, forty-nine percent of the company.'

'Did he, by George? Now that is interesting.'

'Isn't it just?'

There was a distinct sarcastic edge to Gheeta's voice.

'Bannerman must have forgotten to mention that to us; I wonder why? It must have slipped her mind. That size of shareholding makes him a major shareholder and gives him certain rights, such as the right to veto any major decisions, and also gives him full financial access to the books and accounts. And, looking back through the accounts, it seems the company had a tough time in the late nineties, which is when he came in with a cash injection of twenty grand in return for the shares. It's done rather well since, and at today's current turnover and profit forecasts his stake would be worth over a million pounds.'

'How much?' Palmer said in astonishment. 'A million?'

'Correct guv, a million notes. Believe it or not, it has the biggest financial turnover of any agency in the UK. She's a very astute cookie, is Miss Bannerman – that's Rebecca to you of course…'

She pouted her lips and fluttered her eyelids. Palmer smiled.

'Get on with it.'

'Well, she doesn't have a large client list but she does have the cream of the crop; all the big hitters, as you rightly noted from those pictures in the reception area of her offices. The agency had a turnover of just under seventeen million last year, with gross profits of close to three million."

'And poor old Tommy had a stake worth a million in it. I've known people murder for less.'

'A lot less, guv.'

Palmer was beaming.

'Well, that throws a completely different light on things doesn't it? Well done Sergeant, well done. Yes, a completely different light.'

Gheeta took an exaggerated sweeping bow.

'Claire's going to run the Bannerman name through all our business contact programmes to see if we can unearth anymore little gems after lunch.'

She looked at her watch.

'I'm going across to the café; fancy a sandwich brought back, guv?'

'No thanks, not today. I had boiled bacon and pease pudding at half past three this morning.'

He silenced Gheeta's expected question with a wave of his hand.

'Don't even ask.'

'Very posh, h'aint hit my dear,' Palmer said, adopting a posh accent.

They were walking along Russell Square, seeking the offices of Lansbury, Hartnell and Lawson Solicitors; the reason being that Lansbury, Hartnell and Lawson were Tommy Vaughan's solicitors, and Palmer thought it might pay dividends to see who got what in Vaughan's will, in the light of his Bannerman shareholding being worth a million. Claire had come up with the solicitor's name by accessing the Bannerman share documents at Companies house and finding that Lansbury, Hartnell and Lawson acted for Vaughan at the time of his initial investment in the agency, and were witnesses to the share transfer documents.

When they found the offices and made enquiries at the reception desk, Palmer was a little disappointed that they weren't actually going to see Lansbury, Hartnell or Lawson, but plain Mr. Smith instead. He voiced his disappointment to Mr. Smith, who came out to deal with them.

'They all died in the late eighteen-hundreds, but the company kept their names. Some of our clients' families go back that far with us as well,' laughed the rotund figure that Mr. Smith turned out to be. Palmer was reminded of Mr. Pickwick, and could well imagine him in the eighteen-hundreds, patting away at a sweated brow whilst pushing a quill scratchily across a parchment indenture.

He led them into a cluttered, dark-panelled office and sat them in antique leather chairs as he flicked through a large box file, until the document he was searching for came to hand.

'Aha, here we are. Now then…'

He peered closely through the bifocals perched on the end of his nose, his lips moving silently as he read quickly through. He paused and looked over his spectacles at Palmer.

'You must appreciate, Chief Superintendent, as I am sure you do, that this information is only being given to you to assist your investigations into such a serious case; and must remain privy to yourself and your staff at all times, until the official disclosure of the content of Mr. Vaughan's will at the reading of the said will.'

'Quite,' replied Palmer, putting on his serious face.

Smith nodded, and perused the will for a minute or so more until satisfied he had the information he sought. He read aloud:

'Two beneficiaries: the property, that is his house, to include all furniture and contents found therein, to be sold by auction and any moneys gained to be given to the Variety Club of Great Britain to be used at their discretion; the same treatment to be given to any funds in current or deposit accounts in his name in any bank or building society. All shareholdings are to be transferred to Miss Angela Hartman.'

He rapidly scanned the rest of the document.

'That's basically it; all the rest just instructs us as his executors to handle those requests.'

He looked up.

'Is that information of any use to you, Chief Superintendent?'

'It could well be, Mr. Smith, it certainly could well be, sir,' he said, and he and Gheeta rose to leave. 'Thank you for your time, sir; and thank you for fitting us in at such short notice, much appreciated.'

Smith removed his spectacles and shook their hands.

'My pleasure, Chief Superintendent, my pleasure, Tommy was a class act, you know. He always sent a few tickets along for his Christmas shows. Never forgot our children's birthdays. What an awful way to go. Awful.'

'Yes, very unpleasant, sir. Very unpleasant indeed.'

Smith saw them to the large front door. Palmer paused.

'Oh, and one more thing, sir, if you wouldn't mind; not a word about our visit to anybody else who might turn up and show an interest in Vaughan's will.'

'My lips are sealed.'

Mr. Smith paused sharply, as he remembered something.

'Hold on a moment – there was an enquiry; about a week ago, a phone call asking when the will was to be read and acted upon. Just a minute.'

He turned and hurried back into the offices. Palmer turned to Gheeta.

'Who's your money on?'

'Rebecca Bannerman.'

'Not this Angela Hartman woman? She's going to be very rich with those shares.'

'No, how would she know their value?'

'Vaughan could have told her to keep her writing for him, with the promise of the pot of gold at the end of the road?'

They exchanged shrugs as Smith hurried back panting.

'Collins, a Miss Collins made the enquiry. Only got the surname I'm afraid, no address. Mean anything to you?'

Palmer and Gheeta both shook their heads. Palmer smiled at Smith and shook his hand again.

'Not at present but I've no doubt it will do. Mr. Smith, you've been most helpful. Thank you very much again.'

They descended the steps to the pavement as the big door shut behind them. Palmer turned to Gheeta, who had her mobile in her hand, pressing in a speed dial number. She smiled.

'I'm already on it guv.'

She spoke into the mobile.

'Claire? Hi it's Gheeta. Can you run a name through the programmes please? It's just come up and may be significant... Collins, we think it's a female.... Okay thanks, see you later.'

She pocketed her phone.

'I wonder if Angela Hartman actually knows how rich she is, guv.'

'Certainly gives the lady a hell of motive to want him dead if she does.'

'So, next stop Miss Hartman's abode then?'

'All in good time, Sergeant; more important work to be done first. Or have you forgotten?'

'Forgotten what, guv?'

'Golden Sunrise, Sergeant! Is there a B&Q round here, do you know?'

Chapter 9

'Oh, Benji said that, did he?'

Palmer was pacing up and down his office in an obviously angry mood, his mobile phone clamped to his ear, venting his feelings to Mrs P on the other end.

'He did, did he? Well, you tell Mister Know-it-all Benji that some of us have to work for a living, and don't have time to saunter up and down the high street every day like a limp lettuce window shopping, so we wouldn't know the local builder's merchants had a large window display of Golden bloody Sunrise on special offer, would we, eh? And tell him he can buy the biggest tin he can and then he can – no, no, I wasn't going to be rude my dear, I was going to say he can start work on the bloody stairs with it! Seems he's not exactly a busy man, is he? Unlike me...

'No, no I have no idea what time I'll be home, so don't wait up. I'll get a take away... Home- made steak and kidney? Have you? In that case, leave it in the fridge and I'll pop it in the microwave – don't forget the extra gravy, you know what I'm like with your gravy... The gravy's gone where?...What do you mean, Benji's had it – why did you give it to him? Yes, I know he hasn't got anybody to cook for him – he hasn't got anybody to cook for him because he chooses to live on his own. I wish I had all you ladies popping round with pies and cakes like he does – life of Riley, eh?...

'No, no I don't mean I'd rather live on my own – you know what I meant, don't make an issue of it. Anyway, gotta go – see you sometime later... Bye now, love you too.'

The phone clattered back on its rest, and he held his hands out front as if throttling somebody. Gheeta giggled.

'Got a rival for Mrs P's affections have you, guv?'

Palmer sat down at his desk and spoke with contempt.

'Benji, or Frank Benjamin to give him his real name, is our next door neighbour. He is a sixty-something retired advertising executive: bald on top with a ponytail at the back, Ralph Lauren shirts and Gucci tight-fit stone-washed jeans – get the picture? Like your mum says, *mutton dressed as lamb*. On a whacking great pension no doubt, and nothing to do all day except poke his ruddy nose into other people's business. He has an immaculate garden, with a lawn suitable for the world bowls final; every leaf and flower on every plant is perfect, not a weed in sight, probably too scared to poke their heads up. Even the birds that eat and drink from his ornamental solid brass Harrods bird table flit onto the fence when they've had their fill and crap over my side of it. He has a new, top of the range 4x4 every year, the latest mobile phone and kitchen utensils, and four overseas holidays a year, which I swear are a cover for a quick trip to Europe for a nip and tuck to various sagging bits. I hate him.'

'Well, if he ever meets a suspicious end we know where to look first, don't we?'

'And you'll probably be right too.'

Claire entered carrying two CDVs and a time sheet. Palmer looked up.

'Anything on the Miss Collins character yet?'

'Sorry sir, nothing coming up on her. But this is a bit funny.'

'Funny? What have you got there then, a Benny Hill CDV?'

Both Claire and Gheeta looked at him, unaware of who Benny Hill was. Claire dismissed it and carried on.

'It's the CDV discs from the arrivals platform and the pier entrance at Bournemouth, that we sent over to Miss Bannerman for her to take a look at.'

'Aha!' Palmer said, perking up. 'Recognise somebody, did she?

'No. Her office manager brought them back, and said sorry but Bannerman had viewed them and couldn't help us.'

Palmer was deflated.

'Damn. That would have been a nice break, that would.'

Claire wasn't finished.

'Yes but hang on, sir. The discs were checked before records filed them back into the evidence box, and they found the railway platform disc was four seconds shorter than when it was sent out.'

'What do you mean four seconds shorter? Can't be.'

'It can be if you re-master it guv,' Gheeta butted in.

Palmer was lost; the only thing he knew about re-mastering was his AC/DC set of re-mastered vinyl albums. He gave his Sergeant an inquisitive look.

Gheeta took the disc from Claire and examined it.

'Easy peasy, guv: we send her a copy of the platform recordings on a common blank CDV disc which you can buy just about anywhere, she has or buys another one and copies the one we sent her onto it, but edits out the four-second bit she doesn't want other people to see. And being in the entertainment business like she is, I bet they copy and send out show discs all the time.'

'Show discs?'

Palmer was none the wiser.

'Yes, a disc with their clients' act, or bits of him or her in different shows; it's a sort of advert to show off the client. Even money there's a disc copier and editing machine in her office; easy to use, and you can cut or add bits from other discs at the press of a button.'

Palmer was thoughtful, and held up a finger for silence.

'Okay, so if we look at the master disc and see what's missing from the one she sent back, it should show us the person who she doesn't want us to see; and probably it's the person who went to Bournemouth with the *stuff*, and may even be the killer.'

'Case closed?'

Claire was ever hopeful. Palmer had been up too many blind alleys in his career to make assumptions.

'I doubt it Claire, I doubt it very much. But hopefully it will put a name in the frame for a possible Tommy Vaughan killer if nothing else.'

Gheeta slumped back in her chair.

'You think there's more than one killer, don't you guv.'

It was a statement not a question. She knew Palmer's thoughts would be that in the world of criminality, if something good fell into your lap so easily it had probably been put there to send you up.

'I wish I knew Sergeant; I honestly don't know if we are looking for one killer or more than one killer. We can tie everybody together nicely except Lisa James; she stands out from the bunch like a sore thumb. There has to be a connection in there somewhere, but so far it's hiding itself remarkably well.'

He hoisted up a large file with L JAMES writ large on the front.

'Jobs for the rest of the day: me to re-read this lot, and you two to hit your keyboards and find me something on Lisa James we've missed; and, more importantly, who the hell the mysterious Miss Collins is.'

He opened the file and sighed.

'Oh, the joys of being a copper, eh? The Sweeney never had a foot high pile of paperwork to sift through I'll bet.'

Claire turned round at the door.

'Who, sir?'

'Never mind.'

Chapter 10

Detective Sergeant Gheeta Singh couldn't sleep. It was two in the morning, and she stood in her pyjamas looking out from her high-rise Barbican apartment across the shimmering Thames to the twinkling lights on the south side. The apartment had been an investment her father had made when the area had been developed in the late nineteen-eighties and it had paid off handsomely, giving Gheeta a financial stability many of her age had little chance of achieving.

Her parents had come to the UK as immigrants in the fifties, worked hard and made a large amount of money in the electronics business; starting off by making small computer components with imported parts from China on their kitchen table, until the table began to creak and they moved to a small unit in a local East End business park. Now the family business was one of the biggest PC component manufacturers in Europe supplying household name companies with their products. The business was now run by Gheeta's two elder brothers, with her parents taking a well-earned retirement. Gheeta was responsible in an advisory capacity for their IT solutions and systems research department, with her expertise in that area playing no small part in keeping the business ahead of its rivals. She took no salary but had an equal share holding to her brothers; it was family, and she knew that if ever she felt compelled to leave the police, a well-paid senior position in the firm awaited her. And at this moment in time, it looked very attractive indeed.

She sighed audibly. She'd got a problem; a nice sort of problem, in a way, but it needed to be sorted, and if she got it wrong she could kiss goodbye to her police career.

Two weeks ago, when Palmer was on leave, Assistant Commissioner Bateman, their immediate superior officer, had called Gheeta into his office, sworn her to secrecy, and told her that the powers to be were setting up a Cyber Research department south of the river in the Forensic

Sciences Headquarters, and wanted her to take charge and get it up and running; using her bespoke software that was proving so good in the Serial Murders department. She'd have a good budget, and be answerable to the Assistant Commissioner himself. There would be an 'upward salary adjustment' of course; most people would call that a 'raise', but in the public sector the more words you can use the better, and if you can describe something basic in language nobody can understand, even better still.

She sipped from a glass of Malvern water, watching a lone tug pull a barge five times its size slowly down stream, its wake lapping the far river wall like children trying unsuccessfully to scale a gate. Palmer would go barmy. She should probably have told him of the approach straight away, but had been manoeuvred into a corner by the secrecy element. She had wanted to be a police officer for as long as she could remember, and being a police officer in her mind didn't mean being inside all day working with computers; but if she turned it down, was she ending her career? AC Bateman could be spiteful if he'd a mind to be.

The whirring of the street cleaning vehicle's brushes on the road eight floors below brought her back to reality. She took a last sip from the glass and resolved to talk to Palmer about it in the morning, as he'd know how to wriggle out of it without doing any damage to the department or to her prospects. She pulled the blind shut as the barge disappeared from view, and slipped back into bed. When life's going well, why does some arsehole have to spoil it? And AC Bateman was a well-known arsehole.

Chapter 11

Palmer chucked the Lisa James file onto the floor, removed his reading glasses and rubbed his tired eyes. It was the next afternoon, and he had purposely arrived in the office early that day to have one last look through that file. He'd been through it yesterday and found nothing new of interest, and despite sorting through his notes all evening at home, much to Mrs P's annoyance, he found nothing new there either. So, arriving early he'd laboriously gone through every statement, every forensic report, photo and diagram, and found nothing again. Lisa James was a career-motivated lady, with a thoroughly normal and well-ordered life; she must have just been in the wrong place at the wrong time. He bounced his chair back against the wall, swung his feet onto his desk and relaxed.

Gheeta had busied herself with Claire all morning in the team room, re-running comparison software data in the hope of finding a link. It was a little after two in the afternoon when she returned to the office, noticing the MEETING IN PROGRESS DO NOT ENTER sign on the door that Palmer used when he wanted to concentrate on something, or when the front desk had phoned to warn him that Mrs P was on her way up. Not that she had ever taken notice of it; nor had anybody else for that matter.

Gheeta sat at her desk.

'Anything, guv?'

'Nothing, not a dicky bird. Well, at least I'm sure we haven't missed something on Miss James. I just wanted one last go at it after a good night's sleep. Now I am doubly sure.'

'Glad somebody got a good night's sleep.'

'Oh, out partying were we, Sergeant?'

He waved his hands around in the air, like he'd seen kids doing at the warehouse raves he'd busted as a young CID Sergeant and nearly fell off his chair with the effort.

'No guv, not at all.'

She stood and pulled a chair across the floor to the front of his desk, and sat down facing him.

'Guv, can we have an off the record chat for a minute? And I do mean off the record.'

Palmer noted the seriousness in her voice, and swung his feet off the desk, bringing his chair banging down onto the floor.

'Go on.'

She told him the full story of AC Bateman's approach, as Palmer listened intently, getting very angry inside at Assistant bloody Commissioner Bateman, for whom he had little respect or time for. He had the same lack of respect and lack of confidence in all the university graduates, fast-tracked to senior positions in the force, none of them ever having walked a beat or having any knowledge about villains and their ways. When she finished he leant back, hands behind his head, and studied the ceiling for a few seconds.

'Do nothing, Sergeant. Stall him for a few days, and let me have a good think about it. I'll come up with an answer, don't you worry about that; but it will be the right one, one that leaves you where you want to be, and leaves him with no possible excuse for any comeback. We'll scuttle his bloody ship, you wait and see.'

At that moment, Assistant Commissioner Bateman's bald head peered round the door. He smiled at the pair of them.

'Ah good, I hoped I might catch you both. I just wondered if I might have a word with Sergeant-'

Palmer cut him short by jumping up hurriedly, seizing his coat and hat off the stand. Grabbing Sergeant Singh's laptop from her desk he ushered her to the door, squeezing her past a bewildered Bateman.

'Sorry sir, can't stop – just got a very hot lead on the Vaughan case; got to fly. Come on, Sergeant, move!'

He pushed Gheeta out into the corridor in front of him.

'Pop in tomorrow if we're back, sir. Must rush, car waiting down stairs.'

And he was off down the corridor, with Gheeta trying to keep up as she pulled on her jacket that she'd managed to grab on the way out.

At the end of the corridor he ignored the lift, and took the east side stairs down two at a time; behind him, Gheeta swore she heard him giggle. At the next floor down he left the staircase, pushed through the double doors into the CID floor corridor, slowed down to a respectable walking pace along it to the other end, went through the doors to the west side staircase, up that staircase to his own floor, through the doors, along the corridor, and finally back into his own, now empty, office. Then he slumped into his chair and stifled his laughter, while Gheeta sat at her desk and shook her head in disbelief at what they had just done, before collapsing in fits of laughter as well.

Claire walked in carrying a printout, and stopped abruptly when she took in their faces.

'You two look like you've just got away with something wicked. What have you been up to?'

'Nothing, nothing.'

Palmer wiped his laughing eyes and regained his composure.

'The Sergeant just told me a very rude joke.'

'I did not!' Gheeta said, indignant through her giggles.

'She didn't.'

Claire knew Gheeta better than to believe that.

'Anyway, never mind that – this is a little more interesting.'

She put the printout on Palmer's desk, as Gheeta came over to look.

'What is it?' Palmer asked, putting on his glasses.

'Lisa James's birth certificate. I've just downloaded it from the RBDM database.'

'From where?'

'Registrar of Births Deaths and Marriages.'

'And…?'

Claire pointed to a written line on the paper.

'Mothers name is Margaret Collins; got to be the Collins who tried to check out Vaughan's will, hasn't it? Father's name is left blank, but child's name is registered as, guess what? Lisa Vaughan.'

'Lisa James was Tommy Vaughan's daughter then!'

Gheeta was very surprised at that reveal.

'You bet she was!' Claire replied, feeling cock-a-hoop. 'But I don't understand why they registered her as Lisa Vaughan but left the father's name blank?'

'Because,' Palmer said slowly, 'Vaughan had obviously refused to acknowledge the kid was his; remember this is long before DNA testing. So the mother got her own back; it's your child, so it gets your name on the certificate!'

Gheeta couldn't understand.

'Why did nobody make this connection before? Regional Crime Squad would have picked up on it surely?'

Palmer shook his head.

'Not necessarily; they were looking at two different murders, with three months in between them, and Tommy Vaughan was still alive then; he wasn't in the picture at all.'

'Hang on...'

Gheeta was getting lost.

'Why wasn't Vaughan involved in the case? He was her dad!'

Claire smiled smugly.

'Yes, but he didn't know he was.'

She placed another piece of paper on the desk.

'Adoption certificate: Lisa Vaughan was adopted by a Mr and Mrs James, and her name changed by deed poll.'

She placed the last paper on the desk.

'Changed to Lisa James.'

'Of course!'

Palmer's eyes lit up with excitement as he worked it out.

'I bet Tommy Vaughan didn't even know he had a daughter. Don't forget this is back in the sixties, and there was a stigma attached to being an unmarried mum in those days; not like today, where it's a requirement to have popped one out before your seventeenth birthday.'

Gheeta and Claire exchanged false yawns. They were used to Palmer's politics being to the right of Genghis Khan, and his low opinion of modern youth. He ignored them and carried on.

'This young lady, Margaret Collins, would have been at her wits end. It's obvious from the birth certificate that she was positive Vaughan was the father, and if she told him he probably would have told her to take a running jump; probably had lots of girlfriends and one-night stands, being a big star of the time; might even have thought the girl was trying it on. So he just brushed it aside, and forgot about it in his busy life; she must have realised it was pointless pursuing him, and had the child adopted. I think we ought to send a sympathetic victims' support WPC down to Lisa's adoptive parents in…'

He searched his memory.

'Glasgow guv,' prompted Gheeta

"Or maybe not,' Palmer went on. 'They think she was a victim of some nutter, and perhaps it's best we leave it that way. Well done Claire, good work.'

He sucked the end of his glasses whilst thinking aloud.

'I bet Tommy Vaughan had a fling whilst doing a Summer Season; it all adds up doesn't it, eh? He has his fling, and by the time the girl finds out she's up the duff he's off back to the bright city lights and his celebrity world, while she's back home carrying his little gift. See if we can locate the real mother, Margaret Collins; she obviously kept tabs on Vaughan, otherwise why should she be ringing the Solicitors about his will? She could provide the missing link in this case. We really need confirmation that the Vaughan on Lisa James's birth certificate is our Tommy Vaughan. If it is, then he doesn't look such a nice bundle of fun now, does he.'

Gheeta drew in breath and sighed.

'Dig anywhere long and deep enough, and you'll find dirt.'

'Who said that?'

'I did, guv.'

Claire and Lisa laughed.

'Bollocks!'

Palmer rose from his chair too quickly, and grasped his left thigh. Gheeta was worried.

'You all right, sir?'

'Yes, just my ruddy sciatica – lets me know I should have taken early retirement.'

He arched his back.

'Bloomin' discs, teach me to take the stairs two at a time. Right then,' he said, pulling on his coat. 'Time to pay a visit to Angela Hartman; probably a struggling writer in a cramped bedsit in a downtrodden slum area rife with crime, whose life is about to receive riches beyond her wildest dreams, courtesy of the philandering Mr Tommy Vaughan.'

'It's a semi in Ruislip,' Claire corrected him.

Chapter 12

They relaxed in the back of the patrol car on their way to Angela Hartman's Ruislip semi.

'There's a big memorial to the Polish war dead down here somewhere,' Palmer said, peering ahead as they travelled down the Westway. 'Always wondered why it's here. Probably 'cause they were based at Northolt Airfield, I suppose.'

Gheeta couldn't see any point in continuing that conversation. She was re-reading her notes on Hartman.

'This case is a bit like *Alice in Wonderland*, isn't it, guv? Just gets *curiouser and curiouser* as it goes on. Nothing seems to fit together.'

Palmer laughed.

'It's like all jigsaws Sergeant; you just need that one key piece to slot in, and all the rest falls into place. But I know what you mean. This one is a right brain teaser and no mistake.'

'Who's your money on, guv?'

'Who's my money on?' he chuckled. 'Nobody yet; could be we haven't even got the killer in the frame yet – or maybe there's more than one.'

'Yes, but the altering of the CDV points heavily to Bannerman.'

'It does, but what does she stand to gain by knocking off Vaughan? Not getting the shares back according to the will, is she? And it might not necessarily be her arriving at Bournemouth that she cut out of the CDV; she could have recognised somebody.'

'Blackmail?'

'No; a bit far-fetched that one, Sergeant.'

'I know, but I'm struggling for answers and all I get are dead ends. Nothing seems to be going anywhere.'

'It will – just you wait and see.'

Their car pulled up in front of a clean, modest, pre-war semi, with a well-kept front garden in keeping with the rest of the area. They adopted their "police eyes" automatically, checking for any curtain movement in the windows. Palmer held the iron gate open for Gheeta, and carefully shut it after them before following her up the flagstone path to the small porch. He pressed the bell, hoping that it wouldn't be one of those awful chiming ones. It wasn't; they heard it ring inside.

Angela Hartman was in her early fifties; slim, with hawk-like features, glasses, and hair cut straight in the Mary Quant 'curtains' style to the neck. Palmer had a distinct feeling of recognition when she opened the door, and he introduced himself and Gheeta.

Hartman led them through into her front room. It was small but comfortable, with her work station set up in the window bay; two comfy chairs, a sofa and a magazine table completed the furnishings.

'Sit down, please. Can I offer you tea?'

'No, no thank you, Mrs Hartman.'

'Miss, it's Miss Hartman.'

He smiled at her apologetically.

'Sorry, *Miss* Hartman. Well, hopefully we won't take up too much of your time today; you look like a busy lady,' he said nodding towards the workstation. 'We are investigating a series of murders; one of the victims was Tommy Vaughan, and we understand you had a long business relationship with him.'

He stopped, leaving it open as to which road of reply she took. Hartman looked stunned.

'Well, er… yes, I – excuse me. I had heard that Tommy passed away, but not in such circumstances - murdered you said? I'm a little shocked, to say the least.'

And she looked it.

'I'm sorry, we thought you were aware of it,' Palmer lied, having noted Hartman's obvious distress and mentally taken her off the suspects list. She composed herself and continued.

'We – that is, Tommy and I go back – *went* back a good few years, through thick and thin you might say. I worked for him as writer and script editor on his many television shows.'

'How did you two get on? Was he easy to work with?'

'We got on fine; we had our ups and downs, but to still be working with him after forty-odd years we had to be fairly compatible, didn't we? I knew him when he was a five bob a-night stand-up in back-street clubs, and I was still with him when he was at the top of... Oh my God!'

The penny had dropped.

'Do you suspect me? You do, don't you?'

'No, no – we are just trying to get a measure of the man. Was he good to work for?'

She gave a little laugh.

'He could be a right bugger, if you'll excuse the expression – oh, I shouldn't say that, should I? Shouldn't speak ill of the dead, but he was just typical of the entertainment industry; promised everything and gave nothing, like most in that business. You had to chase him for every penny owed; always going to 'see you alright'. God knows how much he actually owes me over the years…'

She laughed again.

'Oh Tommy, you poor darling. What an awful end.'

She dabbed her eyes with her sleeve.

'Interesting work you do, Miss Hartman?'

'Used to be, Superintendent, used to be; not so much now. Mostly after dinner speeches now for ex-MPs and retired footballers. Still, it pays the bills, which is the main thing.'

'Did you have any dealings with Tony Fox or Lisa James at Midland Television?'

'Yes, I'd known Tony almost as long as I'd known Tommy. God, Tony's death was a shock too, poor old chap; no doubt some idiot who didn't get the part he'd been promised and went over the top with revenge. He and Tommy were like twins, you know; like two peas in a pod. Tommy said Tony was the only producer he'd trust not to ruin his career. Lisa James doesn't ring a bell though.'

'Was Tommy on drugs?'

Palmer watched intently for any reaction, but the only reaction was more laughter.

'Tommy on drugs? Good Heavens, no! he was teetotal, you know; occasional cigar, but that was all. I would have known if there was anything else, because he used me as his personal gopher most of the time we were in the studios; Ange, go and get me this; Ange, can you find me that...'

She smiled at the memory.

'What about his enemies? We understand he had a few.'

'Who doesn't, in this business? Not really enemies though, more like jealous people. This business is full of broken promises and broken dreams, Chief Superintendent; they all think they're star quality, and ninety-nine point nine percent of them aren't. Tommy was, and he was also one of the lucky ones who kept going, not a flash in the pan; and to keep at the top, you had to sometimes walk over people, or drop them from the team. There would have been quite a few not mourning his passing, but I can't see anybody actually murdering him – or Tony, for that matter.'

'Can I ask you a personal question, Miss Hartman?'

'You can ask – I may not answer it, but you can ask.'

She smiled, and Palmer returned it.

'Is there any money in what you do?'

She laughed out loud.

'Basically, the answer's no. But it's better than working.'

She laughed again, and then became serious.

'To be honest there used to be, but not now. Luckily for me, I had Tommy and a couple of other 'names' who paid me a yearly retainer; other than that, you'd get one-off contracts for so many minutes of material for sketch shows, and maybe Christmas Specials. I hated those, because you never got repeats. But those days are long gone now. I'm only grateful that I'm at the end of my career now, Chief Superintendent. The house is paid for, and my national insurance stamps are fully paid up, so I'll get by on my old age pension when it falls due; and maybe write my memoirs, eh? Mind you, if I told the truth there'd be a few people who wouldn't want that published. Better have you lot protect me if I do.'

Palmer smiled.

'Not our department, I'm afraid. Did you visit Tommy at his summer season this year?'

'At Bournemouth? No, I sent him a few topical gags once a week; no need for the expense of a visit. He never paid for them either – don't think he will now…'

Both Palmer and Gheeta had picked up on the fact that she had *sent* him material for his act. So out went another contender for the *stuff* carrier.

'What about Tommy's daughter, did you ever meet her?'

He'd fired that one out of the blue for maximum impact, and maximum impact is what he got. Miss Hartman visibly tightened all over.

'D-daughter? Tommy had a daughter?'

'Yes, I'd have thought you would have known that, having been with him all those years.'

Palmer was convinced she knew from the way she had reacted to the question; shook rigid, with the colour draining from her face. He was damn sure she knew.

'Not the sort of thing he'd not have mentioned from time to time, surely?'

'I, err…I had no idea he had a daughter. He never mentioned her – no, never.'

Gheeta's mobile rang and she took the call, while Palmer prodded deeper.

'Apparently it was a long time ago, nearly forty years. Not ringing any bells in retrospect?'

'No, none – I never knew. There were always plenty of pretty girls around Tommy, but I never saw him with a child. A daughter? My-oh-my, how did he keep that from the tabloids?'

Gheeta interrupted.

'Sorry sir, but you ought to hear this.'

Palmer nodded for her to carry on.

'Claire's just had a call from Miss Bannerman. She's asking when are we going to send her the CDV we promised for viewing.'

Palmer was bemused.

'When? What's she mean, 'when?' She's had it and returned it.'

'Well, apparently she hasn't, sir. Claire's checked, and it was definitely delivered by our messenger to the agency office; but Miss Bannerman is adamant that she never got it or sent it back.'

Palmer spoke slowly. 'So some other bugger at her office intercepted it, had a gander, didn't like what they saw, changed it, and returned it.'

Gheeta nodded.

'Looks like it sir, yes.'

He stood up.

'Miss Hartman, thank you so much for your time, I'm sorry we brought a couple of shocks with us, but unfortunately we have to dash off. If we need to talk to you again I'll get my Sergeant here to give you a call; and hopefully there will be no more surprises.'

They hurried out and into the back of the waiting patrol car. Palmer gave the driver instructions and settled back.

'Well, well, well, Sergeant. Somebody at Bannerman's place is playing silly buggers with us, and I mean to find out who it is.'

Angela Hartman watched from the porch as the police car left, not knowing whether to wave goodbye as though seeing off an old friend; she decided not to and hurried back inside, closing the door.

Her heart pumped madly in her throat, and her hands shook. She wasn't cut out for this much excitement. She steadied herself with a few long gasps of air, took the phone off the desk, and dialled the Bannerman Agency.

Palmer was angry; very angry. He didn't take kindly to people who made his job more difficult than it already was, and on top of that list were those clever so-and-so's who had tried to put one over on him.

He turned to Gheeta beside him in the squad car.

'Sergeant, give Claire a call and get her to pull down a list of the Bannerman employees and run it against your existing data fields; see if we can't turn up a surprise or two. I am assuming you do have a way of getting an employee list on the quiet?'

He knew she would have some way of getting it.

'Yes sir, we've a secure line from our terminal to the Inland Revenue mainframe. We'll get the Bannerman Company tax reference number, and that will get us a full list of employees on the books. Be about an hour tops.'

She speed-dialled Claire and relayed the instruction. Palmer lent forward and spoke to the driver.

'Talk about big brother eh?'

He turned back to Gheeta.

'We wouldn't be contravening the Data Protection Act would we, Sergeant?' he said, a mischievous glint in his eyes. 'Because I couldn't possible sanction that you know.'

He was well aware that some of Gheeta's ways of collecting data and information strayed a little from the straight and narrow. She kept a straight face.

'You might think that sir, but I couldn't possibly comment.'

'Hmm.'

'Oh, and by the way sir, Claire said your wife rang to say not to bother about the paint. Benji's got it for you.'

Palmer visibly bristled.

'Bloody Benji, got nothing better to do all day has he, eh? Pottering about, poking his nose in where it doesn't concern him.'

'That's not very grateful. sir.'

Gheeta was on the wind-up trail.

'Seems to me he's saved the day for you, sir.'

'Saved the bloody day? All he's done is buy a pot of paint, Sergeant; and you make him sound like Biggles! Saved the day… I can see the local press headlines now:

"Benji Saves the Day Again! Hero Benji Flies into Save Palmer!'

He put on his best Terry Thomas accent.

"'I say Algy old chap, looks like Benji's saved our bacon once again, old sport!" "Dead right Biffo, he always comes to the rescue when all seems lost!" "What a spiffing fellow Benji is, don't yer think?" "Personally, old boy, I think he's a right little shite"! "Me too old chap!"'

Gheeta and the driver laughed at the accent. Then Gheeta had a question.

'Guv, who is Biggles?'

Chapter 13

Evening gloom was descending fast into night when they reached Knightsbridge and left the patrol car to wait for them round the back of Harrods. Palmer wanted to make an unannounced visit. He wasn't even sure the Bannerman office would still be open or anybody there at this time of day, but Miss Bannerman has struck him as the workaholic type that goes full throttle all day and unwinds in the evening while catching up with the backroom paperwork. He was a kindred spirit in that department; he was thinking about that, and all the times he'd left Mrs P on her own at short notice, working late into the evening to get paperwork up to date while case facts were fresh in his mind.

They jostled their way through the tourists and evening shoppers and into the Bannerman building foyer, when a thought struck him: he hadn't ever asked Gheeta if she was okay to work late. In fact, he couldn't remember one occasion in the past when they'd had a late call out that he'd even thought of asking if she had a previous engagement to go to; the same went for weekends and missed lunch hours. What if she'd got a chap and was going to meet him tonight?

He suddenly felt very guilty; the same feeling of guilt he sometimes got late at night, or in the early morning hours when he crept into bed beside Mrs P. He would lay there, wondering what a better life she might have had married to somebody in a normal job; somebody who came home at regular hours, and had holidays when they wanted them, and spent weekends with the family. But he never said anything to her, because she would only tell him not to be so silly. He didn't say anything to Gheeta either; he assumed she accepted the lifestyle, and embraced it with all its drawbacks. That was the only way they could function as a team. You couldn't plan your day in advance in their line of work.

The foyer of 172 Knightsbridge looked even more dingy and distressed in the worsening light of the evening as they took the stairs, and the old lift clanked past them going down as they trudged up. Gheeta noticed one occupant shrouded in the gloom of its interior as it passed them, somebody else working late.

'I think they call this exercise cardiac vascular, guv,' she panted, as they reached the Agency floor. 'It pumps the blood round fast and clears the arteries. Supposed to be good for you.'

'Why is it that everything good for you hurts,' said Palmer, leaning against the stair rail to get his breath back, 'And everything you like is bad for you?'

The Bannerman Agency Office was in darkness, and the door shut.

'Blast.'

Palmer had hoped for a nose round.

'Nobody working late when you want them to be. I hope the door's not alarmed.'

He pulled a set of skeleton keys from his jacket pocket and started to sort them; not an action strictly within the rules, but then Palmer felt that a slight bending of the rules was perfectly permissible if it led to solving a case quicker than sticking to those rules.

Gheeta put her laptop on the floor and knelt to peer through the large letter box, as he fumbled to sort out a suitable key from the bunch. The interior was quite well-lit by the reflected light from Knightsbridge streaming through the big front windows; well-lit enough for her to see Rebecca Bannerman sprawled face down on the floor of the reception area.

'Guv! Bannerman's in there on the floor – she's not moving guv.'

She barely had time to get her face away from the letter box before Palmer's size eleven hit the door just below the lock and it splintered, swinging open.

Rebecca Bannerman had died from repeated blows to the back of her head by a heavy blunt object. That object was the large glass ashtray from her desk, now tinged red with her blood and lying upside down next to her body.

Palmer bent close and moved around the body, taking care not to tread on or disturb anything in case he destroyed evidence Forensics might uncover: a fallen hair from the killer, an indentation in the carpet from the killer's shoe, or something the ultraviolet might show up.

Gheeta was on the mobile, calling in the troops. Palmer stood upright as she clicked off the phone.

'Well, well, well... and then there were four. Another one who maybe knew something and had to be silenced.

He looked around the main office.

'Or perhaps there was something here that had to be retrieved.'

Gheeta stood beside him.

'*Curiouser and curiouser*, guv.'

'Damn right there,' he said, as he wandered off through the main office and into Bannerman's office. 'Only one half-empty cup of coffee on the desk,' he said, touching it with the back of his index finger. 'And still a little warm, so she was here alone when the killer called.'

He opened a door at the back of the office. It led into a small store room. His voice changed.

'Now then, what have we here?'

His tone caused Gheeta to quickly join him, and they peered into a small editing suite. Palmer switched on the light with a pull cord.

'I would guess that somewhere in this little lot is a machine for editing and copying CDVs?'

Gheeta nodded and pointed.

'That one, guv. State of the art, too.'

'Hmmmmm, I think we'll let Forensics loose in here; but I'd like you and Claire to have a good look through this,' he said, as he turned back and indicated Miss Bannerman's computer on the desk, still switched on with the screen flickering. 'Could be a little gold mine of information, that could. Can you get into it?'

'Take a bit of time, guv; have to alter the modem setting so we can hack in, but having it still on helps.'

She took a USB from her pocket, plugged it into a side port and downloaded its contents onto the computer.

'Okay, that should do it – we'll be able to log in from our PC at the Yard. I've encrypted a log-in password for us to use; I'll need to leave it on, and should be able to download the whole of its contents in about an hour in the morning.'

'Right I'll designate this office a no-go area until you release it; otherwise some prat will come in and switch it off. What about the password – she was bound to have one on certain financial documents surely?'

'Passwords are no problem; bypass them in seconds.'

'So all this scary stuff we get told about changing your password every week is rubbish then?'

'Near enough guv, yes.'

The troops, as Palmer called SOCO, arrived in force: forensic officers, photographers and uniformed branch, plus the pathologist and the undertaker. Gheeta went to organise them, and Palmer wandered around snooping as the crime scene tape went up, cutting off access to the floor, and all the surfaces began to get dusted for prints. By the time they'd taken prints off all the staff tomorrow and eliminated the ones with alibis, the killer could be halfway round the world, thought Palmer. He hoped the ashtray might throw up a rogue print that didn't belong. Bannerman hadn't put up a fight by the look of it, so she probably knew the killer and let him or her in. Or maybe she'd been surprised by somebody waiting after work and hiding? Why oh why was there always more than one choice?

He strolled into the reception area again, which was a hive of activity overseen by Gheeta. He decided to stay out of it, and sat in the receptionist's swivel chair, studying the celebrity pictures on the walls; Bannerman certainly had an 'A' list rosta of clients.

One large photo brought him up sharp. Two faces smiled out at him from deckchairs on a sunny beach: two unmistakable faces, one being the receptionist and the other being Angela Hartman. The thing that really caught his attention was how very alike they looked.

'I knew it!" Palmer shouted out loudly, and most in the room turned towards him. He stood and looked closely at the photo. 'I knew I recognised her! I knew I'd seen those features before.'

Gheeta hurried across.

'Recognised who, sir? What features?'

He pointed to the photo.

'Her face, Angela Hartman's face; when she opened her door I had a feeling of recognition. Look at them, Sergeant, her and that receptionist who works here.'

He tapped the photo to emphasise his point.

'Look at them, they could be sisters – same nose, same sharp features! Damn, why didn't I realise it before?'

'They can't be sisters, sir, or their names would have tallied when we ran the comparison programme of names from the Inland Revenue list.'

'Not if they have different surnames.'

'Can't be different surnames if they're sisters.'

'Can be, if our receptionist is a Mrs and not a Miss, and has a married name,' he said, pointing to her hand in the photo. 'And if my eyes don't deceive me, that's a wedding ring on her third finger.'

Gheeta could have kicked herself.

'Why didn't I think of that? Christ, it's an obvious check to do; married or single. Shit! Sorry sir, I missed that one. Hang on a tick.'

She was off like a shot to Bannerman's office, ducking under the crime scene tape she'd stretched across the door not ten minutes before, and onto the deceased's computer, tapping away at the keyboard. Two minutes later she was back, looking a little pale.

'Our receptionist, sir – guess what? Her name is Collins, Margaret Collins.'

'Well, well, well, so *she* is Lisa James's mother then?'

'She is definitely Lisa James mother.'

'You sure?'

'Positive. Bannerman's password was simple to crack, and they use a basic Sage Payroll programme that lists all the staff: names, job title, salary, national insurance number, everything. Once I had her national insurance number I checked it on the DHS data base, and there she is; single mother, one daughter called Lisa offered up for adoption soon after birth.'

'Address?'

'Got it here Sir,'

She flourished a print out.

'Okay, let's have her into the Yard first thing in the morning.'

'On a murder charge, sir?'

'No, too early for that; we've no proof she had anything to do with this, so just 'assisting with enquiries' will do for now. No doubt she's involved somewhere, but the water's too muddy at present to make any charge that would stand up in court. Anyway, I can't see her knocking off her own daughter, can you?'

He sat back in the chair and swivelled round.

'Four murders now, and even the suspects are getting bumped off.'

Gheeta shrugged.

'Maybe Margaret Collins doesn't know Lisa James is her daughter? After all, she was offered up for adoption at an early age, and no contact since. Could be a one in a million coincidence they've both got mixed up in this together; and surely Angela Hartman would know if her sister's daughter was Lisa James, but she denied knowing her.'

Palmer rose and made to leave.

'Come on, Sergeant, nothing more we can do here. Leave SOCO to do their work; I reckon we both deserve a good night's sleep, as I've a feeling tomorrow will be a very interesting day indeed.'

An hour later, Palmer checked his watch in the moonlight as he silently opened his front door. Quarter to two, early by his standards; Mrs P would be fast asleep, and so would he be in five minutes' time.

He was well-practised in the art of opening and closing his door quietly in the dead of night. He slipped inside and shut it behind him, deftly double-locking the security lock. His faithful hound Daisy raised one eyelid and peered over the side of her dog bed further down the hall, but decided she was far too comfy to get up and offer any kind of greeting; and after last night, when she thought a plate of boiled bacon and pease pudding were on offer, only for Palmer to wake with hunger pains and come back down and eat the lot before she'd got to it, her master wasn't in her good books; so she relaxed back into doggy dreamland.

Palmer quietly took off his shoes and tiptoed quickly down the hall towards the staircase; too quickly, as it was at this point that he stubbed his toes against the heavy five litre tin of Golden Sunrise Benji had placed beside the hat stand. The yell of agony Palmer let out not only woke Mrs P, but most of the street too.

Chapter 14

It was another early morning for Palmer; he'd been at his desk since eight trying to make sense of all the variables the case had now thrown up. Gheeta came in just after nine, struggling with an armful of files, her laptop, mobile, and two coffees.

'Morning, guv. Front desk said you were in early, so I thought you'd like a coffee by now.'

She placed one in front of him. Having worked for some time with Palmer, she knew he'd sit and dehydrate away working on a case rather than break off for a minute or two to get sustenance. Food and drink just didn't seem to appear on his agenda; the best diet she'd ever had was working with Palmer. What she didn't know, of course, was that whatever time he got home at night there'd be a meal of gigantic proportions waiting by the microwave, courtesy of Mrs P.

'Hmm… thanks, very thoughtful of you,' Palmer said, and took the coffee and sipped it. 'That's good. I'm just trying to get my head round things before we see Margaret Collins. I take it they've brought her in?'

'Yep, they've got her in a holding room downstairs. I checked on her when I came in, she seems very cool and calm. Guv, I found a bit of information out that's very interesting. Hang on a tick.'

She opened the laptop and switched it on.

'I went surfin' over breakfast.'

'In the Thames?'

'Oh ha ha…'

She gave a false laugh, knowing that even a non-techie like Palmer was aware of what "surfin'" meant when referring to the internet. The screen lit up.

'I took a long look at the Bannerman computer's hard drive.'

'You went back to Bannerman's office last night?'

'No,' she said and smiled. 'You probably don't remember, but before we left her office I plugged a USB into one of her ports and downloaded a little app of mine, that gives me access to her machine from my machine.

'The only word I understood from that whole sentence was machine, but carry on.'

Gheeta thought about explaining what apps, ports and USBs were, but decided against it.

'Well, it seems from the account payments listed on her computer that Mr. Tony Fox was the recipient of several large payments called 'commission payments' over the last five years, and probably longer. It's only the last five years that are on the computer, so Claire's talking to the Bannerman Auditors to see if any similar payments were made before then. Now, Fox wasn't a client of theirs, and the payments were made quarterly with an annual increase; they were made to a company called Tony Fox Ltd., whose only income was these payments, and whose only directors were Tony Fox and his wife.'

'Do I sense backhanders?'

'I think you do, guv, big backhanders too. These payments were large; the last four totalled one hundred and twenty thousand over the year.'

'Jesus! Let's see if Claire's got anything from the auditors then. Well done Sergeant, nice work.'

He stood and walked to the door.

'What have you done, guv?' Gheeta asked in a concerned manner.

'Eh?'

'You're limping.'

'Oh, that… err… twisted my ankle on a kerb, wasn't watching where I was going.'

Gheeta rose to follow him out.

'Looks more like the kind of injury you'd get from stubbing your toe on a five-litre tin of paint at two in the morning.'

He stopped and turned to see her laughing eyes.

'Mrs P?'

Gheeta nodded.

'She got me on the mobile; said she just had to share it with someone. Said the hardest thing she'd done for months was keeping a straight face at breakfast as you hopped around the kitchen.'

'I knew I could hear her laughing.'

They joined Claire in the team room as she put down the phone.

'Bingo and double bingo! Fox had those payments for the last fifteen years, which is as far back as the auditors go with Bannerman. But this is the big one; the Bannerman Agency is subject to a takeover bid from a company called Universal Management in America, who have, or had, put in an offer of five and a half million quid!'

Palmer sat at a table and leaned back, his hands behind his head.

'Well, there's our motive. But where are our beneficiaries?'

'Obviously Miss Bannerman, for one,' offered Gheeta.

'Now deceased,' added Palmer.

Claire added. 'Well, I've worked out that Tommy Vaughan's shares in the Bannerman Company would be worth near three million if the offer went through.'

'He's also now deceased,' said Palmer.

'But the final recipient of his financial holding, Angela Hartman isn't deceased,' said Gheeta, thinking out loud.

'No,' Palmer agreed, 'She's definitely not deceased, unless something happened to her overnight; so she must be a major suspect now. Amazing how Vaughan's twenty grand investment has rolled up into three million! But we don't think she knows she's in line for it, do we?'

'What about Margaret Collins downstairs?' Gheeta said. 'She worked at Bannerman's, and could have had access to the financial goings on; and, if she is Hartman's sister, we could well have a conspiracy here.'

'We don't know that they are sisters yet,' Palmer pointed out.

Claire flew into a panic.

'Oh shit!'

She rifled through a heap of print outs and pulled one out, giving it to Gheeta.

'Sorry, completely slipped my mind when I went after the auditors. This came in earlier.'

Gheeta read it.

'They are sisters sir – this is from RBMD. The family name is Collins: Margaret has no alteration to that; Angela married at twenty-two, to a David Hartman, but they divorced and she went back to being Collins.'

Claire was a bit bemused.

'That doesn't make sense; she's still calling herself by her married name of Hartman – why do that if legally she resumed the Collins name?'

'It does make sense in the entertainment business.' Palmer explained. 'If she's worked up a good career as a writer under the Hartman name, why change it? That could confuse people, and cost her some work being offered. Right, let's go and see what our prim receptionist Margaret Collins has to say then.'

In the small confines of an interview room at Scotland Yard, Margaret Collins was feeling and looking quite apprehensive. Palmer smiled to try and reassure her that he and Sergeant Singh were not good cop bad cop as portrayed by television, and that he had no intention of whacking her with a rubber-clad lead pipe; although there had been times in the past, when interviewing known villains who were lying through their teeth, that he would have loved to have done so, and at the same time given their pompous "no comment" solicitors a whack as well.

He nodded to the uniformed WPC who was in attendance.

'Hello again, Miss Collins.' Palmer said, sitting down opposite her. 'Or may I call you Margaret?'

The killer smile flashed.

'Yes, yes please do.'

The WPC switched on the recorder.

'Thank you. I am Detective Chief Superintendent Palmer, and this is my deputy Detective Sergeant Gheeta

Singh; also in the room are WPC Arnold, and Margaret Collins. Now, Margaret, you are aware we are investigating the death of Miss Rebecca Bannerman last night at her Knightsbridge office, and the previous deaths of Tommy Vaughan, Tony Fox, and Lisa James. Let me say straight away that this is just an interview situation that is being recorded; that you are not under any arrest situation, and may leave at any time. Do you understand that, Margaret?'

'Yes, yes I do; I just hope I may be able to help you. This is so awful, truly awful. Rebecca was so young.'

'About the same age as your daughter.'

Miss Collins was visibly shocked, which turned into bewilderment.

'My daughter? What do you mean, my daughter?'

'Margaret, we are fully aware of your personal history; and of the child you and Tommy Vaughan had.'

She knitted her eyebrows into a quizzical look.

'I don't understand; that was nearly forty years ago. What possible connection could there be with all these murders?'

She leaned back and sighed deeply.

'In any case, Mr. Vaughan was never aware of the child. In those days there was a certain stigma attached to unmarried mothers, and it was all hidden away very discreetly; by the time our paths crossed again at the Agency, I was long forgotten in his memory. He didn't even recognise me.'

Her eyes widened.

'Oh no, you don't think I killed Mr. Vaughan as an act of revenge, surely? He never knew about the child; how could I possibly hold a grudge for forty years against a man who hadn't the faintest idea he was the father of my child?'

Palmer nodded his understanding.

'But you must have seen him, and presumably talked to him many times over the years. He was a main client of the Agency, so I assume he would be in and out quite a lot; and I find it hard to believe that the pair of you had an affair, and then didn't even acknowledge each other afterwards.'

She smiled.

'An affair? Oh no, Chief Superintendent, it wasn't like that at all. I met Tommy through my sister Angela, who was one of his writers. She took me to Bournemouth one year during his Summer Season there when she had a meeting with him about some television script, and he and I got on very well. I went along to the next meeting and… well, our relationship developed from there. But it lasted a mere two months, hardly an affair; I was just a silly girl, with silly notions about love, and as far as he was concerned he had a new plaything for the summer. When I found myself pregnant, our parents sent me away to relatives in Scotland, and the child was born and adopted there. Tommy never knew and neither did Angela. And that was that; I moved on with my life and I hope the child did too. I have never tried to contact her; it would be so unfair to her adoptive parents.'

Gheeta placed a hand on Palmer's arm urgently.

'A private word, sir?'

Palmer could tell by her manner it was serious.

'Excuse us for a minute, Margaret, if you would. Can we get you a drink?'

'No I'm fine, thank you.'

Palmer nodded to the WPC, and he and Gheeta left the room. Gheeta spread her arms in amazement.

'She doesn't know, guv! She doesn't know Lisa James was her daughter! Christ! How do we handle that?'

'I know, difficult situation. But I find it hard to believe, don't you?'

'Why? She wouldn't have been interviewed about Lisa's death, because the local CID wouldn't have dug deep enough to find out about the adoption before the case was transferred to us; the Bannerman Agency had no connection with Lisa James as she wasn't their client, so there wouldn't have been any contact there either. She's going to have to be told, guv. It could be the whole key to busting this case open.'

'Oh it's the key alright, Sergeant; but I've a nagging feeling it goes deeper than this. Other factors are at work here, and I don't know what they are – yet. Let's have a go from another angle.'

They went back into the room and retook their seats.

'Sorry about that, Margaret; things to be taken care of that had slipped my mind,' he lied. 'Right, where were we? Let's talk a bit about Bannerman's. How long have you been there?'

'Oh, twenty years or so? Seems like forever.'

'And what is your position in the company?'

'Well...'

She thought for a moment.

'I suppose my designated role is Office Manager; at least, that's what's on my employment contract.'

'Which means you do what?'

'Well, I generally keep things on an even keel.'

She laughed.

'Not an easy job, I can tell you.'

'Did Miss Bannerman have a secretary?'

'No, I took care of all that sort of thing for her: sorted the mail, raised the contracts, ran her engagement diary, all that sort of thing.'

'There must have been a lot of confidential material passed through your hands then.'

'I treated it all as confidential, Chief Superintendent; you mustn't let one client know what another is doing, or earning. War would break out!'

She laughed nervously.

'So you knew about the American offer?'

She stiffened visibly.

'Yes, I was aware of it.'

'Was Miss Bannerman in favour of it?'

'I really don't know the answer to that; she kept her cards very close to her chest.'

'Was Tommy Vaughan in favour of it?'

She was a little flustered by that.

'I, err... I- '

'He knew about it, didn't he.'

It was a statement not a question.

'I have no idea; I don't know whether any of the clients knew about it. It was all very confidential.'

'But Mr. Vaughan was a major shareholder in the company, you must have known that; so surely he would be made aware this offer was on the table?'

Gheeta's mind was racing to keep up with Palmer's. She'd seen him do this many times before; Margaret Collins was not proving to be the totally honest and open person they'd expected her to be, so Palmer was on a mission to slightly confuse and harass her, so that her mind couldn't quite keep up with which answer she ought to give so as not to undermine a previous one. It was only a matter of time before the house of cards would topple, and he'd still got the altered Bournemouth Station CCTV recording bombshell to drop on her.

Margaret Collins palms were glistening a little out of view beneath the table.

'I can't recall any correspondence to Mr. Vaughan on the matter.'

'Well, if you'd seen or typed a letter about a five million pound offer for the company I'm sure you would remember it.'

Gheeta made a move.

'Do you use Microsoft Word?'

'Pardon?'

'To type out the mail before printing it off the computer; it's the most common programme, comes pre-loaded in most computers.'

'Yes, yes I think so.'

Gheeta turned fully to Palmer and gave him an unseen wink.

'We can access that, sir, and print off all the letters going right back to when the computer was first installed. Even the deleted ones will be on the hard disk.'

'Good.'

Palmer put on his serious tone, and returned to Miss Collins's questioning.

'How did Miss Bannerman get on with the staff; any enemies?'

'Heavens, no! She was well liked by everybody.'

Her mind was panicking now after the Sergeant's interruption.

'I, err… come to think of it, I do believe there was a letter to Mr. Vaughan about the American offer – yes, yes I seem to recall one now.'

Bingo! Palmer had won round one; now onto round two. He reverted to a nicer tone.

'No matter, Miss Collins; our forensic people will check through all the mail on the computer as a matter of course, so any relevant letters will pop up. Now, what was the Agency's relationship with Tony Fox?'

Another little bomb exploded inside Margaret Collins's carefully rehearsed responses, blowing a hole in her defences.

'He used the agency's clients, as did many other producers.'

'Oh, he did that alright. Our researches into his department's accounts at Midland Television show that the Bannerman Agency accounted for over ninety percent of all his expenditure on artists; a little high, wouldn't you say, for one Agency to get all that business?'

'I really wouldn't know. I had little to do with that side of the business.'

'But you said you typed up the clients' contracts, so you would have noticed most going to Midland Television, wouldn't you?'

'They were standard pre-printed contracts on the computer that I just filled in with the details that Miss Bannerman gave me; then I printed them off and sent them out for the clients' signature prior to their engagement starting.'

Palmer turned to Gheeta.

'Can we look through those on the computer?'

'Yes sir, every one.'

Palmer smiled at Miss Collins.

'The wonderful world of technology; nothing ever deleted, not like the good old days of the shredder; it makes our job so much easier. What were the quarterly payments made to Tony Fox Enterprises for?'

Another bomb exploded in Margaret Collins's head; her mind was beginning to feel like a castle under a continued cannon attack. She sat silently for a while, as Palmer waited for an answer.

'I think I'd like to leave now, Chief Superintendent.'

'Yes, I expect you would, Miss Collins.'

The friendly 'Margaret' approach had gone.

'However, having had this little chat with you, it seems to me that that you were such a key person in that office for so many years, you probably know a lot more about these murders and the reasons why they were committed than you've told us so far. You may well not be aware that information you have is relevant, or indeed that it might be the catalyst that leads us to the killer, so I feel that whilst the murderer is out there somewhere, I must, for your own safety, keep you in custody. I am allowed to do this for forty-eight hours without charging you with anything. You may have a solicitor of your choice brought in to confirm this, or there is a duty solicitor available to you. The officer here will look after you and your wellbeing whilst here, and should there be anything you want to talk to me about, I'll just be two minutes away upstairs.'

He smiled a cold smile at Margaret Collins's shocked white face and left, with Gheeta a step behind him.

The adrenalin racing round Palmer's system had overwhelmed the pain of stubbed toes on a heavy paint tin, and replaced it with the excited anticipation he always felt as the various strings of a case started to knit together. He almost bounced into his office, followed by Gheeta.

'We are nearly there, Sergeant, nearly there!'

He hadn't noticed Assistant Commissioner Bateman, who had been looking out of the window and who now turned to greet them.

'Really? Are you, Palmer?'

Palmer pulled up quickly, his good mood turning to guarded anticipation.

'Oh, sorry sir; didn't know you were in here. But, yes, all the bits of the case are falling into place; shouldn't be long before we crack it now.'

Gheeta slid past and tried to make herself invisible behind her desk.

'Actually, Palmer, I wanted a private word with Sergeant Singh if I could.'

Palmer's brain raced.

'Of course, sir. I'll send her up to your office just as soon as she gets back.'

He handed Gheeta her laptop bag, which she had just put down, and ushered her out of the door.

'Same procedure as last time Sergeant, okay?'

Gheeta gave him a nod.

'Yes sir, same procedure.'

Then she was gone. Palmer turned to the Assistant Commissioner.

'Sorry sir, bit of a rush on at present – strike whilst the iron's hot and all that. What was it you were saying?'

'I was saying, Palmer that I do need some time with Sergeant Singh. It's rather important.'

'Really sir?'

Palmer went all serious.

'May I ask the purpose of this rather important meeting you wish to have with my Sergeant? After all, she is *my* second-in-command, and a very important and key person in my small, overworked and under-funded department; so I wouldn't like to think there were any plans afoot to, maybe, hijack her elsewhere?'

He sat on the edge of his desk, folded his arms in what body language translators call *combative posture*, and fixed the Assistant Commissioner with a cold, questioning glare.

'Well, err… actually, Palmer, we'd like her to set up a new IT Cyber Crime section within the forensic umbrella.'

Palmer slowly rose, walked to the door, and shut it. Then he took a loud deep breath and turned back to the Assistant Commissioner. The look on his face was certainly not friendly.

'Would you like my resignation now or on your desk in the morning, sir?'

This was a dodgy card for Palmer to play. AC Bateman had long nursed the ambition to get rid of Palmer, but due to Palmer's length of service and excellent case clear-up rate, it gave Palmer a slight edge over Bateman's superior rank with the top bosses and Home Office mandarins. But if Palmer went and Sergeant Singh followed, then it would backfire on Bateman as having been mishandled; and those above would not like that at all.

'What?' the Assistant Commissioner laughed awkwardly. 'No need for that, Palmer! We just thought...'

He didn't have time to say what 'they just thought' before Palmer interrupted.

'Detective Sergeant Gheeta Singh is a policewoman, sir, not a bloody administrator. She is a Detective Sergeant – does the word 'detective' mean anything to you, sir? It does to me.'

'Careful Palmer, don't overstep the mark now.'

'Overstep the mark? I think it's the faceless uniformed lot that inhabit the top floor that you refer to as *'we'* who have overstepped the mark – *sir*. My Sergeant has worked her butt off for this department, *my* department; her efforts have probably cut our arrest time by seventy-five percent, and our case clear-up is now one hundred percent – in case you hadn't noticed. I recall how the top floor wouldn't fund me for her research and extra work hours when I brought her into the department; and now the results of her efforts, unpaid in her own time, are so obviously advantageous to this department, you want to take her expertise and dump her in forensics, stuck behind a desk.'

The Assistant Commissioner tried to get in.

'She would have - '

Palmer ignored Bateman; he was in full flow, bit between the teeth, and had no intention of stemming the tide of his hatred of the 'top floor' while he had a good reason to let rip.

'And do you even see how offering that deal to her would totally undermine her confidence as a Detective and dampen her career aspirations, eh? She joined the force to be a policewoman, sir; to catch villains and murderers and bang them up. Same as I did. And now you want to put her into a little office administrating a computer department? Don't you see how that would stifle her completely? Don't you think that if Detective Sergeant Singh wanted to do that she would go and work for a bloody computer company, and earn fifty times what she gets here and have twenty times more free time? Let me tell you sir, and please pass this on to the top floor; Sergeant Singh is going to make a first class Detective Superintendent one day, with more skills than all of the other Superintendents put together, including me. So please, please don't shoot yourself in the foot now and shunt her into Forensics. If you do, I'll bet my pension she'll be gone within six months.'

The Assistant Commissioner tried again.

'We thought that she - '

Palmer wouldn't give way.

'Let me make a suggestion; you get Forensics to come up with one of their bright young things with computer skills, and I'll ask Sergeant Singh if she would train them up on our – *her* systems as we use them; I'll also have Claire involved. Forensics get their IT specialist, I keep the best Detective Sergeant I've ever worked with, you keep the best future Detective Superintendent you're likely to get, and top floor are kept happy. Not that I give a toss about them, sir.'

He relaxed onto the desk again, and awaited the answer. The assistant commissioner turned to look out of the window, his hands clasped behind his back; he thought for a while, before turning back and giving Palmer a nod of his head.

'Your idea would seem to satisfy all parties, Palmer. It could work; I'll run it past the powers that be.'

'And please make them aware of the alternative won't you, sir. Early retirement would suit me and Mrs P down to the ground,' he lied.

'I don't think it will come to that, Palmer.'

'I hope not, sir.'

The Assistant Commissioner nodded curtly and left. Palmer caught his own reflection in the window and spoke to it.

'*Justin Palmer my lad, you've still got it mate. You've still got it.*'

And with a self-congratulatory salute to himself, he fairly bounced out of the office and into the team room.

'You look like the cat that got the cream, sir.'

Claire couldn't help but notice the wide grin across Palmer's face as he bounced in.

'Just once in a while, Claire my dear, you get the satisfaction of turning the tables against the odds, and striking a blow for common sense. Seen Sergeant Singh?'

'Over in the corner sir.'

She pointed to where Sergeant Singh was standing, huddled over a desk with another WPC. Palmer joined them, and Singh looked at him expectantly.

'Should I pack my bags?'

'No, you should not. All sorted; I'll fill you in later.'

It was amazing how Sergeant Gheeta Singh felt elated by Palmer's words. She could give him a big hug; not that she ever would, of course.

'This is very interesting, sir.'

Gheeta pushed a report page across to Palmer.

'WPC Devlin here went to interview Lisa James's foster parents in Edinburgh.'

Palmer nodded hello to the WPC.

'And?'

'They say that Lisa made contact with her real mother about a year ago.'

Palmer sat down.

'Did she now? That is interesting'

WPC Devlin took up the story.

'They apparently never made a secret that she was adopted, right from the age when she would understand what it meant, sir. But it was only about a year ago that she expressed any interest in it, and asked if they would be upset or mind if she tried to find out who her real parents were. They had no objections and even if they had they couldn't stop her legally. Anyway, as far as they know she was able to find her mother and start a relationship, but never found her father. She was quite annoyed that the real mother wouldn't give any information on him.'

Palmer rubbed his chin thoughtfully.

'When you say she started a relationship with her real mother, what does that mean?'

The WPC looked at her copy of the report.

'Well, according to the parents Lisa traced her real mother to London, and usually spent some time with her at the weekend, about once a month. They didn't ask for any details as they weren't too happy about it, but didn't want to upset Lisa.'

'I bet they weren't too happy about it. Well done, Devlin; nice work.'

'Thank you, sir.'

Devlin went back to her desk. Palmer thought for a moment.

'Well, it seems Margaret Collins has forgotten about those cosy weekends with her daughter doesn't it, eh? Why would she want to keep them a secret from us?'

'We could ask her sister, sir?' suggested Gheeta.

'Yes, there's quite a few things I'd like to ask Angela Hartman. Get her brought in tomorrow, under caution.'

'Oh Christ, I nearly forgot!'

Gheeta fumbled through the papers on the desk and pulled one out.

'Forensic report from the Bannerman Office; it confirms the CCTV recording was altered on the Bannerman office machine.'

Palmer nodded.

'Had to be, didn't it?'

A sly smile crossed his lips.

'Those Forensics people are amazing with what they can do these days. Be a nice career for somebody to get in there.'

Gheeta didn't rise to the bait. A whoop of delight from Claire startled the pair of them.

'Got it! The ten-million-pound letter!'

Gheeta leant down to look at Claire's screen. Palmer was lost.

'The what?'

Gheeta explained what she was looking at.

'It's the letter from Bannerman to Tommy Vaughan about the American offer for the business; that Miss Collins had conveniently forgotten.'

The printer spewed out a copy that Palmer picked up and read in silence.

'Damning stuff, isn't it?' he said, quoting from it. *'Delighted to tell you we have received confirmation of the offer we spoke about, blah blah blah… your shareholding in Bannerman will be transferred to blah blah blah… transfer forms for your signature enclosed… regards, Rebecca.'*

'The transfer forms would have been standard share ownership transfer forms,' explained Claire. 'But he never signed them because the Companies House register still has him down as owner of forty-nine percent of the Agency.'

Gheeta had spotted something else.

'Sir, have you noticed the date on this letter? It's the day before we saw him in Bournemouth. So if this was taken by hand to him the next day, the day he was murdered, it could be the *stuff* we are looking for.'

'Of course!'

Palmer clapped his hands.

'Of course it is, and he'd be expecting it too; it says here, *'the offer we spoke about'*, so he knew all along what was going on; and he also knew he was about to become very rich by way of those shares increasing in value.'

Palmer thought out loud.

'So, if we assume Margaret Collins knew about the offer, and knew that he'd left the Bannerman shares to her sister Angela Hartman in his will, she now knew that if he transferred them to the American buyers it would cut out her sister; and possibly her too, if the sisters had talked about it. But, she had the inside information about the America offer, and her sister Angela didn't. Angela wasn't aware just how valuable those shares were going to be; valuable enough to make sure Tommy Vaughan didn't sell them to the Americans himself, pocket the cash and leave Angela out of the picture.'

'Yes,' Gheeta added. 'And if he was dead then the last will he made stands, and Angela would still be his beneficiary for the shares; so she would be the one selling to the Americans and taking the money. It has to be Margaret Collins at Bournemouth, sir, because she would have been responsible for opening the Bannerman office mail, including the one we sent with the Bournemouth station CCTV recordings; and she'd have known that Bannerman would have recognised her, so she altered it and returned it without Bannerman even seeing it. The perfect crime.'

Palmer nodded.

'Yes, but not so perfect because she didn't know we had spoken to Rebecca Bannerman about looking at it; and when Bannerman said she hadn't had it, and we said we had sent it, Bannerman would have asked Miss Collins about it because she dealt with all the post. Collins would have denied they'd received it, having already brought it back to us personally. And then...'

He thought for a moment.

'Either Collins realised the game would be up when we sent another disc over, or Bannerman guessed what Collins had done and gave her some kind of ultimatum on the shares. I don't know which.'

'Well,' Gheeta shrugged. 'You could offer up a host of different scenarios on that one, guv, and they could all be a million miles off course.'

Palmer needed time to collect his thoughts and put things in order in his head.

'Tomorrow is going to be interesting with both sisters in here. Keep them apart at all costs; don't want any collusion on alibis, although I bet Collins has used her one phone call to ring her sister. Hey ho – going to be interesting, very interesting. But now it's time to go home. With a bit of luck, it's Mrs P's toad in the hole tonight; food from the Gods.'

Claire held up a hand to stop him as he went to leave the team room.

'There's one other strange thing that's come up on the artists' residuals, sir; it seems they weren't getting any.'

Palmer had had enough for the day.

'In the morning, Claire; tell me all about their residuals, whatever they are, tomorrow. Goodnight all.'

And he was gone. Claire looked to Gheeta and shrugged.

'Do you want to know about the residuals, or will tomorrow do for you too?

Gheeta smiled and took a seat.

'Go on. I can see you're dying to tell somebody about the *residuals*, so fire away.'

Chapter 15

Mrs P made a lovely toad in the hole; she also made a lovely dumplin stew, and a lovely pease pudding and gammon as well. Palmer sat back in his kitchen chair and looked at his empty plate. All his favourite dishes were probably bad for him, but all were very tasty and devoured with great joy.

Mrs P was out at her Gardening Club evening, which had been re-arranged at another member's house because Mrs P's stairs were, as she told the members, 'being decorated'. So Palmer found his meal waiting under the hot plate in the oven, and had tucked into it with great enthusiasm. A fair dollop of brown sauce and a mug of strong tea had capped it off wonderfully. Nothing beats home cooking, especially when somebody else cooks it.

Daisy the dog looked at him mournfully when shown a clean plate before he washed it. He gave her a 'beef jerky' dog treat, which she accepted ungratefully, before beating him into the lounge and up onto his favourite armchair. She wouldn't have dared jump onto it had Mrs P been around, but Palmer let her be and settled onto the sofa with the local paper to read. The local paper lasted about a minute and a half; full of local council stories, pictures of old ladies complaining about post office closures, bus route closures, surgery closures and more obituaries than a plague could produce.

Palmer didn't want to grow old. He feared it really; when a man passes fifty, a sort of growing fear invades the mind every now and then, with flashes of wheelchairs, walking frames, pills and old folks' homes full of zombie-like skeletons, welded to threadbare armchairs and watching daytime television. Anyway, he didn't feel old; he didn't even feel middle-aged really. He wondered if he was immature; he was always one to look forward to the future, not backwards to the past. Anyway, who cares? As long as Mrs P loved him enough to make him toad in the hole once in a while, he couldn't care less.

Yes, he was definitely immature. He blew a raspberry to old age, and jumped athletically up from the sofa to take Daisy out for a walk, only to be brought up short as his sciatica shot down one leg and reminded him that he might feel young in mind, but just remember how old he was in body.

Chapter 16

'They don't live together, do they?'

Sergeant Singh was thinking aloud. It was eleven o'clock the next morning, and she and Palmer were at their desks in his office; he was reading through the transcript of the tape from the Margaret Collins interview.

'Who doesn't live together?'

'Margaret Collins and Angela Hartman, they're sisters, aren't they? One's a spinster and the other is divorced, so you'd think they might get together. But they don't live together, do they?'

'No.'

'So that means that when Lisa James went looking for her mother, she was looking for Margaret Collins. She would have found the family home at Ruislip, and when she turned up there she found Angela Hartman née Collins, her real mother's sister. That would answer the question of why Margaret Collins was bemused by us asking about her daughter; Lisa's adopted parents thought she was spending time with her real mother, but it was her mother's sister she was staying with. She hadn't contacted her real mother. But was she aware of that?'

'I see what you're getting at; you're assuming Angela Hartman didn't tell Lisa she was her aunt, and let her believe she was her real mother. Let's think this through then, like Angela Hartman would have done. There on the doorstep is a lady who thinks you are her mother; presumably she has asked if you are Margaret Collins…'

'Hang on, guv, one other thing: we are assuming Angela doesn't know about the child her sister had. But, come on; your sister leaves home and goes to Scotland for a year, for no real reason; surely you'd ask questions when she got back, and maybe put two and two together?'

'Or maybe Margaret told Angela about it when the kid was adopted and she came back home?'

'But then why wouldn't Angela put Lisa right when she turned up on her doorstep? Why would she go along with Lisa thinking she was her mother? Got to be a big reason for not saying *'you've got the wrong one, it's my sister you want'*; must be a good reason.'

A light came on in Palmer's brain. 'Exactly, and what bigger reason than a huge amount of money? If Tommy Vaughan had told Angela Hartman he'd left the Bannerman shares to her in his will, to keep her happy after writing stuff for him for little money for all those years, she might think that if a daughter of Tommy comes out of the woodwork, Tommy might be inclined to change the will in that daughter's favour, as a payback to her for all the years of ignoring her!'

Gheeta nodded.

'Or, if he didn't, then that daughter might see fit to contest the will in any case; and in this case, with the support of her real mother and the birth certificate, she would probably win.'

'So Angela Hartman loses the money either way. That's a huge motive for her to keep the daughter and mother from meeting, and in the last resort a huge motive for murder.'

Gheeta couldn't quite believe that.

'Your own niece? Kill your own niece, guv?'

'I've known criminals kill their own mother for much less money, Sergeant. It all ties together nicely. Lisa would have spent odd weekends at Angela Hartman's house, without Margaret Collins knowing and her adoptive parents under the impression she'd found her real birth mother; they'd be none the wiser. Have they brought Hartman in downstairs yet?'

Gheeta made an internal call to find out.

'No, not yet; she wasn't at the house. They're trying to trace her now. I'll go and give them a hand.'

She left the office. Palmer closed the tape transcript folder and pushed his chair up onto its back legs, resting it against the wall, and put his feet on the desk and his hands behind his head.

This was a bewildering case, and no mistake about it. Was he mistaken about Margaret Collins? Was she innocent, or was she very, very clever? Did she edit the Bournemouth recording? Was she protecting someone, namely her sister Angela? And what of Angela Hartman née Collins? She was beginning to look like a wolf in sheep's clothing. One thing was for sure; between them they held the answer to four murders, and between them they possibly committed all four as well! But the mystery of who did what to who, why and when was still to be unravelled.

Gheeta came back in after a few minutes.

'She's working at the BBC Television Centre, apparently recording a game show. Do we pull her out, guv?'

'We most certainly do.'

He swung his feet off the desk too fast, and his chair, and him, toppled sideways onto the floor. Palmer looked up at his Sergeant.

'Rather than standing there, Sergeant, trying, not very successfully, not to break into laughter, you might give me a hand to get up.'

Chapter 17

The Duty Officer at BBC studios held his finger to his lips as he led the pair of them along a corridor to the control room. He pointed through a glass door to where the programme producer and his staff were busily operating various slide switches, watching a bank of TV monitors in front of them that showed the feed from each camera on the studio floor; only the screens showered their light onto the room, which was otherwise in darkness. The Duty Officer indicated a red light above the door.

'When that goes green, we can go in.'

He pointed out the occupants.

'Director, producer, his assistant, vision mixer, runner, script editor; that's Angela Hartman, the one you want to see.'

Angela Hartman was following the lines on a script in front of her with a pen. All inside the room had their backs to the door, and so were unaware of Palmer, Singh and the Duty Officer waiting outside.

Gheeta strained to see what was showing on the screens inside, but each one was the picture from a different camera. She could see what she assumed was the compere of the show; a vaguely familiar face who was waving his arms about excitedly and talking to somebody. Other screens showed the person he was talking too, the audience looking bored, a large fridge which Gheeta assumed was the prize, and a flashing technicolor scoreboard with a human Barbie doll pointing at it. The audience responded half-heartedly to a large APPLAUSE sign being held aloft by a floor manager, and then as the applause died down the people in the control room relaxed, stretched, and flopped about as though they'd just run a marathon.

The red light turned green, and the Duty Officer told Palmer to wait while he went in and had a few words in the director's ear, which he did. The director turned to see Palmer, who took out his warrant card and pressed it against the glass; why he did that he didn't know, as the Duty Officer would have told the Director who he was and why he was there. The director leant back in his chair to look along the line of his staff and called out to Angela Hartman, who looked up and back at him.

He pointed towards the door. She recognised Palmer and gave a smile and a little wave as she gathered her handbag and script. Then she stood up, and as quick as a flash ran out of the emergency exit at her end of the control room. The speed of her exit left Palmer in no doubt as to her motive.

'Shit, she's doing a runner. Come on!'

He was quickly through the door and into the control room, with Gheeta close behind him. In the half light, he stumbled over the staff coats and belongings dumped on the floor behind their chairs, his size elevens leaving their mark on a few iPads and tablets as he made for the door Hartman had used. The more agile Gheeta was past him and through the door first.

Not having a head for heights, Palmer was a bit taken aback as he followed her through the door to find himself on a small steel gantry, at the top of a steel lattice staircase that led from the control room down to the studio floor, a good distance below him. Television studios are a bit like air hangars, with a control room set high in one corner; a thing Palmer had never realised before, having never been inside one. Below him, a bewildered studio audience and floor staff gazed up as Hartman descended the stairs to the studio floor, followed rapidly by Gheeta who was taking the stairs two at time. She reached the studio floor and barged through a line of participants in the show, who weren't really sure whether this was all part of the next game they would have to play for a chance to win the fridge.

Gheeta caught Hartman halfway across the studio, and had her face down on the floor and handcuffed without much resistance. The audience applauded: *was this part of the show?* The confused floor manager was jabbering away into his radio mic, trying to get confirmation that this was for real and not a late addition to the show; the compere fled to the wardrobe room, fearing an attack on his life from some crazed fan he'd probably denied an autograph to at some time earlier.

Palmer reached the studio floor well out of breath, and seeing Gheeta had the situation with Hartman under control, he waved his arms in a calming motion to the audience and told them loudly: 'No need to worry everybody. We are the real police, and everything is under control. Just remain where you are, and the recording will continue in a few minutes.'

He turned to two uniformed security men who were arriving at his side.

'Give us a hand to get this lady out of the studio, lads. There's a patrol car waiting outside.'

They hoisted Hartman up from the floor, and frog-marched her away. Palmer turned to Gheeta, who was brushing down her standard issue trousers with her hand.

'Well done, Sergeant; are you okay?'

'Yes, I'm fine sir.'

'Good, well done.'

Meanwhile the studio had fallen silent, and all eyes were on Palmer. He felt a sort of expectancy from them, so he turned and, for some reason, bowed. And they, for some reason, applauded.

Chapter 18

'Right then.'

Palmer sat down at the table in the interview room, alongside Sergeant Singh and opposite Angela Hartman and her solicitor. She had chosen to have her own solicitor with her rather than the duty one, and as he had been tied up with another case in court, the interview had been postponed for a day until he was free. This had given the team more time to prepare their attack, and had given Palmer time to lounge in a hot bath the night before and get a good night's sleep; safe in the knowledge that the case was fast coming to a conclusion, and a few hours in the interview room with the Collins sisters would unearth all the answers, and tie it all up neatly for the CPS to start prosecutions.

He cleared his throat and switched on the recorder.

'Interview Room Three, New Scotland Yard. Those present are myself, Detective Chief Superintendent Justin Palmer, Detective Sergeant Gheeta Singh, Miss Angela Hartman, and her solicitor. The time is ten thirty a.m. Miss Hartman is under caution in connection with four murders.'

'All unproved,' Hartman's solicitor interrupted.

Palmer ignored him. Palmer didn't like solicitors; in fact, he didn't like any of the so called *professional* classes, which included solicitors, MPs, estate agents, bankers, landlords, consultants and the like. His opinion was that they were all parasites on the working class. He didn't even look at Hartman's solicitor as he sat back, loosened his tie and continued.

'Miss Hartman, if you do not wish to answer any of the questions put to you, would you please say clearly '*no comment*'.

Hartman nodded. He continued.

'Miss Hartman, when did you first find out that Lisa James was your sister's daughter and your niece?'

He hit her hard with his opening question. Angela Hartman looked genuinely stunned.

'What? I didn't know she was!'

She appeared to be taken aback and surprised; but was she faking it?

'Lisa James came to visit you about six months ago, didn't she?'

'She… she may have popped in to talk to me about a script or a show, yes; quite possibly. I can't remember.'

'Miss Hartman, she did not 'pop in' to talk about anything connected with her work or your work. We have checked all the records at Midland Television, and you were not involved in any of Lisa James's programmes or projects; in fact, your name does not appear in any of her paperwork at all. We know that Lisa James was the illegitimate child of your sister Margaret Collins and the deceased celebrity Tommy Vaughan, and that she was given up for adoption at birth. You may or may not have known that prior to her visiting you while she was trying to trace her real mother – her *real* mother being your sister Margaret Collins.

'We know from her adoptive parents that she was trying to trace that real mother; they were party to this and had given their approval. In fact, she had told them that she had succeeded and traced that mother, your sister, and was spending time with her on occasional weekends in London. Lisa James had traced her mother by the surname Collins from her birth certificate, and also the mother's address it listed. That address was previously your parent's address; where you and your sister Margaret were brought up is now your address.

'So, I suggest that one day Lisa James turned up at your door asking for a 'Miss Collins', your maiden name, and you told her you were Miss Collins; which was true, as you are now divorced and use your maiden name Collins on everything except your work, where you are established as Angela Hartman and continue to use that name. Believing you to be her real mother, Lisa announced she was your daughter, totally unaware that there were two

Miss Collinses: you and your sister. You didn't put her right, did you? Why not?'

Hartman shook her head in a disbelieving manner.

'I'm sorry, Superintendent, but this is all fiction.'

'Why did you run away when we came to arrest you at the studio?'

Silence. Then she replied:

'I don't know.'

'Innocent people don't usually run away.'

'It was a silly thing to do, I realise that now. But at the time I just did... I don't know why.'

'I know why. You knew the game was up, didn't you? How do you think a jury will react to your running away – pretty condemning, isn't it?'

Hartman's solicitor whispered into her ear. She nodded.

'No comment.'

'So why didn't you tell Lisa James you were not her real mother? There must be a reason?'

'No comment.'

'You didn't tell her because you knew of her existence all along, didn't you? Maybe your parents told you all those years ago, when Margaret disappeared to Scotland for a year to give birth; or maybe Margaret told you in secret, sister to sister, that she was pregnant before telling your parents? You were, after all, instrumental in introducing her to Tommy Vaughan, and probably knew that a relationship between them was happening. Did Margaret confide in you, Angela? I would imagine finding herself pregnant at seventeen, in an age where such things were frowned on, is the sort of burden she might share with her sister for support. Did she?'

'No comment.'

Palmer exhaled loudly and leant back in his chair.

'Miss Hartman, if you are going to reply '*no comment*' all the time we might as well finish this interview here and now. I will refuse bail, and remand you in prison until a trial where a jury will take your '*no comment'* replies to my questions as '*I have no defence to offer'*, and convict you on all counts.'

He turned to the solicitor.

'Would you like a few words with your client? I'll give you two minutes.'

He spoke into the recorder.

'Superintendent Palmer and Sergeant Singh are leaving the interview room. Interview paused at ten thirty-six.'

He ejected the tape, put into a tape bag which he sealed, got the solicitor to sign across the seal, and left the room with Gheeta. The duty officer looked up and smiled from his desk in the corridor as they approached from the interview room.

'Anything you want, sir?'

Palmer shook his head, as he and Gheeta stood by the desk.

'No thanks, George. Mind you, you a bright light and a rubber-coated lead pipe might help.'

'One of those is she?'

'Well, I hope her brief talks some sense into her; or we'll be here all night at the rate we're going.'

The phone on the desk rang, and the officer answered it before looking up at Gheeta.

'For you, Sergeant,' he said, and handed the phone over.

'Hello DS Singh here... Hi Claire... Has it? Okay, see you in a few minutes.'

She handed the phone back and turned to Palmer.

'The CCTV copy from Bournemouth has arrived; the unabridged version. Shall I take a look, or shall we wait until you're free?'

'Aha!' Palmer said excitedly. 'Well, this will add a new dimension to things one way or the other won't it, eh? No, you go and take a look; and then come back down and fill me in.'

Gheeta left them and Palmer returned to the interview room, where solicitor and client were deep in whispered conversation. He sat down without a glance towards them, put a new tape in the machine and switched it on.

'Interview Room Three, ten forty-five a.m. Those present are myself, Detective Chief Superintendent Palmer, Serial Murder Squad; Angela Hartman; and her solicitor.'

'Jameson, Edward Jameson; of Jameson, Blunt and Company,' Hartman's solicitor identified himself. Palmer ignored him.

'Miss Hartman, I must remind you that you are under caution. You do understand that, don't you?'

'Yes.'

'Good, then let us continue. You had a long business relationship with the deceased Tommy Vaughan, didn't you?'

'Thirty years.'

'I understand from our enquiries that he was a bit of a skinflint; careful with his money. Did he pay you well?'

'Writers don't get paid well, Superintendent.'

'It's Chief Superintendent. What about the shares he promised you?'

'Shares?'

She was jolted a bit by that.

'Yes, we know that he owned a considerable amount of shares in the Bannerman Agency, and you were to have them in the event of his death.'

It was a statement not a question. She nodded, as though a little confused.

'He may have hinted in a joking way at some time about that, but I never took it seriously. He was always going to see me okay, as he put it.'

'Somebody called Collins, your real name, took it very seriously; they tried to get information about his will from Mr. Vaughan's solicitor. That was you, wasn't it?'

'No,' she stumbled over the words. 'No, not – no, it wasn't me. No.'

'So you are implying it was your sister then? She is, of course, a Collins as well.'

Edward Jameson, of Jameson, Blunt and Company held up a hand to prevent his client replying.

'I must protest at that assumption, Chief Superintendent. My client has not said anything to imply it was her sister; she has merely stated that it was not her who approached Mr. Vaughan's solicitor.'

Palmer glared at him, and slowly turned the glare into his killer smile.

'Of course, how silly of me to assume that either of the sisters approached Mr. Vaughan's solicitor. It must have been somebody else who just happened to have the same surname. Now, I wonder why a complete stranger called Collins would do that. Any suggestions, Mr. Jameson?'

Edward Jameson, of Jameson, Blunt and Company fiddled with his watch, somewhat embarrassed. Palmer carried on.

'Miss Hartman, I am putting it to you that you knew full well that Tommy Vaughan had bequeathed those shares to you. Whether he had told you, or your sister, who worked at the agency and would have known what was going on told you, matters not. But one of you made that call to Mr. Vaughan's solicitor to check it out; especially after the American offer came in, which I have no doubt your sister made you aware of?'

'She did mention it, yes.'

'I expect she did, and I expect she also mentioned how much the offer was for. After all, she typed all the letters between Rebecca Bannerman and the American Party's representatives. And no doubt on learning of the amount involved, you would have worked out that should Mr. Vaughan die, those shares would come to you and be worth a few million pounds; but, if Mr. Vaughan was made aware of the dea,l he might be tempted, very tempted to revoke anything in his will and keep the shares for himself. That presents a big motive to wish him dead.'

Palmer was enjoying this; things were pulling together nicely.

'So, let us assume that that was your position; and then out of the blue, who should come knocking on your door but Tommy Vaughan's long lost daughter, looking for her mum. What a threat that was to your nest egg as well, eh? If she actually found her real mum, the next step might well be to find her real dad too; and that couldn't be allowed to happen, could it? No, because Tommy Vaughan might come over all guilty about his parental neglect of his daughter, and make amends by transferring the shares to her once he was aware of their value. Or, if he didn't do that before he died, the daughter would have a very good case to challenge the will in court over who should be the beneficiary of the shares. So that was why you decided to pretend you *were* Lisa James's real mother, while you worked out a plan of action to make sure you kept the shares, wasn't it?'

'No, nothing of the sort.'

'So what other reason is there for pretending to be your sister, and Lisa James's real mother?'

'I… I thought it would hurt Margaret.'

'How? How could it possibly hurt her? She would probably be very excited at seeing her own child after so long.'

'She suffered enough at the time; I didn't want to have it all dragged up again after all these years. I was protecting her.'

'Rubbish, you were protecting your own inheritance. You could see the money slipping from your grasp, couldn't you? After all those years of working for Tommy Vaughan – not a nice man, not a very generous or gentlemanly man, in fact a bit of nasty type so it would now appear; he took you along, on a promise of great rewards in the future, while giving you a pittance at the time. And now you were so nearly there; you could almost reach out and grasp the money; so you had to do something. Lisa James had to be put out of the picture, and quickly; so you murdered her.'

'I didn't!'

Miss Hartman was sobbing uncontrollably as she tried to get the words out.

'I thought – I really thought it best to keep things as they were; keep Lisa in the dark, and then we'd all benefit.'

'No, you didn't.'

Palmer knew she was lying.

'You knew she'd rumble your little pretence sooner or later, or maybe she'd look up Tommy Vaughan; and either way the money would disappear from your grasp. You could easily have been truthful with her, and she might well have shared the windfall with her real mum, and you, her aunt. There would certainly be enough money to keep the three of you in clover for life.'

'I don't know.'

Hartman was trying hard not to break down completely. Palmer rubbed his chin in thought. He thought it time to switch tack to his favourite scenario.

'Of course, on the other hand, maybe Lisa was the bitter one, eh? Bitter that she had been left for adoption, maybe she wanted to find her real parents and confront them; have her revenge. Maybe she had done her homework, and found out that Tommy Vaughan, the big celebrity, was her father? Perhaps she knew already.'

He noticed Hartman was nodding as she sobbed. He'd got there; at last, he'd hit the right vein.

'Maybe she wasn't looking for a tearful reunion; maybe she wasn't the nice little daughter, but the nasty little assassin coming for her bounty, eh? She didn't know about the money, she couldn't have; but she knew how big a star Tommy Vaughan was, and she was going for payback. Oh yes, she'd been abandoned by a rich star who'd dumped her like a toffee wrapper, and now she was going to have her day, was that it? And her day would have finished your nest egg for good, eh? That's the real story, isn't it Miss Hartman?'

'Yes, yes.'

She lost control, and started wailing and sobbing as she let out the truth.

'She didn't know who I really was, she thought I was her real mother. She knew all the facts of her birth and the adoption; she knew Tommy was her father, and she was going to sell the story to the highest bidder; she wanted him destitute and on the streets. She was so angry. I couldn't let that happen; I couldn't let the newspapers get hold of the story, or Margaret would be crucified along with Tommy.'

'And your subterfuge would be found out, and you'd be finished too. So you killed her.'

'No, no it wasn't like that.'

'Oh, it was like that Miss Hartman. You were at the Midland Studios the day Lisa James was killed. We've checked, you were working there. What happened?'

Miss Hartman regained some composure, blew her nose, and sat back dabbing at her tears.

'It was just a normal day at the studios. We were running through a game show format; nothing to do with her. She came over to me during the lunch break in the canteen, and said had I got a minute to talk through something after I'd finished for the day; so I went to her office after we'd closed down - '

'What time was that?'

'We wrap things up at nine, so say about nine thirty.'

'What happened?'

'She was very excited, almost ecstatic. She said that Tommy and I were in good company. She'd found out something about Tony, Tony Fox; something to do with him and the Bannerman Agency; and she was going to, as she put it, blow him out of the water too.'

'What was it she'd found out about Mr Fox?'

'She wouldn't say – she said she'd have his job within a month, and neither I nor Tommy Vaughan would ever work at Midland TV again.'

'So you killed her. How?'

'Superintendent, I didn't mean to kill her, I really didn't. We argued a lot; I kept up the pretence of being her mother; I said we should be building bridges between us as mother and daughter, not being so hateful. Then she slapped me, calling me a… a fucking tart who dumped her baby and forgot it. I could only think of the effect that would have had on Margaret, her own daughter slapping her and using those words. I was so very angry and I don't know why but I hit her back with one of her own award plaques. I lost it, Superintendent, I lost my temper.'

She brushed aside her solicitor's efforts to silence her.

'I just hit her, and hit her, and hit her.'

She put her face in her hands and collapsed forward onto the desk, sobbing.

'Okay,' Palmer said, softening his tone. 'We'll get you some counselling help, a nice cup of tea; then we'll take a break and come back to this tomorrow. One thing I have to know though before I finish with this interview; did you tell Margaret about any of what you have told me today?'

'No, none of it. How could I? How could I tell my sister that I'd killed her daughter? How could I?'

The tears flowed. Palmer checked his watch.

'It is now ten past eleven, and this interview is terminated.'

He stopped the tape and did all the required signing procedure before advising the solicitor of what he was going to do.

'Mr. Jameson, I will be keeping your client in custody overnight, subject to my legal right to do so. She will be charged with the murder of Lisa James, and we will get her before a court tomorrow for a remand hearing. Bail will be opposed.'

Jameson nodded.

'Of course, Superintendent; I understand. May I have access to her and to any relevant paperwork?'

'It's Chief Superintendent, and you may. Once we have her on remand you'll get copies of all the relevant prosecution documents. But I have to remind you that there are another three murders associated with this case, so we may ask the court's permission to continue interviews with the prisoner until we are satisfied as to her guilt or non-guilt in those cases too.'

Jameson nodded as Palmer left the interview room, instructing the Duty Officer to take Angela Hartman to the cells. He walked slowly up the stairs to his own floor, deep in thought. He was having a mixture of feelings. Yes, she'd cracked and had admitted killing Lisa James; but was it just the money? Was it sibling protection? You never knew with the criminal mind; but had she even got a criminal mind?

He barged into his empty office and slumped into his chair. One down and three to go then. But what was it that Lisa James had found out about Tony Fox? It must have been his back handers from the agency. If Gheeta could search the Midland Television Light Entertainment accounts department's files, and find that ninety percent or whatever it was of Tony Fox's bookings were with Bannerman artists, then so could Lisa James; the lady must have thought all her Christmases had come at once. Mind you, she was now a mile away from being the nice lass he'd had in his mind at the start of the enquiry, if Hartman's testimony was to be believed. But then again, was it to be believed? Or would she change it once the severity of a murder charge hit home?

Gheeta poked her head round the door, saw him and came in.

'And...?'

'She cracked in the end; full confession.'

'Well done, guv. Confessed to how many?'

'Just Lisa James so far. Apparently our Miss James knew all about her adoption and who her father was, and was threatening to blow the story wide open to the press; she believed Hartman was her mother and knew Tommy Vaughan was the father, so was about to kill his career and finish the pair of them. Nice daughter to have, eh?'

'It's very confusing, trying to keep track of who thought who was who when you've got Hartman pretending to be her sister, isn't it?'

'It is; and just how do we tell Margaret Collins that her sister has killed her daughter, when she's not even aware that Lisa James *was* her daughter? How do we break that bit of news, eh?'

'We could have a pair of sibling killers here, sir.'

'Could we? How do you work that one out?'

'Because we have now got the missing six seconds from the railway station CCTV; six seconds showing Margaret Collins arriving at Bournemouth station on the day Tommy Vaughan was killed.'

'Have we indeed?'

Palmer thought for a moment.

'Well, that looks like murder number two solved then, doesn't it? Get Margaret Collins back into the interview room for this afternoon, and we'll see what she says to that.'

He stood and stretched.

'Meantime I have to find a florist.'

'A florist, guv? Going to brighten up the office?'

'Anniversary, Sergeant; me and Mrs P.'

'Wedding anniversary, guv? Which one; silver, golden?'

'No, no, not a wedding anniversary; first date. The anniversary of our first date is tomorrow.'

'You remember your first date, guv?'

Sergeant Singh was amazed. Palmer the romantic?

'It took me six months to pluck up enough courage to ask her out, Sergeant, so you bet I remember it. I had a blissful evening in nineteen seventy-two, spent whirling the future Mrs P around the floor at the Empire Ballroom, Leicester square. Swept her off her feet I did!'

Palmer did a little imaginary waltz round his office and banged his knee on the corner of Gheeta's desk, which sent him hobbling back to his chair uttering some mild expletives.

'Hope your sense of direction was a bit better in those days, guv.'

'Ha ha,' he answered sarcastically, as he rubbed his knee.

'I can send flowers for you on the internet; save you a walk to find a florist.'

'No, don't trust it; put my credit card details on the net, and every villain in Asia will be using it within the hour. I've read all about the horror stories.'

'I'll use a secure site, guv.'

She sat at her desk and tapped the keyboard.

'I'll find a local Interflora florist, and they'll deliver today; won't take a minute.'

Gheeta was always amazed at how Palmer was a hundred percent behind the use of IT and social media when it came to crime solving, but totally against it for personal uses. She put it down to a 'generation' thing; swiping a piece of plastic just isn't the same as handing over cash.

'I'll guarantee your card's safety, guv; and anyway the lifts are being serviced, so it's stairs only if you want to go out and find a florist.'

Palmer thought about the four flights of stairs down to street level, and then finding a florist, and then the four flights back up to the office, and the effect on his sciatica.

'Okay, tomorrow; deliver tomorrow.'

He pulled his debit card from his wallet and gave it to her.

'Say around eleven o'clock.'

Gheeta moved the mouse and scrolled down the Interflora listings.

'Here we are, local branches to you. Nothing in Dulwich Village… got one in East Dulwich though; any good?'

'Near enough.'

'Right then, what do you want to send: a bouquet of red roses, a floral display?'

'Floral display? Hang on, Sergeant; I'm on Chief Superintendent's wages, not the bloody Commissioner's! Bouquet of red roses will do just fine.'

'Okay, a bouquet it is then.'

She scrolled down the screen.

'Here we are then, guv… Oh, they look really nice…various sizes… How much do you want to spend; thirty, forty, fifty?'

'No, no, only the best for Mrs P. I'll go up to a whole pound.'

Palmer sent out for sandwiches but didn't really taste them, as his mind was concentrating on how to attack Margaret Collins; to break through the wall of lies, and get to the truth without upsetting her too much. He decided to just go with the flow and treat her like any other hostile witness: attack, attack, attack. But he knew he wouldn't; it just wasn't in his nature.

Back in the interview room at two that afternoon, he took care of the tape procedures, shifted in his chair next to Sergeant Singh, and looked across the table at Margaret Collins and her solicitor. Thankfully the solicitor was the duty solicitor, as Margaret Collins hadn't asked for any specific company solicitor. Taking a deep breath, to give the impression he was getting a bit fed up with all this subterfuge, Palmer went for the jugular.

'Margaret, I have to tell you that we are not at all satisfied that you were telling us everything you knew about the points raised with you in our last interview; or indeed that the answers you did give us were totally truthful.'

The duty solicitor interrupted.

'Superintendent, I must register an objection to that last remark. To propose that my client was not truthful really needs some corroborative evidence in support.'

Palmer smiled patronisingly at him.

'It's *Chief* Superintendent, and that evidence will be coming shortly.'

He turned his attention back to Margaret Collins.

'Miss Collins, you said in our last interview that you were unaware of any correspondence between your workplace, the Bannerman Agency, and Tommy Vaughan about the proposed American take over; and that you hadn't seen Tommy Vaughan for a number of years. Is that correct?'

No response. Typical, thought Gheeta, of a person not sure just how much the police knew, and not wanting to incriminate themselves by giving an answer that would be shot to ribbons. Palmer had the same thought. He fixed Collins with a cold glare, and raised eyebrows that said *'I know more than you think I know.'*

'We have here a copy of a letter from the Bannerman Agency to Mr. Vaughan taken off the computer files, prosecution evidence item number six.'

He passed it across the desk to the duty solicitor.

'It sets out the bid in detail, and asks for Mr. Vaughan's signature on a document to transfer his shares in the company to the new buyers at the appropriate time. Have you ever seen this before?'

She stumbled over her words.

'I, err... I don't recall. I may have, so many passed over my desk - '

'It is dated the day before Mr. Vaughan was killed; and, if you look in the top right-hand corner, can you see what it says there?'

'Yes.'

'And what does it say there?'

'By hand.'

'Correct, it says *by hand*; which I take to mean that this document for signature is so important and urgent that it was to be delivered by hand to Mr. Vaughan at Bournemouth, which is where he was at that time in Summer Season. Am I right in that assumption?'

'Yes.'

'And the very next day, the day Mr. Vaughan was killed, you personally took that letter to Bournemouth to do just that, deliver it by hand, didn't you?'

'No, no I didn't...no.'

Palmer spoke into the recorder.

'I am now passing over four still pictures, taken off the video recording at Bournemouth Station on the day of Mr. Vaughan's murder. These stills show the passengers alighting from the London train at one forty in the afternoon, and clearly show Margaret Collins to be one of those passengers.'

He passed the photos across and pointed at one of them.

'Margaret Collins, that is you, is it not?'

Collins and the solicitor looked. She sat back and made no answer, staring at them. Palmer gave Gheeta a nudge with his knee under the desk. She knew the signal; time to play good cop bad cop.

'Miss Collins,' she said softly. 'Would you like some time alone with your solicitor? It's very important you get advice at this time; you could be facing a very serious charge.'

Collins shook her head. The last thing she wanted was to go away and sit in a cell, then come back and go through all this anguish again. She wanted it all finished one way or the other; she'd had enough. Last night's claustrophobic confinement in a holding cell at the Yard had done the trick, as Palmer had hoped it would. He carried on.

'Must have come as a surprise, to get there and find Tommy had company that afternoon. That company was in fact the Sergeant here and myself; we were interviewing him about Tony Fox's murder. Luckily for you, he was just leaving his dressing room to get some coffees when he saw you arrive, so you never actually came into our view. Do you remember him calling out to you? He said *'hope you've got the stuff'*, the stuff being that letter and the share transfer documents for his signature; the documents that you were determined he wasn't going to sign. The two of you then went off to the café, or somewhere else on the pier where you no doubt got into a heated argument. Probably about the money, but I will never know; unless you want to tell me now?'

No response. Palmer carried on.

'You knew the shares were promised to Angela, and the possibility that his will stated that fact. You also knew what they would be worth having as you had access to the American offer for Bannerman's; and you had a plan to stop him altering the will once he realised how much they would be worth, and a life of luxury could be his by selling to the Americans. What was your plan, blackmail? Did he recognise you after all those years as the girl he had a fling with? He had never seemed to recognise you when your paths crossed in the Bannerman office, had he? Was he even aware of his being the father of your child? But when he told you he had the police in his dressing room asking questions about Tony Fox, that plan went out of the window, didn't it? I expect a certain degree of panic set in, and such was your determination to keep those shares in the *family*, shall we say, that poor old Tommy went over the side of the pier, with knife wounds to the back of his neck; wounds inflicted by you. You murdered Tommy Vaughan.'

The silence was heavy. Miss Collins rubbed the tears from her red eyes and regained her upright posture. Her chest heaved as she took a long breath.

'He read the letter. I told him Angela had confided in me a long time ago that he'd promised her the shares. He ridiculed Angela. I told him he'd made her a promise, and she was relying on it for her retirement. He was awful, sneering that she was just a 'hanger on'.; saying that him giving her work for all those years had opened doors for her. He said she owed him everything, and he wasn't about to throw away the biggest payday of his life on a nobody like her. He said she could get a place in a Variety Club rest home with the other has-beens.'

She moved her head in disbelief at recalling what he'd said.

'Did he recognise you then? Did he know you were Angela's sister?'

She smirked.

'No, people like Tommy Vaughan don't have memories of anything except themselves. I joined the Bannerman Agency ten years after our little... liaison. I saw him quite a few times as he swaggered in and out of the office; I served him coffee, arranged travel and hotels for him, but not once was there a hint of recognition. He had forgotten all about it. There were always lots of rumours in the business, about his various affairs and love children; seems I wasn't the only one. That man only ever cared about number one, Chief Superintendent.'

'You never thought of confronting him?'

'No, never. I got to see him as the arrogant, boastful, selfish and awful man that he really was. No way did I want to admit any relationship with him. It was a forgotten mistake and that's the way I wanted it to stay; buried.'

Palmer took a gamble.

'But you did bring it up with him, didn't you? On the pier that day; you pleaded with him not to break his promise to Angela about the shares, and when he laughed it off and said those things about her you let fly, didn't you? You told him who you really were, and that he had a daughter.'

The silence in the room seemed to last for an eternity.

'Yes.'

It was a barely audible whisper.

'Yes, I did. I was going to kill him if he didn't look after Angela in some way; I'd made my mind up on the on the train journey down. It wasn't just the treatment he'd given her over all those years; it was the way he'd used me as a plaything that summer long ago.'

She stopped to gather her thoughts before continuing, lowering her head into her hands. Palmer stayed silent. She rubbed her eyes and raised her head.

'Chief Superintendent, when I told him, on that very same pier all those years ago, that I was pregnant with his child, seventeen years old and in love, I can still remember what he said to me that day. He said I couldn't prove it was his, and I was probably a little tart sleeping with anyone and everyone.'

She dabbed her eyes.

'I was so stupid in those days. I had visions of him being so pleased; of taking me in his arms and being so happy we were going to have a child. Visions of me as Mrs Tommy Vaughan; a wonderful, sun-drenched life stretching into the future. All stupid; stupid, childish ideas of love… Instead of which he killed me all those years ago on that pier; he ripped out my heart, and now at last I was going to take revenge on the self-same pier.'

She looked up at the ceiling and shook her head in laughter.

'Yes, I told him who I was, and true to form he laughed; he laughed in my face, and said I was as stupid now as I was then if I thought that fact made any difference. He said even if I got DNA evidence he still wouldn't have to pay anything, and he certainly wouldn't let the shares go. He said he wished he'd never fucked me, and then he laughed, told me to 'fuck off,' turned round and leant on the pier railings, laughing.'

'And at that point you stabbed him.'

'Yes.'

'What with?'

'My letter opener, a steel one I use in the office; it folds up very small with a key ring attached. It was a birthday present from Angela for my twenty-first, I always carry it in my bag. I was so angry; all the hate just welled out of me, and I kept stabbing at him for what seemed like ages, until he slid down in front of me to the boardwalk, and I pushed him under the rail with my foot into the sea below.'

'And then?'

'Oh, err… then I went into the ladies and composed myself. I walked back into town, booked into a B &B, and slept. Funny, really; I slept so well – a deep sleep; first time for ages. Then I got the first London train in the morning and carried on as normal.'

'But Rebecca Bannerman knew you'd gone to Bournemouth that day with the papers, didn't she? And she was aware of the murder pretty soon too.'

'I gave the papers back to her, and said I'd been there and Tommy wasn't about; and I'd seen all the police activity and thought it best to come back with the papers rather than leave them for him.'

'But she knew that wasn't true, didn't she? Because she would have read that the body wasn't found until the next morning, so there wouldn't have been any police activity the day you were there.'

'No, no she didn't mention that at all.'

'Really? So she was keeping her powder dry then. With the share transfer documents not signed by Vaughan they were still in limbo. What offer did she make to you?'

'Offer? What do you mean, *offer*?'

'Oh come along, Miss Collins. The whole of this little social circle of Tommy Vaughan knew that he'd promised Angela the shares in his will; he boasted about it, probably to make himself seem like a good chap to others. Rebecca Bannerman would have heard the story, and Vaughan may even had told her he'd left them to Angela Hartman; in which case she would have a new shareholder owning forty-nine percent of her business as soon as the will was executed. However, if it was proved that Angela or somebody else killed Tommy Vaughan in order to get the benefit of those shares, the will would be declared null and void, and with no other relatives around those shares would revert back to the company, to Rebecca Bannerman. So she stood to gain an awful lot if Angela, the proposed recipient of the shares or anybody connected to her, like you for instance, were found guilty in court of murdering him in order to keep hold of those shares. Bannerman knew this, didn't she? She knew it alright, and offered you a deal. What was that deal? She'd keep quiet, and for that she'd get the shares?'

Margaret Collins knew that whatever she said, Palmer knew the truth. He didn't, of course; but that was the impression he gave. She put her cards on the table; she was in so deep now she felt like a rag doll being tossed about in a playground. No point in fighting anymore.

'She wanted the lot, all the shares; she said she knew I'd killed him, it was obvious, and she would keep quiet about it and say I was working in the office the day of the murder if I would get Angela to sign a legal document to sell the shares to her at their old, original price within a month of getting them through the will. Then, once the

American deal went through, we'd get a hundred thousand pounds on top.'

'Which is why Bannerman emailed the American buyers' lawyers to put back the sale date by three months. She wanted those shares in her name by then, so she'd get the full amount to herself.'

He passed a copy of the email to Collins's solicitor and spoke to the tape.

'Prosecution document A13 passed to Miss Collins's solicitor.'

Margaret Collins rested her elbows on the desk with her head in her hands.

'Yes, she thought the will would have been settled and everything through by then, with her as sole shareholder.'

'And then...' said Palmer. 'Surprise, surprise; in came the Bournemouth railway station CCTV recording. Let me see now, is this is how it happened? A package arrives at the Bannerman office by police courier, and being the office manager you open it.'

'Yes.'

'You see what it is, and guess what it shows, namely you arriving at Bournemouth on the day of the murder, which would give Bannerman a very strong hand indeed.

'Yes.'

'So you hid it; and sometime later when the office is empty, you come back and view it.'

'I have a set of keys, so I went back that same evening.'

'And there you are, as large as life on the screen at Bournemouth; which put a different slant on things didn't it, eh? If Rebecca Bannerman sees that, then she hasn't got to provide an alibi for you or keep quiet; or most of all pay out a hundred thousand pounds to you. All she need do is identify you to us, you get convicted of Tommy's murder, and hey presto, the will would be made legally useless and she gets the shares. So you did the only thing you could do; you edited yourself out of the disc and returned it to us with this false note.'

He passed the note over to the solicitor and identified it for the tape.

'For purpose of identification, I have passed prosecution exhibit C5 to Margaret Collins's solicitor.'

He turned back to Collins.

'Is that the note you sent back with the CCTV recording to the police?'

'Yes.'

'Unfortunately for you, you were not aware that at our interview with Rebecca Bannerman we told her to expect the recording, and view it with the hope she might recognise somebody. So when it didn't arrive she contacted us; she actually contacted us asking where it was on the very day we received it back, supposedly from *her*. So, as you can imagine our suspicions were raised, and we checked the copy disc against the master copy and, of course, we found a missing few seconds; and viewing that few seconds on the master disc, we found you. Forensics was able to tell us that the editing had been done on the equipment in the Bannerman office; the equipment that you use for editing and copying what I understand are called 'show reels', promotional discs of the agency artists that you send to prospective employers.

'Right, so let's move onto the night Rebecca Bannerman was killed. What happened?'

Once again, Palmer had led with a question that proposed the scenario that he knew what had happened that night, which he didn't. But Collins was now under the impression that he did, and had to try and put it into a good light for herself.

'She wanted a meeting with Angela and myself; she told us about the recording, and that she was going to contact you the next morning and express an opinion that we planned together to kill Tommy Vaughan for the money.'

'So I assume that her safety net was to get both of you involved in the murder; because if Angela wasn't then there was a chance a jury might be persuaded that you acted alone without Angela's knowledge, and the will would be deemed good and the shares still go to her. So Bannerman had to get Angela implicated into the murder scenario as well. So what happened at the meeting then?'

'I'd known for a long time about the payments to Tony Fox, and said I would make it public if she didn't stick to the original plan and pay Angela the money.'

'The hundred thousand pounds?'

'Yes; it all got a bit heated, and Angela, always the sensible one, told me to go and wait in the coffee bar across the street, while she and Rebecca sorted things out and came to an agreement.'

'And you left them?'

'Yes, yes I did.'

'And then?'

'Well, after about twenty minutes Angela came and joined me, and we both went home.'

'Did she say anything?'

'She didn't say she'd killed Rebecca, if that's what you mean. She said they had reached an agreement of sorts, and it would be worked out in the next couple of days.'

'Okay.'

Palmer rubbed his eyes and stood up.

'I think we'll call it a day at this point. However, I shall be keeping you in custody with a remand warrant that we are applying for this afternoon on the grounds that we will charge you with the murder of Tommy Vaughan, and suspicion of murdering or being implicated in the murder of Rebecca Bannerman.'

Miss Collins couldn't conceal her surprise at the last bit as Palmer went through the security tape procedures. He called in the duty officer to take her to the cells, and trudged wearily up to the fourth floor.

In the office Gheeta was sitting bent over her desk, with her head resting on her folded arms as Palmer walked in.

'My brain is starting to ache with this one, guv; I don't know how you do it without any notes. How do you keep a thread going?'

Palmer laughed.

'I don't, that's the secret. You can't really plan an interview; you never know where the questions are going to lead, because you never know what answers are going to come back from the suspect. So any pre-planned notes would be useless. All you can do is have it in mind where you want to end up. I wanted to end up with a confession, which in the end I got. It's all about intuition, Sergeant; getting to know the kind of suspect in front of you, and never, ever believing the first answers you get.'

'So who killed Tony Fox, guv? I can't figure that one out at all.'

'Jesus!' Palmer said, slapping his forehead. 'Good thing you said that.'

He turned on his heels towards the door.

'Come on, you've reminded me of something I need Claire to check out!'

Chapter 19

Back in the interview room next morning, Palmer and
Gheeta smiled as Angela Hartman and the duty solicitor
entered and sat opposite them. Palmer noted that she'd
ditched Edward Jameson of Jameson, Blunt and Company,
and not before time. A hundred and sixty quid an hour for
sitting on his arse was basically Palmer's impression of
him; actually it was Palmer's impression of most
solicitors. He went through the tape procedure.

'...and those present are Angela Hartman, the duty
solicitor, Detective Chief Superintendent Palmer and
Detective Sergeant Singh, who will be conducting the
interview.'

Gheeta's heart missed a beat, or two. She looked at
Palmer, who smiled back benignly and raised his eyebrows
in expectation, before turning his attention to a wad of
papers in front of him. Swine, thought Gheeta, as she
turned her attention to Angela Hartman, giving her a half
smile as she collected her thoughts. She recalled Palmer's
words the afternoon before: *'it's all about intuition...
never believe the first answer*s...

'Miss Hartman, as you are aware we have interviewed
your sister Margaret Collins, who has now admitted to the
murder of Tommy Vaughan; and in the light of her
answers, I'd like to ask you about the evening you both
had a meeting with Rebecca Bannerman at the Bannerman
Agency Offices in Knightsbridge. Do you recall that
evening?'

'Vaguely I do, yes.'

'You only vaguely recall that evening? The evening
when you, your sister, and Rebecca Bannerman were to
finalise the financial dealings between the three of you
over Tommy Vaughan's shares in the Bannerman Agency;
shares that had been promised to you that could be worth
millions and would make you both very rich – you only
vaguely recall that evening? The evening that also resulted
in Miss Bannerman's death, and you only *vaguely* recall

it?'

The duty solicitor had a word in Hartman's ear before she replied.

'I do recall it, yes.'

'Good, because according to your sister there was a heated argument between the three of you, and you told her to go and wait in the coffee bar opposite while you sorted things out. What was sorted out between you and Miss Bannerman?'

'Rebecca promised to make a financial settlement on me equal to the value of the shares if I let things go through.'

'Equal to the value of the shares at that time? That would be before the American bid was made public?'

'Yes.'

'And you refused; you wanted more.'

'No.'

'No? You accepted the offer, although you knew how much they would jump in value if the bid went through; and you knew you could at least temporarily stop that bid, if not totally finish it. You had a great bargaining tool, Miss Hartman but you accepted her first low, very low, offer?'

'Yes.'

'And you left the building, leaving Rebecca Bannerman probably dancing around the office in delight?'

'I left the building, yes.'

'But your sister told us it was all getting very heated even before she left. I would expect it to reach boiling point after such a derisory offer; yet you say you accepted it and settled it in a cool and collected way, and left.'

'Yes.'

Gheeta threw a wide smile, and raised her eyebrows in a show of disbelief.

'No, Miss Hartman, oh no; you didn't settle anything at all, did you? Your sister Margaret knew all about the agency giving back handers to Tony Fox which had been going on for years, and the pair of you knew if that got out to the media, even the slightest whiff of a financial scandal like that would send the Americans running away and finish the deal off. And there was another little financial irregularity that you wanted settling too, wasn't there; the matter of your residuals.'

Hartman raised her eyes to Gheeta's in a defensive look.

'Residuals? What residuals?'

'The ones Lisa told you about the day you killed her.'

Gheeta had flown a kite on the 'residuals', but by Hartman's look she knew she'd struck gold. When Claire had done an audit on the roster of Bannerman artists that Tony Fox had used, it showed that any repeat fees known as 'residuals' went into the Fox private company, and not to the artist or Bannerman Agency; a scam that must have had Rebecca Bannerman's agreement, and must have been part of the original artist contract they signed; highly irregular, but if the artist wanted to work they had no option but to agree. Gheeta carried on.

'Tony Fox had all his Bannerman artists, including you, on a 'nil residual' contract; in other words, any repeat fees would not go to the artist. In fact, they went to Tony Fox's private company. You knew that you wouldn't get residuals, but you weren't aware that Tony Fox got them, were you? At least not until Lisa told you.'

Hartman lowered her head.

'It was take it or leave it; I didn't have a choice. It appeared Fox was out of the same mould as Tommy Vaughan, just another nasty greedy bastard who misused his power to his own financial advantage. If I hadn't accepted that contract I wouldn't have worked; and there were many other writers who would rush in to take it.'

Gheeta pushed the knife in further.

'And looking at the number of Tommy Vaughan shows that were made, the repeats and overseas sales would have been quite substantial; so the residual payments would have totalled up to a fair amount, all going to Tony Fox, with Bannerman Agency taking their percentage. We have copies of the contracts, and we also know from Midland Television accounts that Lisa James asked for copies to be sent to her office 'for info'. She told you about it, didn't she? And she told you that little scam was the ammunition she was going to use to bring down Tony Fox and take his job.'

Hartman nodded.

'Yes, she hated him; said she'd use it through Equity and finish his career.'

'And before she could, you killed her.'

'I've admitted that already.'

'You have, yes. So what happened after that? I think you waited three months, and then went back and told Tony Fox you knew about his little scam, and wanted your past residuals, and probably something on top, or you'd blow the whistle to Equity.'

'No, I didn't. I didn't even think of that.'

'Oh come along, I can't believe that. It all points to another heated row; maybe it gets out of hand, the red mist comes down, and you kill him.'

'Rebecca killed him. She told us so.'

Gheeta and Palmer were both taken aback by this. This was a turn up for the books that Gheeta's 'flying a kite' hadn't envisaged. She did what every police officer does in a new situation; she shut up, and waited for Hartman to break the silence.

'Lisa James had told Rebecca that she knew about the deals, and tried to come to an agreement that if she got Tony Fox sacked and got his job, the payments would continue, but to Lisa. Rebecca knew that to get Fox sacked, the details of the payments would have to be made public; and if they were not only would Tony Fox be finished, but the Agency would have some awkward questions to answer as well. An obvious point that Lisa hadn't taken into consideration. Rebecca couldn't take the chance, not with the American deal in the offing. Lisa already had copies of the artist contracts and could bring them out at any time, whether they had an agreement or not, and use them against Bannerman. Catch-22; Rebecca would be on a loser either way.'

'So why wouldn't she kill Lisa, not Tony Fox? Then the little scam would still be safe. And even when Lisa was killed by you, you're saying Rebecca Bannerman told you she'd killed Tony Fox, even though the threat from Lisa had gone away with her murder. So why would she kill him?'

'I got the impression he wanted in on the American deal.'

'You got the impression? This was on the night you and your sister went to the Agency, and you told your sister to wait over the road in the café?'

'Yes, as you guessed I was asking for my money from the residuals; I was very angry, and so was she. It was all getting a bit physical; she was trying to push me out of the office, saying I shouldn't try to blackmail her because Tony Fox had made that mistake, and look what happened to him.'

'Meaning?'

'Well, she said he'd tried to get more than his fair share and she'd seen him off, and don't think she wouldn't do the same again. We started shouting and punching, and she was screaming that I was just a two-bit hack and out of my depth, and if I crossed her she'd see that I never worked again and I'd never get a penny.'

She paused and breathed deeply.

'And?'

Gheeta sensed this was the crescendo, and kept the pressure on.

'And then I smashed her head against the wall; again and again… She slumped to the floor, and I still held it and banged it on the floor; the magazine table had been knocked over and the big glass ashtray was beside me, so I used that as well… Oh my God, oh my God, I don't know why; perhaps all those years of taking it from them; being kicked around, promises that never happened, I don't know – something inside just snapped, it seemed so easy; problem solved – just like with Lisa, I'd got away with that one, and I would with this. I felt good…'

She looked Gheeta in the eye, as though asking for an explanation for her actions.

'I felt really good; problem solved. So I put the lights out, shut the office, and went to join Margaret over the road in the cafe'

'You used the lift, didn't you?'

It was a statement not a question, as Gheeta recalled the dark figure huddled in a corner of the dimly-lit lift as it passed, as she and Palmer had climbed the stairs that evening.

'Yes, I heard you and the Superintendent down in the foyer and couldn't risk passing you on the stairs. I was very lucky; if you'd been a few minutes earlier you'd have caught me.'

'He's a *Chief* Superintendent, not a Superintendent; a *Chief* Superintendent.'

Her genuine respect for Palmer brought that out.

'And we *have* caught you, Miss Hartman.'

Gheeta was surprised by the coldness of her own voice.

'What did you say to your sister when you joined her in the café?'

'I made up some story about reaching an agreement, and that Rebecca was going to draw up a legal document the next day. I was very calm, very in control; an amazing feeling really, considering what I'd just done.'

Palmer thought it time to take the reins. He cleared his throat before speaking very softly.

'Well, this is a right mess isn't it, eh? You murdered Lisa James and Rebecca Bannerman, your sister murdered Tommy Vaughan, and you say Rebecca Bannerman killed Tony Fox; four deaths, and all because of a half promise of some shares.'

'It wasn't a half promise, Sup – Chief Superintendent; Tommy promised them to me time and time again. Margaret and I used to work out how we'd cash them in to give us a pension. It wasn't an awful lot of money, but enough to help us retain our standards in old age.'

Palmer nodded that he understood.

'But then with the American interest it did become an *awful lot of money* didn't it, eh? The amount made all the difference; brought in the vultures circling your little pension pot, that now had the prospect of becoming a very large pension pot.'

He paused for a moment.

'You realise that your sister will have to be told that Lisa James was her child, and that - '

Hartman interrupted him.

'And that I murdered her; that I killed my sister's daughter. Yes, yes, I do realise that – and I'll no doubt have plenty of time behind bars to think about it too, won't I?'

'The court will decide that. In the mean time you will be kept here overnight, and transferred to a secure remand home tomorrow to await trial. The Crown Prosecutor's office will lay the charges to your solicitor, who will talk you through them and advise you on your plea. Are you comfortable in your cell?'

'Yes, as much as can be expected thank you.'

'Right then, that's all for now. We may need to clarify some things, and in that case we will make arrangements with your solicitor to arrange a further chat.'

He signed off the tape, and waited while the duty officer took Angela Hartman back to her cell, and brought Margaret Collins from hers. He turned to Gheeta while they waited.

'Where the hell did that stuff about *residuals* come from?'

'From Claire, guv; the day we got the transcript of WPC Devlin's interview with Lisa James's adoptive parents.'

'I don't remember anything about *residuals*.'

'No, I think the thought of Mrs P's toad in the hole waiting at home proved too great a choice against a boring explanation of residuals, guv. You were going to get up to speed on them the next morning, but things motored along a bit fast and you never did.'

'Oh, good job you did then. Well done.'

'I didn't think they'd be as important as they turned out, guv, or I'd have given you a heads up on it.'

The duty officer brought in Margaret Collins. She sat opposite them with the duty solicitor; her fingers entwined on the desk, a faint smile on her lips. Knowing what they were about to tell her, neither Palmer nor Singh smiled back. Gheeta really didn't want Palmer to foist this one onto her. The tape was set, and Palmer took a deep breath and broke the silence.

'In my long career as a police officer, Margaret, I have had to do some pretty rotten things. I have had to tell people that their loved ones have been killed, tell parents their child has had a bad accident, or worse; and, Margaret, I have something to tell you that I find particularly heartrending, even taking into account this whole nasty mess that we are now involved in. I must ask you to be prepared for a nasty shock.'

Tears welled up in Margaret Collins's eyes, and one slid down her cheek. She whispered very softly and slowly:

'My sister murdered my daughter.'

Gheeta was rocked by this, and taken by surprise that Collins already knew. Palmer kept his composure, nodded slowly, and reached across the table to cover her hands with his in a gesture of comfort.

'Yes, yes she did.'

Margaret Collins sobbed for a full minute before regaining her composure, to a certain extent. She spoke between tears.

'I'd guessed – too many coincidences, your questions about Tommy and me; it all began to add up in my mind. I didn't want it to, but it did; each part of the awful jigsaw slotting into place… My poor child was killed by everybody in this awful game of greed – and now the jigsaw is nearly complete.'

She collapsed forward onto the table, wailing like a wounded animal. Gheeta hurried round and held her in comfort, while Palmer went outside and asked the duty officer to get a medic.

They sedated Margaret Collins and had the doctor take a look at her, before settling her down in a cell for the night; a video camera keeping watch and a WPC sitting in with her, just in case she tried anything stupid in her hours of grief.

Palmer and Gheeta took the stairs up to his office in silence. She grabbed two coffees from the machine on the way, and they sat sipping them. Palmer spoke first.

'The paperwork on this bloody case is going to be horrendous.'

'Well at least we've got confessions, guv; on tape too, so the briefings for the Crown Prosecutor should be fairly easy. Imagine trying to make this prosecution into an easily understood and coherent case for a jury if they hadn't confessed!'

Palmer laughed.

'I'd like to see anybody make this one coherent; more twists than a judge's wig. Where have all the easy ones gone? The ones where you wait outside the building and the villain walks out with a smoking gun or bloody knife and says, *It's a fair cop…it was me what dun it, guv.'*

Gheeta laughed along.

'Well, when you think about it that is basically what happened here, only not quite as quickly.'

Palmer took the last sip of his coffee.

'I needed that; tasted foul, but I needed it. And by the way, your Hartman interview was very good Sergeant, very good. You handled her well, and got a result, can't ask for anything more. Well done.'

'Thank you, *Chief* Superintendent.'

'Yes, I did notice that too.'

He smiled at Gheeta, stretched, and stifled a yawn.

'Early night I think. Long hot bath, and sleep.'

The door opened and in came the Assistant Commissioner, followed by Perky. Perky, real name Cyril Perkins, was the maintenance foreman of the Yard; he was in his usual paint-splattered, baggy boiler suit, pencil stub parked behind his right ear and notebook in hand. The Assistant Commissioner gave Palmer and Gheeta a smile.

'Ah, glad you are both here. I understand congratulations are due; good confessions on all the murders. Well done.'

Palmer smiled back.

'Thank you, sir. Hello Perky, what brings you here? New desks coming in? Chairs with cushions, maybe?'

His voice was tinged with sarcasm. The Assistant Commissioner smiled back an embarrassing smile.

'Sorry Palmer, nothing like that. Cuts in funding, you know.'

Palmer widened his eyes questioningly.

'Really? I could have sworn I saw a couple of nice new coffee tables going up to the 5th floor last week. Must get my eyes tested.'

The Assistant Commissioner ignored it.

'Perky – I mean Mister Perkins, has been trying to get in to give this office a lick of paint, but I've kept him away while you two have been involved in the Vaughan case.'

Perkins looked round, mentally measuring the amount of paint needed as only decorators can.

'Twenty litres and a day's work at the most, Justin; my chaps will be in and out so quick you won't notice them.'

He gave the room a once over.

'This is the tattiest office in the building, you know.'

Palmer took umbrage at that, and bristled.

'Well what do you expect? Last time it saw you was Royal Wedding Day, 1981 – and then you only came in to get a good view with your missus and a free packed lunch! This office is the sharp end of police work, mate; this is where crimes are solved and criminals caught, so Mr, and Mrs Perkins can sleep soundly at night.'

Perkins ignored it.

'What colour do you want it? Same again, magnolia?'

A smile slowly crossed Palmer's face and grew into a beam. He looked towards Gheeta and then back to Perkins.

'Golden Sunrise.'

'Golden Sunrise?' Perkins repeated.

'Yes, Golden Sunrise.'

'Well, that makes it easy then; we've just done out the whole of the fifth floor in Golden Sunrise, and there's loads left over.'

Chapter 20

By mid-morning the next day things were getting into shape. Gheeta had somehow sourced two administration clerks from the typing pool to help Claire put all the case papers and statements into chronological order and type out the interview tapes; Palmer had cast his eye over each as it was filed, and collated the crime scene photos and pathologist reports into the growing pile of evidence; the Crown Prosecution Office sent over a barrister who got down to familiarising himself with the case and all its twists and turns, copying the main confessions and placing them into an abbreviated file, just in case either of the sisters retracted and pleaded not guilty.

This was the piece of police procedure work Palmer hated: book work and reports; and to be honest he shifted it onto Gheeta whenever he could. He was the same at home. Mrs P looked after all the household bills, and kept things such as council tax payments and utility bills up to date; she wouldn't let him near them as he'd do half the job, get bored, question why it cost so much, put it aside, and forget it. If something didn't interest Palmer, he couldn't be bothered with it; and there was no kind of paperwork that interested Palmer. He was already hoping for a call that would take him off on another case, and away from this paper hell.

The call came, but it didn't take him off the case. It was Gheeta's phone that rang; she took it without taking her attention off the paperwork that she was working on. A few words from the caller and she dropped the papers.

'Be right down.'

She put the phone back onto its base, and turned to Palmer.

'Guv, there's been an accident. Hartman's been hurt; badly hurt.'

'What? Where?'

'The cells.'

'Oh no, I hope it's not what I think it might be,' Palmer said, already half out of the door. 'Come on.'

Chapter 21

In the basement cells corridor, all was silent. Several officers including a firearms officer were waiting expectantly as Palmer and Singh arrived; they pointed for them to go on through the open exit doors at the end of the corridor, where a prison van was stationary in the courtyard with all its doors closed. The duty officer was kneeling on the courtyard tarmac, with medics attending a young civilian prisoner escort officer whose shirt was red with blood, and his arm heavily bandaged.

'What's going on, George?'

Palmer sidled up to the duty officer.

'What happened?'

'Bloody civilian contractors, sir, that's what's going on. Prison service should never have brought them in; they can't do the job.'

'Yes, yes,' Palmer interrupted. He was impatient and wanted to know what was going on. 'What happened to this lad, and who is inside the van?'

'Your two killer sisters are inside, and they aren't locked in the cubicles.'

'What!'

Palmer was shocked.

'What are they doing inside it? They should be in separate cells inside the building, not in a bloody van!'

'No room, sir; all the cells are full and we had instructions to keep them separate, so we made arrangements to take them to Wandsworth for the night. We were getting them into the van when the Collins lady produced a knife, and started slashing at everything in sight. She went barmy, as you can see,' he said, nodding towards the injured escort officer. 'I've got a marksman at the ready, and sent for a can of tear gas to drop inside the van; so don't you go doing anything to put yourself in danger s,ir before I'm good and ready; one officer down is enough.'

'Don't worry George, I'll be okay. I'll see if Collins will listen to sense. You have that marksman loaded and ready. If I'm attacked, I'll drop to the floor and he can have a clear shot at her, okay?'

'Well no, not really. I - '

Palmer didn't wait for clearance. He knew that to do it by the book meant waiting for a SFO (Senior Firearms Officer) to arrive and cede control to him; but with Collins apparently gone mad with her letter opener, slashing people in her time of great grief, he had to try and calm the situation. He slowly approached the back doors of the van; all was quiet, no sound coming from inside. He turned to see the marksman knelt ten meters away, with an HK417 rifle covering him. Palmer gave him a nod; the marksman nodded back. He was primed.

Clearing his throat, Palmer spoke loudly but warmly.

'Margaret, Angela – can you hear me? This is Chief Superintendent Palmer, can you hear me ? You can't both stay in there forever; they'll drop a tear gas canister inside shortly, and that's not a very nice experience I can tell you. Best you both come out now… Margaret, you've injured a civilian here; but whatever you have done has been done now, and we can't alter that. So let's clear up this mess and get you out of there; come along, open the door please.'

It seemed like an eternity before the door handle was slowly turned from the inside. Margaret Collins's trembling voice talked softly from inside.

'It's open now, Chief Superintendent.'

Palmer glanced back to make sure the marksman was in position; he was. He stretched forward slowly and pulled the door open at arm's length, using it as a shield as it opened in case Collins was about to rush at him. She wasn't; inside, at the end of the narrow steel walkway between the two rows of cells, Margaret Collins knelt behind the lifeless body of her sister Angela Hartmann, lying awkwardly like a discarded rag doll. Both were covered in blood. Collins held her trusted steel paper knife in one hand, its blade a shiny scarlet.

'Oh Margaret, what have you done?'

Palmer spoke softly, like a loving father.

'What have you gone and done now?'

Margaret Collins looked him straight in the eye. She was as cool as a cucumber. Palmer had seen that look in killers' eyes before. It said *I know what I have done, and I believe I was right to do it.*

'I'm completing the jigsaw, this awful family jigsaw of death, Chief Superintendent. My daughter is dead, killed by my own sister; how could she murder her niece? How could she do that? My daughter's father Tommy Vaughan is dead, and I killed him; and do you know, Chief Superintendent, I actually enjoyed killing him. And now my sister is dead too, because I couldn't control my anger towards her for killing my daughter; and it's all because of an old promise of some money, a promise that probably wouldn't have been kept in any case. Bannerman and Fox are dead too. So where does that leave me, Chief Superintendent? I'm the last awful piece of this jigsaw, aren't I?'

She smiled and shrugged her shoulders.

'So I'm just completing it.'

And with that she cut her own throat.

Chapter 22

'Oh God, how awful!'

Mrs P looked quite shocked when Palmer described the ending of the case.

'She must have been mentally unstable to do that.'

'We will never know now, will we? Every one of the people in this case had a dark side.'

Palmer sat in their kitchen as Mrs P dished up his evening meal. He looked at the plate of fish and chips from the local chippy.

'I thought it was your home-made moussaka tonight? You got one out of the freezer this morning, I saw it on the side before I went to work?'

'Benji had it,' she said, in a very matter-of-fact way as she put the tomato sauce bottle in front of him.

'Benji had it?'

'Yes.'

'All of it?'

'Yes.'

'Why did Benji have all of my moussaka?'

'He had an unexpected guest arriving, and hadn't time to go to the shops or cook anything; you know what he's like when he gets a bit flustered. So I helped him out.'

'With my moussaka.'

'And mine too. He did help us out with the tin of paint.'

Palmer thought it best to just eat and say nothing else. The fish and chips was quite nice really, but he kept his '*I'm not happy*' face on all through the washing and wiping up ritual, and then retired to the lounge to see what was on telly. He was quite surprised to find the new series of *Ray Donavan* about to begin on Sky; it was one of his favourite US dramas, so he settled back into the sofa as Mrs P brought him a coffee and Daisy the dog curled up by his feet. Time to relax and wind down; and that didn't happen often in Palmer's life.

Then the phone rang.

End

CASE 2
THE FELT TIP MURDERS

Chapter 1

Hamilton Jarvis permitted himself a smug little smile of self satisfaction. The reflected purple hue from the floodlighting of St Paul's Cathedral dome a hundred yards away, but on the same level as his third-floor city office windows, gave the room a nice warm feel on this chilly, dark, February evening. The staff had left for home, and he sipped his favourite whisky in peace. No interruptions.

His accountancy business was flourishing. Ever since he'd branched into tax evasion advice, or as he preferred to call it 'wealth management', his client base had grown nicely, with several very rich celebrity 'names' now on his list. So, taking everything into consideration, life at sixty years old was pretty good.

It had been a good day, too. A late, long, lunch with a corporate client, and then a slow browse around his favourite sports shop, where he had picked up a new Browning B725 20-Gauge Over and Under shotgun that he'd ordered for the new shooting season; both he and his wife were active members of the local Clay Pigeon and Target Shooting clubs. Then he'd had a long chat with the shop staff about salmon flies and lures, before picking a couple to add to his collection. Hamilton Jarvis gave everybody the impression that he was a sporty country gent, an impression Hamilton liked to give.

He cast a long look around his plush, luxury office, as he eased his deep leather chair back a few inches and swung his patent brogues up onto the mahogany desk. Yes, he'd done well. Prestige premises off St Paul's; forty-two members of staff; a rising turnover; and, of course, the thing his ego liked best, a rising status in the city's financial community. Personally he had a very healthy bank balance, plus another in the Cayman Islands known only to himself. Yes, the world was a nice place for Hamilton Jarvis. He had just turned sixty, and his only son Archie was well established in the business, destined to take over in five years when Hamilton was looking forward to many years of retirement spending his money and living a life of luxury with his wife Margaret; or maybe without his wife Margaret.

He'd thought about divorce or separation; he'd thought about it quite often lately. It had become a recurring theme in his thoughts. He could well afford to split his wealth in two with Margaret; after all, he'd still have the Cayman's money to himself, as she knew nothing about that account. He smiled at the thought, and took another sip of his whisky. Be nice to buy one of those young nubile Asian brides he'd seen on the internet, or even play the field through one of the dating sites; he could do it too, with his money. He and Margaret hadn't been 'man and wife' for fifteen years, and neither had much respect for the other any more; she knew about all his little extra-marital wanderings, and he knew about hers. They'd kept up the façade of a happily married couple to the outside world, for the sake of the family, but now Hamilton's views on life were changing as he grew older and the years left were dwindling; and they seemed to be dwindling with increasing rapidity.

So very deeply wrapped up in these thoughts was Hamilton, that when his office door opened suddenly he was quite surprised, as he thought he was the only one left on the floor. He squinted through the gloom, faintly recognising the figure approaching him quickly and silently across the deep pile carpet.

'Can I help you?'

Those were his last words, before the metal bar his assailant wielded split Hamilton's skull and left him slumped in his opulent leather chair, the whisky from the dropped glass soaking into his waistcoat. He was dead. Another furious blow to the temple made doubly sure.

His murderer had one or two things to do before leaving, and taking out a thick black marker pen, set to work.

The accountancy firm of Peter Mouse and Co. was smaller in comparison to Hamilton Jarvis's, and concentrated on handling the affairs of doctors and medical professionals. Founder Peter Mouse had sold out two years previously, during the period of hectic growth between the top five competitive accountancy firms in the City of London as they battled to be top dog, achieving their growth by acquisition of other firms, followed by staff redundancies and asset stripping. Peter had held out until he was sure he'd got top dollar on the offer, and then taken the money and run; well, not exactly run, more of a leisurely stroll down to the bank. He'd followed up the sale of the business with the sale of his London central flat; then, when all the financials were done and dusted, he had driven sedately in his Rolls Bentley to his country house in the unspoilt Cotswolds, to set about giving his new found leisure time to his great love: gardening. He'd lost his beloved wife Jennifer five years previously, and managed with a daily housekeeper from the local village who cooked and cleaned; plus an aged gardener who he rigorously controlled in a military manner so that the three acres of lawns and flower beds were planted with what Peter Mouse wanted, and not what the gardener would plant for ease of maintenance.

A portly man of sixty-five, Peter had an envy of the obvious fitness of his seventy-two year old gardener, and secretly he had installed both a rowing and a running machine in his bedroom to try and work off the extra three stone his years of plenty had accumulated around his frame. He took regular check-ups, paid for by his health insurance plan, and had heart check-ups twice yearly as an extra precaution; both his parents had both died from heart attacks, and his brother suffered with angina. He felt he had worked hard to attain his wealthy lifestyle, and wanted as many years as he could get to taste the fruits of it in his retirement.

The evening sun was casting long shadows across his lawn as he settled back on his gently swinging recliner, admiring his light Cotswold stone manor house set against the backdrop of colourful shrubs and full-leaved copper beech trees, interspersed with silver birch. He truly loved this area, but the parish council, on which he was, of course, a leading light, was beginning to lose the fight against investment bank-funded developers, and small enclaves of 'executive estates' were springing up as the local farmers took the money for their land, and ran with it to the bank. He had thought a few times of doing the same; his gardens were just over three acres, and quite a few 'executive homes' could be built on that. The thought of a Spanish villa was very appealing, especially when his rheumatic knees played up in the English winter. He and Jennifer had not been blessed with children, so there were no family ties to keep him in the UK.

He was shaken from his thoughts by the sight of a figure coming out of the large shrub bushes to the side of the lawn. The one thing that had nearly put him and Jennifer off buying the place originally was the public footpath running alongside the west of the property; it was a favourite route for ramblers, and the peace of many a relaxing day in the garden was often interrupted by the intrusion of lost souls asking directions. Mind you, it was a bit late in the day for a rambler to be starting out now, and this figure was wearing a normal jacket and trousers. Peter reached down beside the recliner for his spectacles, and put them on as the figure approached.

'Hello Peter,' the voice said coldly. 'Remember me?'

Peter did have some vague recollection of the face, but his mind struggled to put a name to it.

'Because I remember you Peter. Oh yes; I remember you, you bastard.'

The iron bar did its work once more, and the lifeless body of Peter Mouse slumped onto the recliner, before sliding off on to the lawn. Another furious blow to the back of the neck made sure the job was done, before the assailant knelt over the body, taking a broad felt-tip pen from a jacket pocket.

Being a corporate banker had not been Richard Johnson's priority in life. He smiled to himself as his pass key let him into the private apartment block where he lived, and the lift took him up to the third floor. He'd wanted to make a fortune on the stock exchange, and to that end had gone straight from university into banking; and here he was, eleven years and several banks later, sitting pretty at Capel Barclay and Hanson, one of the leading investment banks in the city. He'd never quite clicked with the speed of the dealing room, or the inner sense needed to play the futures markets, and had ended up in the core business of the corporate business department, the place where most of the *would be* high flyers, who couldn't fly quite high enough, tended to crash land.

A more subdued and leisurely climate existed here. Richard had a portfolio of roughly thirty businesses of varying sizes, each generating a turnover of three million a year plus; and his job, although he and the bank would never admit it, was to squeeze as much capital out of them and into the bank's coffers as he could; in fees, interest payments on loans, loan swaps, and any other derivatives that only bankers seemed to know how to apply. Richard's yearly bonus, which was a sizeable one of twice his salary, depended on him being able to do this successfully; and so he had not the slightest interest in his clients' business, other than being able to screw them financially.

Today had been a successful day, in the 'screwing' sense. The morning had been spent at a fabric wholesale client's warehouse in Great Tichfield Street, on the pretence of it being the 'half-yearly' business review, which basically meant asking irrelevant questions about expected future sales and trends, which in today's fast moving economy and ever-changing fashion trends was *totally* irrelevant. This was followed by a good meal in an expensive watering hole, paid for by the client, and then on to the next 'mark', an electrical retailer in Charing Cross Road; there to repeat the futile future sales and trends questions, before taking a taxi back to the office to register a four hundred pound charge against both clients' accounts for 'time and advice'. Nice work, if you can get it. His smile was changing into a smirk as he recalled the day, a smirk that said *'you mugs, you stupid mugs...'*

The lift came to a halt at his floor with a small bounce, and the doors opened, interrupting his thoughts about what he was going to spend this year's bonus on. He walked down the plush carpeted corridor to his apartment door, where he fumbled for the key with one hand while clutching his heavy briefcase in the other. He'd ring his girlfriend Suzy, and get her to accompany him to Silverstone this weekend. Richard Johnson had a passion for fast cars, and had overpaid for a pair of top-price tickets for the F1 Grand Prix. Suzy would be impressed, and as his intention was to marry her, and thereby, he hoped, gain entrance into her father's small but successful merchant bank, anything he could do to impress was well worth the money. He reckoned on another six months of wooing, and then he would be the son-in-law; the father would undoubtedly want him in the family bank, as there were no brothers to carry on the business, and he would be sitting pretty for life.

He put his key in the lock. The future looked good for Richard Johnson; very good.

The blow that crushed the front of his skull into his brain, causing instant death, was dealt with such force that the assailant had to wiggle the iron bar a bit to remove it.

Things didn't look good for Richard Johnson anymore.

Chapter 2

'I'm pissed off.'

It was a fortnight later at New Scotland Yard, and Detective Chief Superintendent Justin Palmer, head of the Serial Murder Squad, sat at his desk; he was not a happy man. He pushed his standard, government issue wooden chair back on its wonky rear legs against the wall behind him, dislodging a further small amount of plaster from the hole that this repeated action had gouged out over the years. He then swung his feet up onto the old standard government issue metal desk, knocking several report files from a stack so that they spilled onto an already congested floor beneath him.

Palmer surveyed the mess and exhaled loudly. The three red files he held in one hand he tossed onto the now clear desk space.

'Very pissed off.'

'Yes guv, you're pissed off.'

Detective Sergeant Gheeta Singh sympathised with her boss's mood, without lifting her gaze from the computer screen on her desk.

Palmer swung his legs off, wincing a little as his sciatica stabbed his left thigh, rose and picked his way across the littered office floor, to gaze out of the large picture window onto a busy Victoria Street four floors below. Fifty-nine years old, and days like this made him wish he'd not agreed to continue working on after the standard police retirement age; but he knew retirement would never have worked for him, and really he was glad he'd stayed on. What would he do every day, other than get under the wife's feet, take the dog for a walk, and get bored? Anyway, he loved his job; he had never wanted to be anything else but a copper, joining up straight from school into the old Cadet Force, working his way up from there. He was still pretty fit, but a few aches and pains every now and then were a reminder that he wasn't twenty-one anymore; and the ever-increasing grey hue to his thatch, which seemed to him to be getting greyer every day, only underlined it.

He really enjoyed his work though, and it had taken on a new and exciting appeal with the advent of information technology, which had opened up a whole new world of crime detection. He had embraced the modern technologies with open arms, and having noted the skills in the Cyber Crime department of young Detective Gheeta Singh, he had pulled in favours and had her transferred permanently to the Serial Murder Squad, giving her a free hand to install any and every programme that might be of help in solving crimes. His department now had a bank of computers in his team room on the other side of the corridor from his office, and Detective Gheeta Singh had soon been made up to Detective Sergeant Gheeta Singh, becoming his number two. She had then persuaded Palmer to add a civilian helper, Claire, to the team. Gheeta had met Claire purely by accident in the Yard's restaurant where they had got talking one lunch break, and she'd found that Claire was working in the typing pool but had obvious skills in computing, and was taking evening courses on HTML programming. Bingo! The team was complete. In two years they had installed every and any programme that could possibly be of help in crime detection, and Gheeta had written and added a few herself where there was nothing in the market capable of doing the job she wanted done.

But even a bank of computers couldn't help Palmer with the problem he could foresee coming his way from *'her indoors'*, or Mrs P as she was known to one and all. He spoke to his reflection in the window.

'What do I tell her eh? Sorry love, but we can't go on the cruise I promised you, the cruise we've waited five years for, because I've got three bodies and no killer, and apparently my team are the only ruddy team capable of tackling it in the whole of the Met!'

He turned to Gheeta.

'You'd think we were the only team in this building capable of solving serial murders.'

'We are, guv. It's what we do.'

'It's what *any* detective is supposed to do, Sergeant, and there's plenty of them in this building doing sweet nothing!'

'Yes sir, but *we* are the Serial Murder Squad, and the case does involve *serial murders*. You're the only one that has the experienced team, guv; the only one with a wonderful Detective Sergeant, namely me, who has built you a wonderful computer system, mostly in her own time I might add, that will solve this crime in no time at all. Then you and Mrs P can sail into the sunset, G & T in hands.'

'When I tell her this lot has landed on my desk, I'm more likely to be sailing down to A&E with my head in my hands.'

The office door opened, and the balding head of Assistant Commissioner Bateman sheepishly peeked in.

'Aaah, you're in, Justin. Sergeant.'

He acknowledged Gheeta, who had stood up when he entered; she didn't know why she stood though, as nobody else did. Must be a throw back to her childhood, where you stood if an adult entered the room; a time past of good manners and deference, a bye-gone time in the UK, but still adhered to by some Asian families, including hers. The Assistant Commissioner shut the door behind him and continued.

'I understand this triple murder case has fallen in your lap at a bad time, Justin.'

'Yes sir; slightly. In fact, to be blunt, it couldn't have happened at a worse time. Ruby wedding anniversary is in three weeks, and Mrs P and I are booked on a cruise. First time ever, and really looking forward to it she is, sir; especially after having spent last Christmas on her own, due to me having to work on the Baxter case.'

This was a neat reminder to his boss that he'd spent the twelve days of last Christmas cooped up in surveillance vans and interview rooms nailing a certain Mr. and Mrs Baxter, whose main occupation in life had been to befriend wealthy elderly people who had no family and divest them of their life savings and property, before arranging their 'accidental' deaths.

'Yes, well…'

The Assistant Commissioner didn't really have a clue what to say to this. He looked towards Sergeant Singh for support, but Sergeant Singh kept her gaze firmly away from his.

'Well I'm sure you'll have this one all sewn up before very long. Keep me informed.'

He nodded to them both, before beating a hasty retreat. Palmer sighed and went back to his desk and chair. He picked up the first red folder from where he'd tossed it down earlier.

'Right then, better get on with it then, eh? I shall swat up on these crime reports tonight; and you, Sergeant, will go home, get an early night, and be prepared for a long day tomorrow. I want a team of twelve, including two with a good knowledge of accountancy and banking. Team meeting eleven tomorrow morning. Oh, and be an angel – on your way out pop into the pizza place round the corner, and get them to send in a ham and pineapple with anchovies on a thin base, and a large coffee.'

He handed Gheeta a ten pound note.

'Good night, Sergeant; sleep well. This case has got to be done and dusted in a fortnight, or '*she who must be obeyed*' will throw a fit; and when she throws a fit, it usually hits me on the back of the head!"

Chapter 3

Detective Sergeant Gheeta Singh is a very attractive thirty-something Asian cockney, born in the East End of London after her parents fled Idi Amin's Uganda and sought refuge in the UK in the 1970s. They had lost their business in Uganda, but managed to transfer enough money to start again in the UK; that business was now one of the largest IT wholesale companies in England, run by Gheeta's two elder brothers, and if she wanted it there would always be a senior director's position in the company for her. But at an early age, she had made up her mind to enter the police force.

Her father had made sure she completed her education, and both before and after graduating with an IT degree from university, Gheeta had turned down several offers of employment in the banking industry to pursue her choice of the police force as a career. Her skills in the computer sciences had soon marked her out as '*one to watch*' by the senior officers, as she worked her way through the outdated IT systems and brought them up to speed. Palmer, being a man of action, and sometimes taking the action before thinking through the consequences, had requested her for his department, and pulled in a string of favours to secure the transfer after she had been sent to repair a cyber fault in his department's HOLMES terminal, managing to sort it out in thirty minutes; outside security-vetted contractors had quoted three days.

Being always on the lookout for new ways of beating the criminals, Palmer had long been aware that the power of computing was going to be an essential part of police work in the future. It was the best move he had made in a long time; Gheeta had basically thrown out a majority of the slow, out-of-date terminals and replaced them with fast modern servers and programmes, many of which she had written herself, and some of which Palmer was sure were not entirely within a legal framework; but they worked, and so a blind eye was turned.

Gheeta liked Palmer; she liked him a lot. They had now cracked three serial murder cases and she felt comfortable with him. She felt very much an integral and important part of the team, as Palmer was always looking for her input to quicken things up. He encouraged her interest in using computers to solve crimes, and made sure she got as much time off as she needed if an 'outside' course came up that she felt would benefit herself or the squad. She had spent countless hours of her own time working on making programmes bespoke to the needs of the department and installing them securely. Palmer was on a winner, and he knew it. Not being a child of the computer age, most of it went way over his head; but he could see the great advantages it brought to detective work, and the savings on man-hours for his department.

Yes, Gheeta liked Palmer; so much so that she had the pizza house add a slice of his favourite chocolate brownie to his order. Palmer always tried to restrain himself, as well as the temptation of his second favourite: raspberry jam doughnuts. Well, in truth he tried to resist, but often the resistance was futile, and he gave in; another battle lost in the war against his ever-expanding waistline. Men are so vain, thought Gheeta, as she left the pizza house, knowing full well that every pair of male eyes in the place was firmly fixed on her shapely uniformed bum. So she swayed it just that little bit more.

Chapter 4

Palmer put the office phone down. Mrs Palmer had indeed not been a happy bunny at the news. He'd promised her he'd get the case out of the way before the cruise date, promised her faithfully; but he knew that she knew that he was a copper through and through, and the case, any case, would always come first. She'd married a copper forty years ago, and nothing had changed.

'Love you lots, sweetheart.' He'd ended every phone call for forty years with those words, and he still meant them. Tough on the outside, Palmer was a bit of a softy when you dug down a bit. And he knew he'd married a gem. They'd had their moments, rowed and shouted at each other; and once or twice he'd had to deflect a flying piece of crockery. But over the years they seemed to have bonded almost into one person; each could read the other's mind, and each knew what the other's reaction would be in certain situations. The bottom line was that they'd die for each other if need be.

Palmer had first set eyes on his gem as a young Detective Constable, when he'd gone round to her house to arrest her dad on a minor theft charge. The family were a well-known bunch of South London petty villains from Camberwell, with her three brothers seemingly inheriting the father's criminal genes. Palmer spent so much time calling round to pull one or the other of them in to 'assist with enquiries', that the very attractive daughter, who was to become Mrs Palmer, had suggested he might move in. It was a tongue-in-cheek offer, but their ongoing banter each time he called developed into something more, and both were well aware of it. When he did at last ask her for a date, 'I thought you'd never ask' was not the reply he'd expected; within six months, they were man and wife. He had obviously alerted his superiors to the situation, and all police work to do with her family was delegated elsewhere. There had been a few raised eyebrows at the time, and several side bets laid as to the length of the marriage. How he wished he had taken them on; the winnings would have more than paid for this damn cruise.

He stretched his arms and loosened his tie. Picking up the folder marked Hamilton Jarvis, he spread the pictures of the late Hamilton Jarvis, prostrate by the garden swing, across his desk, and started to read the pathologist's report, the forensics report, the crime scene report, Jarvis's medical history, his business history, and a host of other information on the deceased. He knew that somewhere in amongst that lot was the key to solving this crime; in every case Palmer had ever solved, the clue was in the victim's past. Pretty obvious really, but it would be in there somewhere. He just had to find it.

He'd finished the Hamilton Jarvis folder, and was about half way through the Peter Mouse one when his pizza arrived. So engrossed was he in trying to find a common link between the two, he ate the slice of chocolate brownie without a thought as to how it had found its way into the box.

At twenty past two in the morning, he finished reading all three folders of reports and put his notes aside. He yawned loudly, grabbed his Prince of Wales check jacket and his battered trilby from the standard government issue metal hat-stand, and made a call to the front desk to get a squad car to drop him off at home in Dulwich.

The journey only took twenty minutes at that time of night. Bright moonlight lit the house as he quietly let himself in; he let Daisy the dog out into the front garden where she peed on the lawn knowing that this would turn into a dead patch, and have Mrs P. cursing next door's cat. Mrs P would have a fit if she knew Palmer let Daisy out into the front garden for a pee every time he came home in the early hours; the dog had two walks a day for that kind of thing, and her front lawn was her pride and joy. Palmer had thought of telling her that cat pee doesn't actually kill grass, but that would put Daisy firmly in the firing line, so he didn't. He slipped a couple of dog biscuits into Daisy's bed, gave her a pat, and crept upstairs, where he put his pyjamas on and slipped softly between the sheets next to Mrs P. He fell quickly asleep, dreaming of a cruise with blue oceanic skies and calm seas; the strange bit was that the ship seemed to be made of chocolate brownies.

A hundred and forty miles away in Worcester, Ian McDougal, a forty-seven year old fork lift truck driver was murdered as he walked home from the late shift at the Cosworth factory where he worked. His killer wiped the iron bar on McDougal's overalls, and took out a thick black felt-tip pen.

Chapter 5

Palmer had been first in the office the next day, his mind
buzzing with the ifs ,whys and wherefores of the case. He
ordered enough copies of the victims' folder reports from
the print room for each of his team, outlined his immediate
action plans to Sergeant Singh, gulped down a cup of
coffee from the vending machine, grimacing at the taste of
it, and strode into the team room across the corridor where
his team were assembled, on an assortment of
uncomfortable standard government issue steel and
wooden chairs around various distressed desks and tables.

'Morning, all.'

He smiled round the room, feeling secure as he
recognised tried and trusted faces from other cases he'd
led.

'Here we go again, people. I trust you've kissed the
kids goodbye and brought your jim-jams with you, 'cause
I want this one wrapped up and on the Crown Prosecutor's
desk in record time.'

He turned to two new faces seated at the front beside
Gheeta.

'You all know each other, except we have two new
officers with us this time. Detective Sergeant Gilbert and
Detective Sergeant Burbage, who are from the Business
Fraud Department of the City of London Police Force,
whom I have asked to be seconded to us for this case as it
involves bankers and accountants from their patch.'

Groans came from the team. Bankers and accountants
were not anybody's favourite people. Palmer continued.

'It involves bankers and accountants being
murdered.'

Cheers from the team at this. Palmer silenced them
with a wave of his hand, and moved on.

'On the desks in front of you, ladies and gentlemen,
are three victim files. If you would open the one for
Hamilton Jarvis, we will get the ball rolling.'

Much turning of pages and shuffling of files ensued, until all the team had Hamilton Jarvis's file open in front of them.

'Right, well; briefly, what we have here is, to all intents and purposes, a well respected sixty-year old accountant who gets bludgeoned to death in his office for no apparent reason. Nothing stolen, valuable paintings left on the wall, wallet undisturbed in his pocket. I want to know everything there is to know about this chap. Team one?'

He looked around the room. Two hands were raised.

'You two get into his personal life; his habits, friends, clubs, close colleagues, neighbours. Who's he trodden on lately, has he sacked anyone recently, who benefits from a will if there is one. Make a bloody nuisance of yourselves, and stir up the hornets' nest until one flies out. Team two?'

Two more hands went up.

'Same goes for you, but you're working on Peter Mouse, file number two. Retired chap, on the face of it an ordinary bloke, well provided for, widower with no dependents; so who did he upset so much they had to kill him, eh? Take his life apart, and find his enemies; and if he hasn't got any start again, 'cause he must have at least one. Team three, where are you?'

Another two hands shot up.

'You've got Richard Johnson, file number three. Different kettle of fish this one; very much a jack the lad, city whiz kid banker, loads of dosh, and probably loads of hangers on too. But he was a corporate bank manager, so there'll be potential enemies galore. Has he bankrupted anybody, refused loans, or stitched them up with swap deals; find me somebody with a grudge big enough to murder for. Team four?'

Nods from the two new detectives in the front.

'Welcome, gentlemen. You two will have access to all the files, and do a forensic accounts job on each victim. Check their bank statements; look for unusual withdrawals, offshore accounts anything out of the ordinary in their finances. Oh, and you might keep an eye on the expenses and overtime sheets these other buggers in the team send in, eh?'

He winked at them, as the other officers moaned loudly.

'Right then, as you can see from the photos of the bodies we do have one very interesting lead. Each one had the letters PBT written on their forehead in thick felt-tip. So remember those initials, and see if we can't come up with somebody they all knew who had those initials, or maybe part of a car number plate, anything. They are very significant letters, or why would the killer write them on each body? My old bones tell me they are the key to the case; plus, and this doesn't show on the photos, each victim had a new one pence coin in their mouth, obviously put there by the killer; but why? We know all three worked in the financial services industry, and the PBT gesture is probably highly relevant to this; but how it is relevant, we don't yet know. So, if you get anything on this, like it being something done at some ritual. like the Odd Fellows or Masons, let me know.

'Right people, let's get to work; all the information you get you will put onto the iPads Sergeant Singh will be dishing out, and then upload to our mainframe each day through the app already programmed on them. Claire will collate it all, and hopefully our programmes will cough out some matches that tie the victims to each other in some way; as well as to their killer, fingers crossed. You are all experienced coppers in this room, or you wouldn't be on my team, so as well as the iPads and programmes doing their bit, if any of you get a hunch, a feeling about something, I want to know about it. As usual, the route to me is through Sergeant Singh, who will be pulling the strings together and handling the administration. Okay, let's go get the bastard.'

Chairs scraped the floor as the team stood and left the room, fired up by Palmer's obvious trust in them. Truth be known, they liked to be on *his* team; he hadn't one unsolved on his CV, he treated them all as equals. and hr gave them their head to go out on a limb, so long as he was kept in the loop. Most of them had been hand-picked by him from the uniformed branch over the years he had been running various teams and squads, and if somebody gets you off the uniformed beat and into the detectives' room for a couple of weeks, you owe him. You owe him big time.

Half an hour later, things were buzzing. The computer terminals in the team room were alive, their LEDs flashing as Claire uploaded the information from all the reports on the murders, and the programmes Gheeta had written sifted through them, looking for any similarities. Palmer sat in his office, mulling over the day's schedule in his mind, while Gheeta sat working out schedules, transport and paperwork.

'Well, I think I managed to fire them up a bit, eh Sergeant? I think they all get an adrenalin rush at the first case meeting; I know I do. It's like the start to a treasure hunt; the clues are all there somewhere, you know they are. It's just a matter of finding them.'

He opened Richard Johnson's file and spread the crime scene photos across the desk, repeating *sotto voce*: 'Just a matter of finding them.'

'There's something here you know,' he said, louder this time. 'I know there is, but… I can't get to it. Why should our murderer knock this guy off in a public corridor outside his flat, where he or she could be seen, and Johnson could call out for help? Why not wait a few seconds until he opens the door, and then barge in and do the job in the relative safety of his flat? It doesn't make sense to me.'

The phone on his desk rang, and he motioned Sergeant Singh to take it.

'It'll be Mrs P wanting to give me a shopping list to get on the way home,' he whispered. 'Tell her I'm in a meeting."

'No way, guv; I'm not going to tell lies. And why are you whispering? I haven't answered it yet!'

'You're a copper, Sergeant; you've got to learn to tell lies. Didn't you know that?'

He picked up the phone himself, keeping his hand over the handset.

'If I get a list of half of Morrisons stock to get on the way home, I'll have you back out on the beat forever and a day…..Brick Lane night beat too.'

He raised the handset to his mouth.

'Hello, Palmer……'

A huge smile crossed his face.

'Hello Dickie, how are you? Yes I'm fine, and you? How's the countryside these days, still chasing runaway cows and illegal muck spreaders, eh? And you… tut tut Dickie, your language hasn't improved has it, old mate – what can I do for you? Lost the Tamworth two again have you? No, I won't let you forget that… Go on then, what have you got for me?'

Palmer's demeanour changed to serious, as he listened to his old pal Detective Superintendent Richard Hart of West Mercia Police, Birmingham Division describe the murder of Ian McDougal, a fork lift driver, killed by blows from a blunt instrument to the head. But more significant to Palmer was the description of the letters PBT in felt-tip on the deceased's forehead; Superintendent Hart had seen Gheeta's *'all forces for information'* email describing the very same *modus operandi* used in their cases. But this was a spanner in the works. What possible connection could there be between a factory worker in Birmingham, two city accountants and a banker? It broke the neat circle, both logistically and demographically. West Mercia would send their file down to Gheeta on the ISN line. Palmer asked to send two of his team to Birmingham to dig around a bit into McDougal's life and times, and upload their findings to the team room. Superintendent Hart wasn't too keen on having a couple of London rozzers stomping all over his patch, but was persuaded when Palmer told him that the two he'd send were already working on the case, and would therefore be more likely to spot any similarities. He was very persuasive when he needed to be.

He put down the phone after a few minutes' reminiscing with Hart, and put Gheeta in the picture.

'Spreads it out a bit doesn't it, guv.'

'It certainly does, Sergeant. On another subject, why do you sometimes call me 'guv' and other times call me 'sir? I'm not bothered either way, but it interests me why you use one and then the other?'

Gheeta sat back and smiled.

'Protocol; I call you 'guv' because it's sort of nice and friendly, while still being respectful; and I always call you 'sir' when there's a third party present, as deference to your senior rank. But if there's not a third party present and I call you 'sir', it means you've really pissed me off – guv.'

They both laughed, and she continued.

'What's the procedure with the McDougal end of things, then?'

'Take one of the lads from team one, and one from team two. Brief them after you've had a look at West Mercia's crime report, and send them up there; that'll mean we have one with knowledge of the Hamilton Jarvis case, and one with knowledge of the Peter Mouse case, so if anything turns up remotely connected or of significance to those investigations, bells should start ringing. Right, time to meet the family I think.'

He opened the Hamilton Jarvis file and glanced at it briefly.

'I think we might pay a visit to the grieving Mrs Jarvis. Give her a bell and tell her we'll be round about two-ish.'

A thought struck him.

'I take it she does live in town?'

Gheeta tapped her keyboard and checked the screen.

'Bromley.'

'That'll do nicely.'

Chapter 6

The leafy London suburb of Bromley made a pleasant change from the hustle and bustle of Victoria Street. Palmer and Singh were comfortable in the back of an unmarked Range Rover 720 as it slipped effortlessly over Vauxhall Bridge, through Brixton, Herne Hill, over Crystal Palace, and down into Bromley.

'Who are we meeting, just the widow?'

Palmer liked to know who, or what, was waiting behind the door. Sometimes in cases like these he'd turn up and find all the widow's near and distant family had moved in, together with the doctor, vicar, and uncle Tom Cobbly and all.

Gheeta referred to her notes.

'The widow and the son, Archie.'

'Archie; unusual name.'

'He works in the family business, guv; not known as a high flyer but respected within the financial profession, and also a director of the family company.'

'Nice pads out here, aren't they?'

Palmer nodded out of the car window, towards the detached houses behind security gates with front gardens the size of Wembley Stadium.

'Not many coppers live round here, I'll bet.'

'A few bent ones maybe, guv.'

Sergeant Singh got a withering look for that remark.

'Tut tut, Sergeant. Such cynicism.'

'Can't think where I get it from, guv.'

The car slowed down as the driver checked the house names. He pulled into the drive of a large elegant Victorian-built six-bedroom affair, and slid the car silently to a stop on the tarmac outside a large porch. Palmer opened the door to get out, as a rather portly double-chinned man in his late-thirties strode from the porch; he at once reminded Palmer of Billy Bunter, a fictional sticky bun-eating character from Palmer's early reading days at primary school. Very round, very red faced, and very bouncy, with thin-rimmed spectacles perched on the end of his squat nose; all he needed was the bun.

He peered over the specs and offered a hand. Palmer half expected it to be sticky.

'Detective Palmer?'

'Detective *Chief Superintendent* Palmer.'

Palmer had worked hard for nearly forty years to get that title, and he was proud of it. His hand was pumped up and down with such ferocity that he nearly stumbled.

'Sorry yes, Detective Chief Superintendent Palmer. I'm Archie Jarvis, Hamilton's son.'

He was obviously family, as the dark suit and black mourning tie were in evidence.

'Do come inside and meet mother.'

Archie strode off, but Palmer stayed put. He had always got hot under the collar when the 'workers' of the world were ignored; he felt that the key personnel in a supermarket were the shelf-fillers and checkout staff rather than the management, and the most important people in any team were the grafters, not the managers. Archie was four strides away when Palmer spoke loudly.

'Mr.. Jarvis, this is my Sergeant, Detective Sergeant Singh.'

Gheeta had joined him from the other side of the motor. Archie stopped and retraced his steps, and sheepishly shook Gheeta's hand.

'I'm very pleased to meet you, Sergeant.'

'And me you, sir.'

They filed through the porch, which was about the size of Palmer's living room, into a wide oak-panelled hall with a large open staircase leading up to a circular first floor balcony. Palmer removed his trilby as Archie led them down the hall and off right into a rear lounge, off which a conservatory led to the rear gardens. The afternoon sun was streaming in through large French doors.

Mrs. Hamilton Jarvis rose from her armchair, and Archie made the introductions. In her late-fifties, and a slim, fragile looking lady, she wore a black trouser suit and dark glasses; as she removed them, her red eyes bore the obvious marks of having shed a few tears. Palmer made a few nice remarks about the house and gardens, together with his condolences on her loss. He declined the tea and biscuits offered, and set about the business in hand.

'You'll forgive me, Mrs Jarvis, but I have to be blunt in these matters. I'm not here to upset you or your son, or cause you any discomfort or any more grief than you have experienced already; but I am dealing with a murder case, involving more than one victim.'

Both were visibly shocked by this. Mrs Jarvis was first to speak.

'M...mm....more than one? I don't understand, Superintendent; my husband was alone in his office when he was attacked.'

Palmer chose his words with care.

'He was alone, yes. But there are significant characteristics in the murder of your husband that tie in with those found in another three recent murders.'

He let that sink in for a moment.

'Two were in the financial area that your husband worked in, another accountant and a banker; and one was totally different, involving a factory worker in Worcester.'

Archie was mystified.

'How were they tied together, Superintendent?'

'I am coming to that, sir.'

In other words shut up and listen, thought Gheeta, who was doing her job of carefully monitoring the body language of Archie and his mum. It was quite normal; no sweaty palms, fidgeting, or eye contact avoidance. They weren't killers, she was sure of that. Archie's hand was trembling a little, but many people behave in the same way in stressful situations; and sometimes just the presence of the police can have that effect on the most law-abiding citizen.

'First of all,' Palmer continued. 'May I ask what might seem to be a few impertinent questions?"

'Of course, Inspector.'

'Chief Superintendent, mother; he's a Chief Superintendent, not an Inspector,' Archie corrected her, with a big smile towards Palmer, who wasn't sure whether he was being helpful or sarcastic.

'Right then. When you first learnt of this horrible crime, did any name spring to mind?'

Both shook their heads. Mrs Jarvis was emphatic.

'No, no none at all. Hamilton had plenty of business rivals, as do all successful businessmen; no doubt he trod on a few toes from time to time, but then he got trodden on himself, too. But nothing ever lasted, no grudges were held. It was all over and forgotten, and onto the next fight.'

'Fight?'

'Not in the sense of fisticuffs, Chief Superintendent,' Archie explained. 'But there is a lot of rivalry in the accountancy business, and most big companies have a three-year contract with an accountancy firm, so at the end of the three years other firms make their pitches for the job. Being in '*the fight*' is just a term we use for it.'

'I see,' Palmer said; he was learning something new every day. 'And how about outside of the business, in your husband's social life; any enemies there?'

Mrs Jarvis was stumped for an answer.

'We both play, or rather played golf at the local club, but that's about the extent of his social life; although we did a little clay pigeon shooting now and again, and Hamilton went salmon fishing in the season. But we aren't really involved deeply in anything, not on any committees or anything like that. Didn't have the time really; Hamilton worked very long hours, so we valued any time we could spend together.'

She brushed away a tear.

'Do you have any friends or relations with the initials PBT?' Palmer asked, hoping against hope that the answer would be 'yes'.

Both wife and son shook their heads.

'Can't say those initials ring a bell with me,' Archie answered first. 'Do they with you, mother?'

She shrugged her shoulders.

'No, I'm afraid not.'

'Any clients of the business with those initials, individuals or companies?'

Palmer addressed the question to Archie.

'Well, not that come to mind immediately. But I'll search our database in the morning, and let you know one way or the other.'

'If you would, that would be very helpful,' Palmer said. He rose and looked through the open French doors. 'What a lovely garden, Mr.s Jarvis; you must spend hours on it.'

Her mind taken away from her immediate grief, Mrs Jarvis smiled and joined Palmer.

'It's my hobby, Inspector. It's so relaxing.'

Gheeta raised a hand to stop Archie from correcting his mother again.

'Do you like gardening?' she asked Palmer.

'Mrs Palmer takes good care of it, I'm afraid. She's got the green fingers.'

He was going to go on and say that everything he planted seems to die, but thought better of it in the circumstances. And in any case, it was all just a ruse to get to the next part of the interview.

'My Sergeant here has a beautiful garden; grows all her own vegetables, too. Would you let her take a little look around your garden, Mrs Jarvis? I only ask because she'll give me ear ache on the way back if she doesn't get a peep. You keen gardeners are all the same, always spying on each other!'

Mrs Jarvis beamed at Gheeta, taking her by the arm and leading her out into the garden.

'Of course you can look around. Come along, my dear.'

'Don't give her any cuttings,' Palmer shouted after them. 'I can't afford to let her have time off to plant them at the moment.'

Sergeant Gheeta Singh lived in a 5th floor Barbican apartment, with no garden; not even a window box or a pot plant on the balcony. She had no interest in horticulture of any sort, but knew Palmer had used the ploy to separate mother and son. She'd been used as a decoy in his little scenarios before, and knew exactly what he was up to.

When they'd left, Palmer sat back into a chair and smiled at Archie.

'You're a director of the family business sir, aren't you?'

'Yes, indeed I am, as is mother. Although obviously she is a non-executive director; hasn't any real say in the day-to-day running of it.'

'I only ask because in a crime of this severity we explore every angle, and so I hope you won't mind if I ask a few questions that I thought were best asked without your mother being present?'

'Oh, right, yes, fine. Fire away.'

'Business okay, is it? No financial worries?'

'No, none; we've never been stronger. We have an excellent and growing blue chip client list.'

'Any staff been sacked lately?'

Archie gave a little laugh.

'Our problem is keeping them, Chief Superintendent, not sacking them. It's a very transient business, with head hunters ready to pounce on anybody making a name for themselves, luring them away with promises of mega salaries and bonuses at the big firms. But I know what you're getting at, and I honestly can't think of anybody who's left in a nasty way. We just have to accept that we can't match the offer being made to them and wish them well.'

'Did your father have a mistress?'

Archie looked stunned.

'Really, Chief Superintendent!'

'I'm sorry, sir, but I have to ask these questions. You understand now why I didn't want your mother present. Was there a mistress or lady friend?'

'No; no, definitely not.'

He slumped back in his chair.

'Good heavens, the thought has never occurred to me – and I'm sure it never occurred to father either; he worshipped mother. Please don't ask *her* that question.'

'I have no intention of asking her, sir, no intention at all. Sorry if I upset you, but so many murders are simply a result of relationships going wrong, and I have to find these things out to discount them.'

Palmer wondered why Hamilton Jarvis worked so many late nights if he worshipped his wife so much. All those late nights couldn't have been necessary, surely? Not for work, anyway.

'One last point, Mr. Jarvis. We have a couple of our own fully trained forensic accountants in my team, who I'd like, with your permission, to come in and have a quick nose round the company.'

'Well…'

Archie wasn't altogether happy at this.

'We do have confidentiality clauses in the contracts with our clients, which could prove a problem.'

'We won't breach them, sir, it's all just routine; staff lists, client lists, engagement diaries, things like that. The force is subject to the Data Protection Act.'

Archie was relieved.

'I will make sure they get all the help they need, Superintendent.'

'Thank you,' said Palmer and stood up. 'Well, if I can get my Sergeant away from your mother's lovely garden, we will leave you in peace. I'm sorry we had to disturb you at such a time.'

He looked Archie in the eye, and his tone hardened.

'We will get this bastard, sir. I promise you that.'

Chapter 7

'He's got no trousers on.'

Palmer was looking at the crime scene photos of the Ian McDougal murder, sent down the line from the West Mercia force and printed out.

'No pants either,' Sergeant Singh commented, stating the obvious.

After leaving the Jarvis home, Palmer had gone back to the Team Room at the Yard and sat with Gheeta and Claire as they ran the input material coming from the teams in the field through comparison programmes in the computers; nothing was pairing up, except the obvious. Palmer wandered round the room and slumped into a chair. If the case plodded on at this rate, Mrs P would be going on the ruby wedding cruise with her sister, and not him. Something had to break soon. He went back to Gheeta's table and spread the photos out.

'Well, that's clearly our link, isn't it.'

He pointed to the photo, showing McDougal's forehead with PBT writ large across it.

'Any coin in the mouth?'

'Nothing in the crime report, and the post mortem report makes no mention of one either.'

Palmer eyed her questioningly.

'They would have checked the mouth, wouldn't they? The coin is very small.'

Gheeta skimmed through the report.

'Deceased had false teeth, so they must have removed them; they would have noticed anything else like a coin in the mouth.'

She hurriedly looked through the rest of the post mortem report.

'Stomach contents consisted of last known meal – no coins.'

Palmer sat down and thought aloud.

'So McDougal is obviously a victim of the same killer as our other three; but the killer's signature is changing. He's dropped the coin bit, but but still uses the

PBT letters. Why would he or she do that? Sending us a clue? It's like he, or she, wants us to solve it.'

'Could be,' Gheeta replied, thinking along the same lines. 'But the new signature also has the victim with no trousers or under wear; very strange.'

'Correct. So the PBT bit is a constant in the killer's mind, while the absent coin and bare bum bit are only relevant to this victim.'

Gheeta continued the thread.

'Which could indicate the reason for the person being a victim.'

'Okay…'

Palmer was on a roll now.

'So the reason for the first three was to do with money, hence the coin; and McDougal was… clothes?'

'Or lack of them.'

They both laughed.

'Hmmmm…' Palmer mused, stroking his chin. 'It makes sense logically, but it doesn't make sense in any credible way. But I bet it will; I just bet it will in time.'

Gheeta's phone rang and she took the call, as Palmer settled back to read the West Mercia reports in more depth, hoping for a little pointer to fly off the page and hit him between the eyes. Gheeta put her call on hold and interrupted his thoughts using her scribbled notes.

'Team two have unearthed a certain Peter Brian Tradlett.' she said, looking up from her notes. 'PBT; currently working for Hamilton Jarvis's company, and previous to that for Peter Mouse; until Mouse sold out, and he was made redundant by the new owners.'

Palmer chucked the reports onto his desk.

'Bingo! Any connection to Johnson?'

'No, none come to light as yet.'

'Right, tell team two to totally concentrate now on this guy; all the resources. I want everything we can get on him; background, family, a total life history. And get the chaps that are going into Jarvis's office to get a copy of Tradlett's engagement diary for the periods covering the murders. But tread lightly, we don't want to frighten him away if he is our killer.'

'I can't imagine he is, guv. I mean, he must be a super cool and cheeky guy to go round and put his initials on his victims, while still working for one of them. Bit obvious, isn't it?'

Gheeta was right; Peter Brian Tradlett hadn't gone round signing his initials on dead people's foreheads, or on anything else for that matter. Peter Brian Tradlett was a very competent and respected MBO – Management Buy Out advisor; four years away from retirement, and with cast iron alibis for all the relevant dates. In fact he never even suspected that he'd had a brief two days of fame in the squad's office as a serial murder suspect, as Palmer's team checked him out secretly and concluded that Peter Brian Tradlett was plain Mr.. Ordinary. Shame really; it may have made his rather boring and repetitive life a little more exciting if he had known. Either that or given him a heart attack.

The facts and cross references built up steadily on the computers' databases as the teams uploaded more and more information, and dug ever deeper for clues. There were six companies that were, or had been, clients of both Jarvis and Mouse; but only one of these, Hanniger Tools, had dealings with Johnson as well.

'Why should a company employ two accountancy firms?' Palmer asked DS Gilbert and DS Burbage at the team meeting on day eight.

'Jarvis was a limited company,' Gilbert answered. 'So one set of accountants would do the books and assess tax liabilities, and the other would do the audit, which is basically checking that the first lot hadn't missed anything.'

'And where would Johnson come into this?'

Burbage took up the reigns.

'In this case, his was the principle bank: the bank at which the company has its current account, and from which account all other banks and funds that have lent money to the company are paid out from.'

'What is this company? What do we know about them?'

Burbage continued from his notes.

'Hanniger Tools Limited, a machine tool company; makes lathes and other machinery, and exports them world-wide; accounts are up to date at Companies House, finances seem sound. Good CR with Dunn and Bradstreet – '

'CR?' Palmer interrupted.

'Credit Rating. No apparent debt other than an overdraft facility, which is quite usual. Good equity in the company, three factories on industrial estates in Birmingham, Walsall and Worcester; head office and accounts office in Worcester.'

Chapter 8

The boardroom of Hanniger Tools was very plush indeed. Charles Brackley, CEO and George Cartwright, the Finance Director, welcomed Palmer and Singh.

'Can we offer you any refreshment?' Brackley asked with an enquiring smile. 'Please do sit down.'

He indicated a leather corner unit that offered views of Worcester Cathedral and the old bridge over the Severn through a completely glass wall.

'Thank you sir, we won't be taking up too much of your time,' Palmer said, making himself comfortable, even though these modern low sofas that cuddled you like a giant marshmallow wreaked havoc with his sciatica. 'I appreciate you fitting us into your schedule at such short notice.'

Gheeta sank into her half and prepared to take notes on her laptop, quietly flicking on the camera and audio as backup.

Palmer cleared his throat as the two top men sat opposite, in firmer chairs which kept them higher than Palmer and Singh; an age-old power play that interviewers used to distinguish their exalted position over the one being interviewed. Palmer wasn't fazed, as he used it himself in the Yard's interview rooms.

'Well, I don't want to alarm you in any way, but we are investigating a series of nasty murders; each of which has a tenuous connection to Hanniger Tools.'

He let the shock sink in for a moment before continuing.

'Your company – this company, has had business dealings with the accountancy firms of Hamilton Jarvis and Peter Mouse, am I correct?'

Brackley looked at Cartwright, who responded.

'Yes, yes we employ both those firms as our accountants.'

Palmer nodded.

'And you bank through the corporate arm of Capel Barclay Hanson?'

'Yes, we do.'

'With Richard Johnson as your business manager there?'

'Yes, yes he is; Richard has been our man at Capel Barclay Hanson for over three years...'

He broke off, as a light came on in his head.

'What has Richard done, Chief Superintendent?'

'He's gone and got himself murdered, sir; as have Hamilton Jarvis and Peter Mouse. And all, we have reason to believe, by the same person.'

He let that news sink in. Brackley eventually spoke first.

'So you being here, Chief Superintendent, would indicate that you think we, Hanniger Tools, are somehow involved?'

Palmer smiled.

'Not personally sir, no; but you see, the only connection we have found so far between these men is that they each had dealings with this company. What I'd like to ask for is your permission to do some investigative work here, which is basically to talk to any staff who would have dealt with any of the deceased.'

'Well, that's basically me,' said Cartwright, who had gone white. 'I had all the day to day dealings with them, being the financial side of the company. I can't believe this...'

He stood and went to the water cooler at the side of the room, poured himself a tumbler and returned. Gheeta noted his hands were shaking a little.

'This is awful news.'

Palmer agreed.

'It is awful, yes. Did you know or socialise with any of them, Mr. Cartwright?'

'No, not at all; any business was done here. I met with Richard once a month for a quick check on the finances, and to plan our capital needs for the next couple of months. I only ever met Hamilton Jarvis the once, when he originally pitched for our account; most of the work and contact from then on was with his son, Archie. Same with

Peter Mouse; in fact, Mouse had sold up and left the company prior to them starting to work with us.'

'How did Richard Johnson strike you? Likeable lad, was he?'

'Yes, very. It's not always easy for an old fuddy-duddy finance director like me to get on with these present-day investment banker types, all Gucci suits and cockney accents; they hardly seem to be out of their prams, most of them; but Richard was very easy to work with. We are a very long established and rock solid company, Chief Superintendent; not the sort of company a bank has to worry about. We own all our factories outright, which gives us security value well above any borrowings we may have, and we have a steadily rising earnings against share price ratio.'

'I'm glad to hear it, sir.'

Palmer hadn't a clue what Cartwright was talking about.

'Did Johnson seem strange or other than ordinary the last time you met? From his diary we noted he saw you just three days before he was murdered.'

'No, quite the opposite.'

A smile crossed Cartwright's lips for a fleeting moment.

'He'd just got hold of two tickets for some racing car meeting, and being a fast car fanatic – I think they are called 'petrol-heads' – he was over the moon.'

'Didn't mention any problems with a girl friend or awkward client, nothing of that sort?'

'No, we didn't really talk about personal things much; and it would be very unprofessional of him to discuss any dealings with another client, whether good or bad, with me. Even when we were first introduced to Richard, I found it strange that afterwards he never once mentioned Robert; that's the chap who introduced us to Richard's bank, he was one of Richard's clients, and one of our suppliers. Even when the chap went bust it, was never mentioned by Richard.'

The hairs on Palmer's neck stood on end, and a shiver ran up his back. Sergeant Singh's fingers froze on the keyboard, sending row after row of lower case b's across the screen.

'When he went bust, sir? This would be the Robert chap?' Palmer said, looking at Gheeta as he slowly put the question to Cartwright.

'Yes, poor chap; known him for years. He was probably one of, if not the oldest supplier we had; provided us with specialist hardened bearings for the big lathes. He had a very good business too, a market leader in its field. Far as I can recall, he had some good contracts with a lot of solid companies.'

Gheeta needed more.

'Then how did he go bankrupt, sir?'

'The last recession, Sergeant; it took most of us by surprise. Luckily we had enough capital to ride out the storm, but we lost a lot of good manufacturing companies; and Robert Damon – that was his name, I remember now – Robert Damon was one of them. He'd just invested in new machinery on borrowed money from the bank; he was very excited about it, too. I seem to remember it was over a million and a half pounds' worth, and would have put him well and truly at the top of the pile. Then the work dried up as his clients fell by the wayside, and that was it. Bank wants its money back, forecloses on the business and sells the assets; anything left is split between the major creditors, who are lucky if they get a penny in the pound.'

Gheeta pushed for still more.

'So just to be clear, sir, Robert Damon's company was also with Capel Barclay Hanson?'

'Yes.'

'No, no he wasn't,' Brackley intervened. 'If you remember correctly, Richard Johnson was with Royal Irish Bank in those days, and when he moved to Capel Barclay Hanson we went with him. We felt at the time that our relationship with him as our business banker was very good, which is not always the case in dealings with banks, so we elected to transfer our account with him to CBH.

Robert would also have been with Royal Irish, but I don't think he transferred with Richard to CBH.'

'When did you transfer from Royal Irish to CBH?'

She didn't know why, but Gheeta had an inkling this date was going to be important.

'January 24th, 2010.,' Carter said precisely. 'I'm bound to remember that date, it was my silver wedding anniversary.'

Palmer laughed.

'My ruby's in a fortnight, taking the wife on a cruise, hopefully. It's all booked and paid for, so got to wrap up this nasty little state of affairs by then, or it'll be her sister going up the gangplank with her – and me probably walking the plank!'

They all laughed.

'Right, gentlemen, if I could bother you for the last known address of Robert Damon and his business, we will take up no more of your time.'

'Do you think *he* did it?'

Brackley obviously didn't.

'I wouldn't have thought it of Robert; from what I remember of him he was a lovely man. I must say that talking about him today has made me feel guilty about not keeping in touch with him.'

Danger signals flashed in both Palmer and Gheeta's heads. They exchanged a glance. Palmer took the initiative.

'Well, I would ask you, both of you, not to contact him just now, if you wouldn't mind. Perhaps after we have eliminated him from enquiries would be a better time for a reunion.'

His tone left them in no doubt that this was an order, and they nodded in agreement.

'My Sergeant will contact you when the time is more convenient.'

Palmer ended the meeting with the perfunctory thanks, as he struggled to extricate himself from the sofa's grip, Gheeta offering a helping hand. Brackley got Damon's last known address from the Hanniger Tools accounts department, then they bade their farewells and left.

Palmer was hardly able to contain his excitement as they settled into the back of the squad car to make their way back to the Yard.

'It fits! It bloody well fits! This Robert bloke – '

'Damon, Robert Damon,' Gheeta said.

'Yes, Robert Damon. He hasn't shown up on the records of the two accounts firms or on our software because he went bust and they probably deleted him; and he wouldn't show up on Johnson's client list because he didn't follow him to the new bank from Royal Irish. Why didn't we think to look at Richard Johnson's previous employment, eh?'

'Because we didn't know he had any, guv.'

'But we didn't look to find out, did we Sergeant? Make a note to give team three a rollicking for not looking.'

'But team three weren't told to – '

Palmer cut her short.

'Initiative, Sergeant; they should have used their initiative. Not up to us to nanny them.'

'No, guv; and guv?'

'Yes?'

'Before you ask, *'rising earnings above share price ratio'* means the company is worth more than all its shares added together.'

'I knew that.'

'No you didn't.'

'No, I didn't.'

They both laughed.

Chapter 9

'Bloody Kew Gardens isn't it, eh?'

Palmer stood in the doorway of his office with hands on hips, surveying the dozen or so large container-grown garden shrubs that covered the floor space, and the three that reached up to the ceiling. Sergeant Singh opened the delivery note left by the nursery's delivery driver and read it aloud.

'My dear Sergeant Singh, thank you so much for your sympathy and company in the garden the other afternoon. I thought you might use these in your own garden.'

She turned to Palmer.

'They're from Mrs Hamilton. Guv, I haven't got a window box, let alone a garden.'

'You have now,' Palmer giggled, edging his way through the foliage to his desk. 'Probably a lost tribe in here somewhere.'

'What am I going to do with them, guv? I can't send them back.'

'Your dad got a garden, has he?'

'No, he's got a patio with a barbecue thing on it.'

'Hmm, got a problem then, haven't you?'

Palmer was enjoying this.

'You could have them, guv? You've got a large garden, and Mrs P. loves gardening.'

'Actually you're right, she'd love this lot.'

'Right, that's settled then. I'll scrounge a wagon and get them sent over.'

'Better not be any bugs in them; if they get into her vegetables, you'll be for it.'

He scooped his folders from the desk and fought his way back towards the door.

'I wouldn't be surprised if Neanderthal man popped out of them.'

Assistant Commissioner Bateman peered around the door.

'Talk of the Devil...'

Bateman was taken aback.

'Good Heavens! Having a garden fête, Palmer?'

Chapter 10

In the team room, Palmer looked down at the single sheet as it clicked off the printer.

'Is that all there is?'

Claire turned from her terminal.

'That's it, sir. He seems a model citizen; no previous, other than two parking fines before 2010, and then after that loads of County Court Judgments and bailiff warrants.'

She pointed to the computer screen.

'And if you look at the Companies House records here, they all tie into when his business went bust. You've got a summary of the business accounts for the four years before that at the bottom of the paper.'

Palmer took in the figures.

'He had a good business until then didn't he, eh? Blimey, four million gross profit in 2008! That can't be bad. Can you download the complete accounts from anywhere?'

Claire smiled.

'I think we might manage that, sir.'

Palmer knew that smile.

'Oh, I see. One of Sergeant Singh's bespoke programmes, eh?'

'Yes, sir. Give me half an hour and I'll have them. It's an encrypted line.'

'A *what* line?'

'Encrypted, sir. I'll get this information from Companies House, but it's not generally available; you need a password and we haven't got it. It's guarded by an ever-changing code that mashes everything into numbers, dots and dashes; that's called *encrypted*.'

'And we have a programme that can get through that?'

'We have, sir.'

'But it's not legal.'

'I couldn't possibly comment, sir.'

'We haven't had this conversation, have we Claire?'

'No, sir.'

'Okay. When you've got them, give them to DS Gilbert and Burbage; get them to take a look and then to talk to me when they're done.'

Palmer was well aware that some of Gheeta's programmes were not totally within the law, but she was always able to provide him with the information he wanted so he didn't ask questions. He turned for the door.

'Right then; let's find my Sergeant, and then I think we'll pay Robert Damon a visit…'

He looked down at his sheet of paper.

'In Tooting? Not a very exclusive area for someone who had four million coming in, eh?'

'The operative word being *had*, sir.'

'Yes, you're right there. That's a big chunk of money to lose from your wage packet; could make you a very bitter person that could; very bitter.'

Gheeta entered, and a big grin appeared on Palmer's face.

'Ah, look who's just come in; the Monty Don of the Serial Murder Squad! Grab your fork and spade, Monty; we're off to Tooting.'

Chapter 11

The large red brick Victorian residences that border Tooting Bec Common had long since lost the majestic look of opulence their original Victorian owners used as a sign of their wealth. Now they looked faded and tired in the afternoon drizzle from an overcast threatening sky, their insides bashed about by cheap 'developers' to make numerous low rental bed-sits of no quality; and yet they still managed to somehow hold onto a little pride from their magnificent past, like an old soldier bent and withered with age, but still with the row of tarnished medals on his chest telling of past glories.

'I used to play Sunday League football here when I was a boy.'

Palmer pointed from inside the squad car towards the threadbare grass pitches, as memories of the smell of embrocation and brown lace-up leather boots flooded back.

'You and Tom Brown was it, sir?'

Gheeta permitted herself a smile, as did DS Bryant and DC Chapman from team three who were in the back.

'Bollocks.'

Palmer looked out of the side window.

'Changed a lot this place has; it used to be really posh round here, a very upper class area.'

'All bedsits and petty crime now, sir,' DS Bryant spoke up from the back. 'I did six months with Regional Crime Squad out of Streatham Hill a couple of years ago; mainly lots of minor drug teams and break-in boys, a hard area. I bet we've been clocked a few times already, and mobiles are ringing in the street dealers' pockets warning them.'

Gheeta pointed to an imposing five-storey pile coming up on the left.

'That's Damon's place. Flat three.'

The car pulled up just past the building.

'Right then.'

Palmer was first out, rubbing his sciatic thigh as the others joined him.

'Bryant, you get round the back and cover any fire escapes; I don't want our man doing a runner that way. Chapman, take the front door. Sergeant Singh and myself will go inside. Once we are in, nobody comes in or out, OK? Lock it down. With a bit of luck our man will be in, but if he's out he may have unfortunately left his door open…'

There were knowing smiles all round at this.

'So I don't want to be disturbed. If anybody arrives get me on the walkie-talkie, understood?'

The once well-tended front garden was now a wilderness, peppered with broken brown furniture and split rubbish bags where the feral cats had searched for a meal. Palmer pushed the gate, which scraped open. A sprightly-looking elderly lady walking towards them from further down the road stopped, looked, took in the action for a moment, and decided to cross onto the common and watch from a handy bench.

Gheeta saw her, and thought that police activity in the area was probably a regular occurrence, a spectator sport for the locals, and noted that the lady would be a safe distance away should anything untoward occur; the last thing they wanted was a fracas with a suspected serial killer in which a member of the public got involved.

The front door was open, and the bells on the splintering frame numbered eleven; flat three had no name. They edged into the hallway, squeezing past two dilapidated pushchairs parked on the bare floorboards, and mounted the wooden uncarpeted stairs on tiptoe. The light switch didn't work, making the area fairly dim.

Palmer knew DC Bryant was quite right about the area's reputation, and guessed that most of the doors would be heavily secured on the inside; they were probably being watched through the peepholes as they went by.

Flat three on the first floor had an old and heavily oak-panelled door, whose paint had long since done a runner; dents, grooves and splits to the frame gave a hint that forced entry had been tried a few times in the past, most probably by daytime opportunist thieves. Palmer listened for a moment, then put his eye to the peephole, fully expecting to stare straight at someone looking back out. Instead he saw a small hallway, with a solitary coat hanging from a wall hook to the right. He rattled the letterbox a couple of times, keeping an eye to the peephole just in case somebody grabbed the coat and went the other way fast. Instead a figure emerged from a side room, and came to the door. Their eyes met through the peep hole, and Palmer drew back.

'Who is it?'

The voice was firm.

'Police,' Palmer replied, using his stern voice. 'Open the door please; we'd like a few words with you, sir.'

The door opened a few inches, and two clunky security chains were visible. An eye looked through the gap

'Mr. Damon? Robert Damon?'

'Yes?'

Palmer pressed his warrant card to the gap.

'Chief Superintendent Palmer, Scotland Yard; this is Detective Sergeant Singh.'

Gheeta showed her card.

'I wonder if we might come in for a few minutes, sir. We believe you may be able to assist us in an enquiry; much easier to talk in private than on a communal landing, sir.'

Nobody wants to talk to the police in public, especially when you don't know the reason for their visit. Damon went to shut the door, so as to release the chains, and found Palmer's foot placed firmly 'twixt frame and door.

'Oops. Sorry sir, old habits die hard.'

He removed his foot; the door closed, the chains slipped off, and the door opened again. They went in as Robert Damon shut and chained the door behind them. He was forty-eight, and looked fairly fit; well-groomed, dark hair with grey streaks, and about five foot ten. His appearance certainly didn't fit that expected of a typical resident of this house; he looked more like a well-to-do businessman, in dark well-creased trousers, open neck check sports shirt and patent leather shoes.

'After you, sir.'

Palmer waved Damon past them in the narrow hall, and they followed him into a sitting room. A very nice sitting room, thought Gheeta; well-kept, tidy, and clean, with no dust; the usual three-piece suite in buttoned green leather, a flat screen TV, two ladder back chairs and an old mahogany dining table. No clutter. The lace-curtained windows gave a wide view of the playing field below.

'Please sit down.'

Damon indicated the sofa, and sat in an armchair. Palmer took a ladder back and sat with his back to the window, while Gheeta sat between Damon and the door; all good training manual stuff, Damon was now unwittingly in an interview scenario where he couldn't see both officers at once, which gave them the opportunity of exchanging glances and signs. Palmer had also made sure he was in a higher chair than Damon, which put him in the *'power'* position.

'How can I help you then?' Damon said. 'Another robbery downstairs? Thank my lucky stars I managed to get an upstairs flat.'

Palmer shifted a little forward on the chair, removed his trilby, and became very serious.

'It's a bit more serious than that, sir. I'd like to ask you a few questions about some old business acquaintances if you don't mind.'

Damon looked surprised.

'Really? Well, it's quite a time since I was in business, Chief Superintendent, but go on.'

Palmer smoothed the brim of his hat.

'Can you recall when you last saw Ian McDougal?'

Damon looked confused, thought Gheeta.

'McDougal?'

Palmer held his silence, a trick that entices a further response from the other party.

'I don't know any Ian McDougal; I'm sure I don't.'

Palmer nodded.

'How about a banker called Richard Johnson, does that name ring a bell?'

Damon's mood changed.

'Oh yes, indeed,' he said, his recognition tinged with sourness. 'He was my bank manager at Royal Irish when I was in business. What's he done. run off with the bank's money? That wouldn't surprise me at all.'

He smiled, and Palmer smiled back.

'What about Peter Mouse and Hamilton Jarvis?'

'Those two as well, eh? That makes a trio of *spivs in suits* if ever there was one. Johnson, Mouse and Jarvis; what have they been up to, Superintendent?'

'It's *Chief* Superintendent; and they've all been murdered, sir.'

Palmer hit below the belt. Damon stiffened.

'Oh my God… Are you kidding? Murdered?'

'When did you last see Johnson, sir?'

Damon's mind was racing.

'Chief Superintendent, do I need a solicitor here?'

Palmer smiled, noting that Damon had got his title right this time.

'No, sir. You're not under caution, just assisting in enquiries as they say. And the last time you saw Johnson was?'

'Ages ago. I'm afraid the business fell victim to the recession and… that was the end of the line.'

'And you've not seen or heard from Johnson since?'

'No; and to be quite honest, Chief Superintendent, I wouldn't want to. He wasn't exactly helpful in my time of need.'

'Banks do have a tendency to take away the umbrella when it rains, sir.'

'Johnson never provided an umbrella to start with.'

Damon was obviously still very angry about whatever had happened.

'I just hope to God that all bankers aren't like that little shit; I don't like to talk ill of the dead, but I can't find any sympathy for him. When the chips were down he didn't only jump ship, he looted it first; he pulled the financial rug from under us, when any fool could see we would have gotten through with a little help. His bloody bank got everything, all the assets; even my car.'

He relaxed for a moment, and then stiffened again.

'Oh God, you suspect me, don't you?'

'I wouldn't go that far, sir. We are just talking to people at the moment, trying to get a picture of the chap and the other two victims; trying to fit the jigsaw pieces together. Do the initials PBT mean anything to you, now or then?'

'PBT?'

'Mmm-hmm'

'No, no I can't say they do. Why, should they?'

'No, not necessarily; just another piece in the jigsaw.'

Gheeta had noticed Damon's attitude had changed; he was now guarded and abrupt in his manner, sitting forward on the edge of the arm chair, not relaxed sitting back into it. She cast a cursory glance round his immediate area, looking for anything he might grab as a weapon if he made a run for it. Palmer, too, had noticed.

'Do you have a job, sir? What did you do after the business failed?'

'No, I don't have a permanent job; I do factory work through agencies, and I get benefit payments when not working. The higher you are, the further you fall, Chief Superintendent. Are you going to caution me now?'

'I hadn't thought it necessary, sir; as I said before, we are just doing preliminary enquiries. How about Peter Mouse, when did you see him last?'

Robert Damon sat in silence as his brain told him exactly what was going on, and exactly why these officers were here, with probably more outside. Four murders, and he had known three of the victims, all of whom had been part of his business collapse; he *was* a suspect, no doubt about that. Palmer's eyes bore into his until he looked away.

'I'm not answering any more questions until I get legal advice.'

Palmer stood and looked down at him. He put his trilby on and turned to look out of the window, thrusting his hands in his pockets. Either Damon was the killer, and the questioning had made him realise the police were onto him; or he was innocent, and thought the circumstances of his bankruptcy could be twisted to make him *look* like the killer.

'Sergeant, caution Mr. Damon please.'

If that's how you want to play it, then that's the way we will play it, thought Palmer.

Sergeant Singh gave the caution from memory, and asked Damon if he understood. He did.

'Right then.'

Palmer swung round and strode to the door, looking at Damon as he did so.

'Robert Damon, I am arresting you on suspicion of the murders of Richard Johnson, Peter Mouse, Hamilton Jarvis and Ian McDougal and taking you into custody, where you will be provided with a lawyer. Is there anybody you'd like us to call before we leave?'

'No.'

Chapter 12

Sergeant Singh was going over her notes on her iPad when Palmer strode purposefully into the office later that afternoon. He threw himself into his chair, banging his feet up onto the desk with two loud thumps.

'Bastard won't say a word; not a bloody word. If we have to prosecute on circumstantial and motive, this could take months to put together. By the time it's put to bed, the bloomin' cruise ship will be back in dock, and Mr.s P. will be passing round the photos – photos of her and her sister! I need to get a confession on this one, and quick.'

He swung his feet off again and paced the room. Gheeta put her notes down.

'Who's his lawyer?'

'He's using the duty solicitor, Ernie Fredericks from Braxton's.'

'That doesn't help, does it?'

Palmer grunted in agreement. Good solicitor though he was, Ernie Fredericks was slow, one of the old school solicitors; pushing seventy, and refusing to retire while his faculties remained bright, Ernie Fredericks was determined to keep the awful scenario of 24/7 retirement boredom that he had seen envelope some of his contemporaries well away, for as long as he could. He knew the ropes and all the tricks. He kept to the letter of procedural law, and insisted on pausing interviews if he felt the need to confer with his client, and retiring to a private room with them. Most solicitors would do it then and there in the interview room and carry on, but not Ernie; Ernie was paid by the hour.

Gheeta was scrolling through her notes.

'You know, he was completely unruffled until you mentioned Mouse and Jarvis. He's either a very good liar, or totally innocent; there was no recognition in his voice or body movement when you mentioned Ian McDougal. He was quite prepared to talk about Johnson in terms verging on hatred, until he realised he'd talked himself into being a suspect, and then he clammed up when Mouse and Jarvis were mentioned.'

Palmer nodded, rubbing his sore eyes.

'If he's innocent, then why just shut down like that? Get the team to start working on him; times and places, where's he been, what's he been doing since his business failed. Oh, and get the address of his old factory; it might be worth having a look at, if it's still there. I think I'll be stuck in the interview room with him and Fredericks all day tomorrow at the rate we're going. Take a look at it in the morning, but take a couple of the team with you, Sergeant. Could be more bodies hidden there.'

'Do you think he's our serial killer then, guv?'

'Well, he's certainly got the reasons. But to be quite honest... I just don't know,' he said, as he rose to leave.

'Hang on,' Gheeta said, looking up sharply. 'You just said there might be *more* bodies hidden at the factory.'

'Don't tell me you're scared?'

'Of course not, but that's not the point, guv. None of the bodies were hidden, were they? No attempt to conceal them. Strange, that.'

'Not really, not if the killer actually wanted them found. But I don't know why. Was he or she sending a warning to others that he was after them? I don't know.'

He sat back down and tipped his chair back against the wall, leaning his head back into his hands and staring at the ceiling.

'Sergeant?'

'Yes, guv?'

'There's a snail on the ceiling which I believe belongs to you, courtesy of Mrs Jarvis.'

Chapter 13

Palmer kept Damon in the cells overnight and continued his interview at nine the next day; by eleven, he had had enough. He cut short the interview and motioned Ernie Fredericks to leave the interview room with him. In the corridor he turned on Fredericks, ready to explode.

'What are you playing at Ernie, for Christ's sake? No comment after no comment!'

'He won't even talk to me, Justin. I can't make him speak.'

'Yes you can, you're his bloody solicitor! You are there to advise him, Ernie; so go in and advise him to talk. I am going to break for half an hour – half an hour, Ernie, and that's all the time you've got to get him talking and answering my questions. If he doesn't I will sling him in a cell, and on the basis of his being a hostile witness I'll get an extension to keep him there until I do get something. Understand that, Ernie? He's a suspect on two murder charges now, and maybe a further two to come. You explain to him that I have enough circumstantial evidence to prosecute, and I will ask for a prison remand until the trial, which could put him inside for a year at the rate our court system grinds along. He doesn't look the kind of chap that would enjoy being banged up; and he'd enjoy it even less if somebody let slip to the other prisoners that he was up on paedophile charges.'

'But he's not!'

'I know he's not, and I've no idea how such rumours start; but somehow they do. Half an hour, Ernie; half an hour.'

He made his way back up to the Team Room, hopeful that Sergeant Singh might be having better luck. But Gheeta was downbeat when she returned from Damon's old factory premises.

'Nothing, guv; just a boarded-up factory on a small derelict industrial estate waiting for re-development. Ground floor only, couple of offices, remnants of old machines, bits of tangled metal the scrappers missed, and, I'm glad to say, no bodies.'

She removed her hat and sat next to Palmer in the Team room, where he was watching Claire input new material data.

'Never mind Sergeant, worth a try; could have turned up something. I've given Ernie half an hour to get Damon talking.'

'Is he still playing hard to get then?'

'Yes. I said I'd sling him in remand if he didn't open up.'

'You'll be lucky; the Assistant Commissioner will never let you hold him without charge.'

'The Assistant Commissioner won't know, will he?'

Palmer took a gulp of coffee from the machine in the corridor.

'Yuk! This is awful – must contravene the Trades Description Act if they call it coffee.'

He grimaced as he put the cup down.

'We need a breakthrough. We've actually got nothing concrete so far, have we? No fingerprints, no witnesses, no DNA, no murder weapon; just one suspect and a lot of circumstantial.'

'And a partner.'

Claire turned from the computer screen, smiling broadly.

'What partner?'

Palmer turned towards her quickly, and in doing so knocked over the coffee onto his hand.

'Shit, that's hot!'

Claire continued as he grabbed a cloth from a drawer and mopped up the spillage.

'We've downloaded all the information on Damon's accounts from CH – that's Companies House…'

'I know, I know,' Palmer said, blowing on his hand.

'It tells us that at the time of Robert Damon's company going bust, he wasn't a sole trader but a partnership with another party.'

'Who?'

'His wife.'

Palmer and Gheeta looked at each other. The thought of Damon being married hadn't occurred to them; the flat had given the distinct impression of being a bachelor pad.

'He's married?'

'Or maybe they divorced since the Company's downfall,' Gheeta suggested. 'That flat was definitely not for two.'

Claire was busy on the keyboard again.

'Give me five minutes and I'll have the answer. I'll start at Somerset House BDMs and work through.'

'Births, Deaths and Marriages,' Gheeta answered, before Palmer had even asked the question.

'Here,' Claire said, reaching over to take a sheet off the printer as it buzzed it out. 'The address of Mr. and Mrs. Damon taken off the CH record.'

Palmer took it from her and looked with interest.

'Harrow; a bit of a come-down from there to a bedsit in Tooting Bec. Let's take a trip out and see if the wife is still there.'

He was about to don his trilby when he remembered his half-hour promise to Ernie Fredericks.

'Damn, I can't leave Ernie in limbo. I left him quaking in his pinstripes, so hopefully I should get a result there.'

He passed the sheet of paper to Gheeta.

'Probably better if you go. Softly softly, be very formal; could be a bit of a shock to be told her hubby might be a serial killer.'

'Ex hubby, sir,' Claire said, sitting back from her terminal. 'Married in 1976, divorced in 2010.'

'Well now,' Palmer said, as he rubbed his hands together. 'That does add some weight to his motive doesn't it, eh? Not only can Mr. Damon blame the victims, if they are his victims, for his business failure, but he can also blame them for his marriage failing as well. He must be a very bitter and twisted soul inside, mustn't he?'

'I'll have to tread carefully, guv; if his ex has re-married or got a new partner living with her, I can't really barge in. She may not have told him about her past?'

Palmer considered Gheeta's point.

'Yes, you're right; if she's got a new life going, which is highly probable after fourteen years, the last thing she wants is this little lot rearing up its ugly head. But she'll have to be put in the picture sometime, because we do need to talk to her. If we go to prosecution she'll undoubtedly be called as a witness; so what we need to do is have a quiet word off the record now to brief her, and bring her up to date. You'd better also warn her that being a serial murder case, once it goes public the press will be all over her like flies on – '

Gheeta interrupted him quickly.

'Jam, guv; and it's bees.'

'Exactly. Mind you, if the divorce was a bitter one she'll probably sell her story and make a fortune. Anyway, whatever she does is no concern of ours; but she needs to be interviewed, so have a lovely afternoon, Sergeant. Meanwhile, I'm off to make Mr. Damon's life a bit worse for him.'

He patted Claire on the arm.

'Well done, Claire. Information technology, the future of crime solving!'

And he left the room with a new-found bounce to his gait. Gheeta stood, and addressed the wall.

'Good afternoon Mrs. Damon, or whatever you call yourself these days. I'm Detective Sergeant Gheeta Singh from the Serial Murder Squad at New Scotland Yard, and I'd just like to make you aware that the husband you shared thirty years of your life with has recently bludgeoned to death some of your old business advisors. I wondered if we might have a little chat?'

She turned to Claire as she left the room.

'I get all the easy jobs, don't I?'

Chapter 14

Palmer wasn't in a good mood. He'd realised by the expression on Fredericks's face when he entered the interview room that no progress had been made with Damon, and the suspect was still firmly shut up like a clam; a slight shrug from Fredericks confirmed the situation to Palmer. He keyed up the interview tape, and then sat silently for half a minute looking unblinkingly at Damon before talking in a soft, resigned manner.

'Mr. Damon, your solicitor Mr. Fredericks has informed you of the range of charges that can be brought against you. He has no doubt underlined the severity of all those charges, because they are for murder, Mr. Damon, and each will carry a life sentence if the court brings in a guilty verdict. In other words, sir, the rest of your life will be spent in a cell less than the size of this room, and probably shared with two other men who you may not find very appealing. Now, just in case Mr. Fredericks has not made you aware of the recent changes regarding suspects remaining silent during interviews or giving *no comment* answers, let me put you in the picture. The courts look upon both as an admittance of guilt.'

He gave Fredericks a look that froze him into silence, if he had been about to contest Palmer's twisting of the law.

'Therefore, by common deduction your actions here today will undoubtedly bring about a direction to the jury from the judge to find you guilty of all charges.'

He checked his watch.

'Interview ends 12:16.'

He switched off the tape, took it from the machine, bagged it and stood, arms folded, as Fredericks signed across the seal. Damon remained inert.

'Mr. Fredericks,' Palmer said, in a softer tone of voice. 'As you will be aware, I am within my rights to put your client in a remand cell for forty-eight hours, which I intend to do while I apply for a court order to remand him indefinitely to prison. However, in the vain hope that your client might come to his senses and make a full confession that could improve his chances of leniency in his sentence, I will leave you for a further hour.'

He took a deep breath.

'As far as I am aware, your client has no previous criminal record, and with your expert advice might possibly convince a jury of the need for psychiatric tests in a secure environment; which, in turn, might possibly convert a prison sentence into one of detention in a suitably secure institution.'

He opened the door and beckoned the duty officer.

'Put a man in here please, and see that Mr. Fredericks and the prisoner get any refreshments they require.'

He nodded to Fredericks.

'Right then, I will see you in an hour.'

In the corridor, he shook his head at the duty officer.

'What do you make of him, Geoff?'

'Not helping himself is he, Justin?'

Sergeant Geoffrey Bleadon and DCS Palmer went back a long way, both having come out of the cadet corps at the same time.

'No, he's not, which is baffling. If I was up on four murder charges, I'd be squirming every which way to try and get out of it. But he just sits there like a statue.'

'I reckon he's innocent. I was watching through the mirror; he's innocent, mate.'

They leant against opposite walls of the corridor, Palmer with his hands thrust deep into his pockets.

'Circumstantial points to him, Geoff; and it's good circumstantial.'

'I'll give you odds that he's clean.'

'How good are the odds?'

'Ten to one.'

Palmer raised his eyebrows.

'That good, eh?'

'Justin, that guy in there is *not* a serial killer.'

'So why the silence then?'

'No idea; crack that and you've cracked the case, mate. He could just be scared shitless, or on the edge of a breakdown; I've seen that before. I mean, just look at him.'

They both looked through the one-way glass window in the door to where Fredericks was in earnest conversation with his client.

'He's a regular bloke getting on with his life, and then bang, he's up on murder charges. He hasn't even made a phone call; not even to the wife.'

'Ex-wife.'

'Family then.'

'Hasn't any that we can trace.'

'Okay, but you'd ring somebody, surely. Somebody will be wondering where he is. He must have some commitments; at work, meetings, social life...'

'So this silence is overriding all that isn't it eh?'

'It is.'

'So what's he gaining from it then?'

'Dunno, time maybe?'

'Time for what?'

'I've no idea; perhaps time for something to happen that clears him. Or time for an accomplice to get away, if there's more than one killer.'

'Yes, but if he's innocent and wants to clear his name, all he has to do is give us some alibis. Four murders, Geoff! He must have an alibi for one of them if he's innocent, surely?'

'You'd have thought so, Justin. Okay, so he doesn't want to clear himself.'

'Maybe he does, but not just yet... but then why not yet?'

'Give his accomplice time to scarper.'

'No, there's no accomplice. When we first spoke to him at his flat and mentioned the victims' names, he spoke of them in the present tense; he thought they were still alive, and made it obvious that he didn't like them. He shut up as soon as I told him they'd been killed. I thought it was all a pretence, you know, talking about not liking them so we'd think he wasn't the killer.'

'So why wouldn't he carry on that way then? Why shut up?'

Palmer was working it out. He spoke very slowly, as his thoughts juggled themselves into place.

'Because up until a certain point he thought we were investigating his old business contacts for their own financial crimes; embezzlement, stuff like that. As soon as he cottoned onto the fact that they were the victims, that they had been murdered, he shut up...'

Palmer's voice trailed away as the pieces fell into place in his head.

'Of course! He shut up because he'd guessed who the killer was – and by staying silent we'd keep working on him, thinking it was definitely him. He's protecting someone, Geoff! Shit! It's got to be the ex-wife; here we are piling up all the motives against him, losing the business, being bankrupted, marriage breaking down, and they can all apply just as well to the ex-wife who was a partner in the business!'

He kicked the wall in self anger.

'The bastard shut up to keep us concentrating on him rather than her. Oh Jesus! My Sergeant's gone round to see her this afternoon!'

Chapter 15

Sergeant Singh got out of the patrol car and gave her tunic a cursory brush down with her hand, flicking off the crumbs from an almond slice she'd managed to eat on the way to stop her stomach rumbling during any interview she would be carrying out with Mrs. Damon. Palmer didn't seem to get hungry during the day, so you had to grab food and drink when you could when working in his department.

55 Marmott Road, Harrow was nice; very nice. A detached four-bed with front and rear gardens, and an integral garage to the right; probably 1930s-build, with a pebble drive leading up to the porch and garage. Gheeta crunched her way up the drive to the porch and pressed the bell, hearing it ring somewhere inside. After a few seconds, an elderly lady in her seventies peered through the glazing, saw the Sergeant's uniform and warrant card being shown, and opened the door.

'Hello? Can I help you?' said a stern commanding voice.

'Mrs. Damon?'

'No, she's out at the moment. Can I help? I'm her mother. Is everything all right?'

'Yes, Mrs...?'

'Raynes, Dorothy Raynes. Is my daughter all right? Has she had an accident?'

The voice was now worried, and Gheeta gave her a reassuring smile.

'No, nothing to worry about Mrs. Raynes. I just need to have a chat with her.'

'Oh, well err...'

She stood back and beckoned Gheeta in.

'Do come in. She won't be long, just popped down to the shops. I've just made a pot of tea, would you like a cup?'

'Love one.'

That would wash down the almond slice a treat, Gheeta thought. Mrs Raynes led her into the front sitting room.

'Do sit down.'

She peered through the net curtains to where Gheeta's patrol car was parked.

'Would your colleagues like a cup?'

'There's only me, Mrs.Raynes. But thank you for the offer, it was very thoughtful of you.'

Mrs Raynes smiled.

'Manners don't cost a penny dear, do they? I think I've some assorted biscuits somewhere too. My daughter should be back any minute; now make yourself comfortable.'

Chapter 16

Palmer was pacing round the operations room in the bowels of New Scotland Yard like a caged panther. Around him dispatchers were busy with their radios, and giant wall screens plotted the GPS signals from the mobile units throughout London. It was a busy place.

'Why won't she answer? Isn't the signal getting through?'

The ops manager was stood beside a seated operator, who was continually calling Sergeant Singh's call sign.

'It's getting through, sir; she's just not answering. She could be parked in a dead spot.'

'What about her personal radio?'

'No answer on that either, sir.'

'Pull the nearest car to front reception to pick me up and get me to Harrow; and get any cars in the Harrow area round to that address I gave you, and tell them, softly, softly, no sirens; just get close and observe. I want anything that happens relayed to me in my car, okay? And keep trying to raise her.'

He rushed from the room and took the stairs up two at a time, which he immediately regretted as his sciatica sliced through his right thigh like a burning needle. At his fourth-floor office he grabbed his jacket and trilby and hurried back down, grunting and oooing as the sciatic pain stabbed at him again. He ran out of the building and into the waiting car, where he rubbed his leg hard as it sped into the afternoon Victoria Street traffic, siren wailing and blues on. He was worried about Gheeta; really worried.

Everything looked normal, and all seemed to be serenely quiet from the outside of 55 Marmott Road, Harrow. Palmer stood beside the squad car, sixty yards up the road from the house and out of view; sixty yards the other way, a marked patrol car sat watching too.

'How long have they been here?' he asked the four local officers in a marked car parked in front of his.

'Two minutes before us, sir. Ten minutes tops,' replied a young constable behind the wheel.

Palmer held out his hand.

'Give us your radio for a minute, Constable. What's their call sign?'

'Tango two eight, sir. We're Tango two seven.'

Palmer pressed the radio on and spoke to base control.

'Tango two seven to Base.'

'Go ahead, Tango two seven,' came the crackly reply.

'This is Detective Chief Superintendent Palmer, with Tango two seven, Base. Could you patch me through to Tango two eight please.'

'No problem, sir, they already receive you. You have full comms with all the local cars and officers. Go ahead, sir. Base out.'

'Thank you, Base. Tango two seven to Tango two eight, anything to report on the premises, any movement?'

Tango two eight came back, a female voice.

'Two eight to two seven, Sergeant Lewis here, sir. Nothing happening as far as we can see, no movements whatever; the place looks empty. There is a side alley between it and number fifty-seven, where we could get to the rear of fifty-five unseen, Two eight out.'

Palmer thought for a moment.

'Yes, good observation, Lewis. Put two lads down it to the rear, with extreme caution though; we think we are looking for a middle-aged white female who could be very dangerous, as well as my Detective Sergeant, who will be in uniform and possibly being held in a hostage situation. Her safety is paramount. I'm authorising CS gas and taser if needed.'

'Understood, sir. We will make our way to the back.'

Palmer and his team watched as two officers quietly slipped from the far patrol car, one being Sergeant Lewis. Both scrambled along under cover behind the front and side hedges at number 57, up to the house front, and then quickly disappeared into the side alleyway to the rear.

'Right then lads, let's see what we can find. Two with me, two guard the front, and same thing goes for you; be careful, and use spray or taser if you think an attack is coming. I'll take the flack if the IPCC get shirty afterwards.'

Palmer had no time for the Independent Police Complaints Committee; an overpaid quango whose members had never had to take on a weapon-brandishing thug or nutter, so they hadn't the right to judge an officer's actions in a live situation, that was his view of them.

He and two uniformed officers strolled to the front of the house, trying to look relaxed and calm while inside them every reaction was on standby should something nasty happen; the lids were off their CS spray cans, and their tasers were off lock. Palmer's eyes scanned the ground and upstairs windows for any sign of movement. He reckoned there would be plenty of eyes watching them from the neighbours on either side and opposite; it was that sort of suburb, full of retired persons now sitting on a fortune in bricks and mortar, whose kids were probably hoping mum and dad would pop their clogs before the property bubble burst. They crunched up the short drive and Palmer pushed the bell, hearing it ring inside. The Sergeant had positioned himself behind Palmer, his finger firmly on the CS gas cartridge button, but out of sight to anyone opening the door. There was no answer, so Palmer rang again. Warrant card in hand he waited. An age seemed to pass.

'Check if Sergeant Lewis has anything.'

He nodded to one of the officers to use his radio, which he did.

'One zero five to Lewis.'

'Go ahead one zero five,' came the reply.

'Superintendent would like a status report, ma'am.'

Palmer was impressed by the deference; who said coppers were sexist?

'All quiet this side, One zero five. No movement at the back of the house at all; seems empty from here. Lewis out.'

'Tell her we are going in, and to stay put,' Palmer ordered, moving forward under the porch to examine the lock as the message was relayed. 'Damn, it's a five-lever mortice; need a locksmith to get through one of those.'

'We have a ram in the car boot, sir.'

'No, better not; cost a packet do these doors, not your usual B&Q plywood job. Let's have a look at the windows.'

He moved to the front bay window, peering through.

'Window locks, damn. Oh well, looks like we'll need the ram after all, Constable.'

The constable's radio crackled into sound.

'Zero two seven car to Palmer. Looks like you have company, sir.'

They all looked round as a dark green Honda CV drew into the drive, crunching the pebbles like a fast tide on a stony beach. The engine stopped, and the ex-Mrs. Robert Damon hurried from the driver's side towards them, clearly worried at the sight of three men, two in police uniform, trying her windows.

'Excuse me, can I help you? This is my house. What's going on?'

Palmer stepped forward, warrant card to the fore, taking in this rather petite middle-aged lady in blue trouser suit and matching clutch bag.

'Detective Chief Superintendent Palmer, New Scotland Yard. And you are?'

'Angela Damon, I live here. Is it mother? Has she had an accident?'

She was searching her bag for a key.

'Your mother? No, no actually we came here to talk to you.'

'Me? Why on earth would you want to talk to me? And why are there so many of you?'

She was all fingers and thumbs, and starting to nervously shake. Palmer took the key off her when she pulled it from the bag.

'Allow me, ma'am; perhaps we'd better go inside. No need to worry, purely a routine matter.'

'I can't help it, I'm sorry. It's a nervous condition; any stress and I go to pot, start shaking like a leaf. I've pills inside; I'll be alright in a minute.'

Palmer opened the door and preceded her inside, doing a quick visual check just in case. 'Come in, come in.'

Mrs. Damon had gone into the sitting room and was hurriedly opening a blister pack of pills from a drawer, throwing two into her mouth and swallowing them.

'Sit down, please; I'm fine now. The magic of modern medicine; a pill for everything.'

The officers had positioned themselves, one by the front door and one by the sitting room door, while Palmer sat on the sofa. Mrs. Damon took an armchair.

'Now, how can I help you?'

'Mother; you mentioned your mother just now?'

Palmer was fishing.

'Oh God, Mother!'

The stress showed again, as she hurried out to the hall and called up the stairs.

'Mother, are you there? Mother, where are you? MOTHER!'

Palmer thought it about time he took charge of the situation. This lady was an obvious bag of nerves, and no more a serial killer than his dog Daisy was; although once Daisy had been left for an hour in one of his grandchildren's play rooms, and wreaked havoc amongst the stuffed toys. He told the officers to search the house, then took Mrs Damon gently by the arm, guided her back into the front room, and sat her down on the sofa. He pulled up a dining chair and sat facing her.

'Your mother has probably just popped out, to the library or the shops; she'll come back in a minute and wonder what all the fuss is about. Now, can you confirm for me that you are the ex-wife of Robert Damon?'

It was the wrong question. Palmer realised that as he watched the colour drain from her face at the mention of the name.

'Robert? Oh God, what's happened to Robert? Has he had an accident? Is he all right?'

'No, no, no; now please calm down, Mrs. Damon. Can I call you that?'

'Yes, yes I still use my married name. No reason to change it.'

'Okay. Now look, you must calm down and stop jumping to conclusions. I told you there is nothing to worry or fret about, and I just want to ask a few questions, all right?'

'Yes, yes, I'm sorry. I can't help it, I just get so easily into a panic with my nerves. I had a bad time in my life some years ago, and it left its mark.'

'A bad time, ma'am?'

'A business failure, it took a lot out of me. We lost everything we'd built up over twenty years; it put a strain on my health, broke up my marriage. It was an awful time. Robert was far stronger than me, but it all still fell apart. I haven't seen him for a number of years, so when you mentioned his name I just assumed that something bad must have happened to him.'

Palmer looked around.

'Was this your marital home?'

'No, this is mother's house; we started off our married life here, but had our own place after a few years. Then we lost it to the damn bank, they took everything. We came back here after the bankruptcy. You might expect to start off your married life living with your mum, but you don't expect to end it that way. It didn't work out; we got divorced, and I had nowhere else to go after that; so here I stayed.'

'And Robert?'

'I think he rented a place in south London somewhere.'

Palmer sensed she was now calmer and in control. The pills had worked.

'Mrs Damon, I don't want you to jump to any conclusions or wrong ideas with what I have to tell you; so let me finish what I am going to say first and you'll get the whole picture, and then we can take it from there. Understand?'

'Yes, yes of course. I feel fine now.'

'Good.'

Palmer relaxed a bit, and gave her one of his killer smiles.

'I am investigating a rather serious matter that concerns some people who you and Robert would have known when you were in business. It would appear that – '

He halted, as the serious expression on the face of the officer who entered the room froze him in mid sentence; he feared the worse.

'Found something?'

'Upstairs, sir; there's a separate flat.'

Palmer was relieved with that answer.

'It's mother's,' Mrs Damon explained. 'We separated the house when Robert and I came back here after the business went bust and we were basically on the streets; Mother took the flat and we had the rest of the house. It gave us a little privacy, and it's stayed that way since. A god-send really, as I'm sure mother and I would murder each other if we couldn't have our own space and some private time.'

A thought struck her, and she turned to the officer.

'Oh God…is mother up there? What's she done, is she alright?'

'No, no ma'am,' he reassured her. 'It's empty. I just thought the Chief Superintendent might like to take a look.'

It was a broad hint that Palmer *should* take a look. Palmer took the hint.

'Right, I'll be two shakes of lamb's tail, Mrs Damon. Why don't you make a nice cup of tea? I'm sure we could all do with one. The officer will help you; then I'll tell you the whole story. Don't let him near the biscuits though; they'll disappear in seconds.'

He gave her his killer smile again, and left the room to meet Sergeant Lewis coming in from the back.

'Nothing out back, sir, all neat and tidy. We checked the shed and small greenhouse, but nothing you wouldn't expect to find.'

'Good. Apparently there's a flat upstairs we ought to look at, come on.'

He took the stairs two at a time, until his sciatica reminded him not to and he reverted to singles. A good old fashioned wide staircase with polished wood banister, which he felt like putting a leg over and sliding down, like his grandkids did at his place; but of course he didn't. It was a nice house; the sort of place that needed a family to keep it alive, not a middle-aged divorcee and her mum. Good sized rooms, plenty of space. He paused on the landing, which was large enough to accommodate a half circular rosewood table with a satinwood inlay veneer, and a rather large foliage plant drooping from a central pot.

'Up here, sir.'

The second officer was leaning over the banister, at the top of a further but smaller staircase leading off the landing to the second floor. Palmer and Lewis went up and into the self-contained flat. The officer pointed to an array of locks and bolts on the inside of the door.

'Whoever lives here likes their privacy, sir.'

'What have you found then?'

Palmer walked into a living room cum kitchen. It had all you need: a TV, music centre, fridge, microwave; presumably Mrs Raynes did her cooking downstairs in the proper kitchen and just had snacks up here. A heap of women's magazines and last week's papers littered a corner sofa. The only other furniture was a high back chair and low central coffee table.

'This is the interesting bit, sir.'

The officer led them through into a bedroom; a normal bedroom except for one wall, which was covered in letters and various pieces of paper. Palmer walked over, putting on his glasses.

It was a paper trail, each piece connected to the next by a thick black felt-tip line. Starting on the left was an invoice from Hamilton Jarvis Accountants, demanding payment for an overdue account. The black line from it led to a letter from Peter Mouse, advising Damon to change banks and giving an appointment time for a meeting with himself and Richard Johnson of Capel Barclay Hanson. The black line led on through a letter cancelling CBH's overdraft facility with immediate effect, followed by a letter calling it in for immediate payment. Palmer was getting the gist of this trail as it moved via the black line on through a repossession order from the High Court on behalf of the bank on Damon's house, then a High Court Bailiff's possession order for their household items and cars. Towards the end of the trail was a picture of the Damons on their wedding day; the photo had been cut in half to separate him from his bride, and the black line led to him. But the final piece of paper sent a shiver down Palmer's spine. It was a newspaper page, with a photo of the ex-Chancellor of the Exchequer Neil Ledbury, above a story detailing the upsurge in small business failures since the ERM debacle and resultant interest rate rises which Ledbury blamed for the recession. Palmer's brain was working overtime. If this was a plan of victims, which it was, then Ledbury was in the frame to be next. The clincher was above the papers. Written in six inch high black thick felt-tip were the words PAY BACK TIME. Of course, PBT, thought Palmer. The jigsaw pieces had fallen into place at last.

'It's the mother. Christ, the fucking mother of all people.'

Remembering his manners, he turned to Sergeant Lewis.

'Sorry Sergeant. Don't usually use that sort of language in front of the ladies.'

'It's okay sir, I've heard worse.'

She smiled at him, considering it unusual for a bloke to apologise for bad language.

'Right then, seal the room Sergeant; nobody, but nobody gets in until forensics arrive. Then get on the radio and order them here in double quick time, and in numbers. There's an officer missing, believed to be in the hands of a serial murderer; and get onto my office. Speak to Claire, put her in the picture, and tell her to get as many of my team that are available and get down here with them now. Get me a radio too, please. I want a description of the mother, Mrs Raynes, out to every officer in the Met and City forces. This lady is dangerous, bloody dangerous; three murders so far, and possibly a fourth. The description goes out with an extreme caution note; don't approach, if seen just call it in. See if Mrs. Damon has a picture of her mother, preferably a recent one, and if she has get that out on the wire immediately. Put a press blackout on the case, and get me through to the Political Protection Unit. I think Neil Ledbury is in great danger. Put them through to me as soon as possible.'

He realised he'd just loaded Sergeant Lewis with a heck of a lot of work.

'You okay with all that, Lewis?'

'Yes sir. I'm female, we can multi-task.'

She smiled, then went to work on her radio putting Palmer's instructions into play. Palmer made a mental note to keep an eye on the career of Sergeant Lewis; so far, he was impressed.

He turned back to the wall and sank onto the bed as he followed the line through again. If the sequence on the wall was true, then Robert Damon was to be her next victim; but he was in custody, safe and sound in a cell. The downside was that perhaps he wasn't the next victim now, as circumstances had pushed Sergeant Singh into the possibility that she might need to be the next one in the mind of Raynes. But there was something wrong. He stared at the wall and went through the trail again, travelling through the sequence of events in chronological order and matching them mentally with the paper trail. Then it hit him! McDougal wasn't there; Ian McDougal wasn't on the wall at all. Perhaps he'd been an afterthought; an old enemy of Raynes that she'd tagged on as she got into the swing of revenge killing. Why not? It was a known fact that serial killers get high with success, and go on to kill beyond their original plans.

He left the room, with Lewis still busy on the radio and the other officer barring the door with crime scene tape. He took the stairs down slowly to rejoin Mrs Damon, plus tea tray, in the front room. She was about to have a family tsunami hit her. He hoped she had plenty of her nerve pills left.

Within the hour the place was buzzing with activity as the various teams moved in; SOCO were photographing the flat and taking away everything in sealed bags, in the hope of finding fibres or DNA samples from any of the victims. House-to-house along the street was being conducted by Palmer's own team, in an effort to establish that Sergeant Singh had indeed visited the house. Had anybody seen her, or her car? Two positives had come forward almost at once, who remembered her patrol car outside Raynes's house.

Palmer had commandeered the front room and stood at the window, thinking hard. Mrs. Damon was still in the chair, with a medic by her side just in case the pills wore off. Claire had arrived and taken over the table with her laptop, which was up and running and connected to the team's mainframe at the Yard via a modem through her phone. Palmer had asked her to check something.

'Yes, she's here sir. Company Secretary, Louise Raynes.'

Palmer swung round from the window.

'That would be your mother, wouldn't it Mrs Damon? She was your company secretary at the business.'

'Yes. She was a bookkeeper by profession, you see, so it seemed obvious for us to have her keep ours.'

'So she would have had access to all the financial figures, and would have seen the money problems coming down the line.'

'Oh yes, she was very aware of them, and handled all the confrontations with creditors and the bank; she kept us at arm's length from them. Richard and I were really concentrating on sales and trying to work our way out of the troubles by getting as many orders into the system as we could, to prove to the bank that we were sound, and that they should back off for a time and give us a chance to trade our way out of our financial position. Accounts can take up so much time, and we didn't have it. She was a real rock for us.'

She shook her head.

'I really can't believe that mother would even think about doing the things you say, let alone actually killing somebody. I can't believe it, I really can't.'

Palmer was more intent on getting Gheeta back safely than in what Mrs. Damon did or didn't believe about her mother.

'The evidence upstairs would seem to prove otherwise, Mrs Damon. We can only assume that your mother watched as you and your husband's lives were brought to financial ruin, and over the years this has festered into hatred for those she thinks responsible; and then one day something went bang in her head and... well, that was it.'

'She signed off the accounts through all the bad years, sir,' Claire spoke up. 'So she would definitely have been aware of the financial positions.'

Sergeant Lewis poked her head round the door.

'Six positives now, sir, on Sergeant Singh's car being outside the premises; and two on Mrs Raynes and a policewoman leaving in it, with Raynes in the back seat.'

'Right, see if there are any CCTV cameras in the area that might have picked up the car. See if we can find which direction it went in.'

'Will do,' Lewis said, leaving the room.

Palmer seated himself back on the dining chair facing Mrs. Damon.

'Where would your mother go, Mrs Damon? She's got a police officer as hostage and needs to find a place of safety; a place we wouldn't think to look.'

Mrs. Damon was without an answer.

'Even the thought of my mother with a hostage is preposterous, Chief Superintendent; quite ridiculous.'

'But yet quite true. Any relatives live nearby?'

'No, none.'

'Any property, like a garage or a flat?'

'No, nothing like that.'

'The warehouse!' Claire shouted out as she hit the keyboard. 'She owns the warehouse!'

Palmer sent his chair reeling as he rushed to peer over her shoulder at the screen. Claire tapped a few keys, and a printout stuttered out from the underside of the laptop.

'This is the assets and debts list from the company's bankruptcy filing,' she explained. 'One of the creditors was the landlord of a warehouse; the landlord was called Raynes Trust. It's too much of a coincidence isn't it, sir?'

'Damn right it is.'

They both turned to face Mrs Damon.

'It was my father's. He had an import business in the fifties, and when he retired the property was put into a trust; the rent was to secure a pension for mother. It had been empty for years before we took it. I thought it had been taken by the bank?'

'No, they wouldn't have been able to touch it,' Claire explained. 'It wasn't owned by you; it was owned by the Trust. Here, look.'

She showed Palmer the Raynes Trust accounts on the screen as it printed out.

'It's still owned by the Trust, but no income from it since 1955. It's been financially dormant; in other words, empty.'

'That's it then!'

Palmer grabbed the printout and was flying out of the door.

'That's where they've gone! Lewis, come with me; I need your local knowledge.'

He shouted for his team to follow him, and then he was running down the drive and into the nearest squad car that had a driver. He thrust the warehouse address in front of the driver as Lewis jumped in the back, and they were off, sirens blaring and lights flashing as he radioed in for a firearms officer and dog team to meet him there. Looking towards the heavens, he just hoped that they'd be in time.

Palmer didn't vent his feelings often, but Mrs. P. would tell you that there was a deeply emotional man underneath the hard public servant exterior; she'd seen him quietly shed a tear at an old romantic movie, or "Land of Hope and Glory" sung at the Last Night Of The Proms on TV. On Remembrance Sunday he'd always busy himself down the bottom of the garden for those poignant sixty seconds when Big Ben struck eleven, before returning misty-eyed afterwards. Palmer had lost three uncles in the war; he'd never known them, having been born after the war, but his parents had photos of three happy-looking young men in uniform taking pride of place on the mantelpiece when he was a kid, and he felt their loss anyway.

Right now, his eyes glistened over as he faced the thought that he might not be in time to save Sergeant Singh.

Chapter 17

Sergeant Gheeta Singh had undergone basic training in hostage negotiation, and been on two courses on criminal psychology and self preservation in subversive situations. But when an elderly lady sweeps into the room with a vicious looking double barrel 20-gauge sawn-off shotgun aimed at you, rather than the expected tea tray and biscuits, it kind of sets you back on your heels.

'I have no wish to kill you, Officer, but I will if you try anything. I haven't finished my work yet – and I *do* intend to finish it.'

'Oh my God…' Gheeta said, her brain overloading as she realised her situation. 'It was you; you killed them, didn't you, not your daughter!'

'Angela? She wouldn't kill a fly. She's a nervous wreck, a shadow of her old self, and all because those bastard bankers and accountants caused her so much stress that she went through a terrible breakdown; before that, she'd have murdered them with her bare hands. But you can't get at them, can you? They hide behind solicitor's letters and bailiffs and won't take your calls or meet you, the bastards!'

She spat the words out.

'They killed her, mentally and nearly physically killed her too. Took everything she and Richard had built up, and when they couldn't get any more out of them, they dumped them out on the street.'

Gheeta was controlling her anguish, quietly taking deep breaths to get oxygen into her blood; a trick they'd taught her at Police Training College, and it was working. She was calm and collected, and in full control.

'Lots of people suffered in that recession, Mrs Raynes. I don't think – '

'And who didn't, eh?' Raynes snapped back. 'Who didn't suffer, eh? Who made fortunes out of it, eh? The damn Banks and bankers, that's who! They made millions out of the misfortune of others, and so did the accountants in cahoots with the banks, heaping charge upon charge for

stupid, worthless advice; not to mention the bastard
government ministers on their big salaries and big
expenses. Did any of them go to the wall? No, no of
course not. Even when they admitted afterwards that they
had got it wrong, they still carried on in their big well-paid
jobs, or retired on massive pensions, and got a non-
executive position with… guess who? With the bloody
banks they supported, that's who. They should all be
strung up!'

Gheeta stayed quiet. This was real hatred spitting out
that wasn't about to be calmed. Raynes carried on.

'I haven't finished, you know. Oh no, not yet ; and
now it doesn't matter, does it? I'm a murderer, and will be
locked away for life; so a couple more won't make any
difference, will it?'

She laughed out loud. Was this really the same person
as the frail-looking elderly lady who had opened the front
door a few minutes before?

'And the more I kill, the better the story for Angela to
sell to the papers. You see, I'll get our revenge on the
bastards for all those years of misery, and Angela will be
set for life financially; and they'll have paid for it. Sort of
ironic really, isn't it?'

'And what are you going to do now, Mrs Raynes?'

Gheeta could see it was pointless to try and talk her
into putting down the gun, so the next best thing was to try
and find out her intentions and plan ahead.

'My turning up here has upset your plan a bit, hasn't
it? My boss knows I 'm here, and will be worried in a little
while if I don't check in.'

'You won't upset my plan one bit, my dear. What I
am going to do now is kill Neil Ledbury.'

Gheeta was startled, and showed it. This was off-plan.

'Neil Ledbury, the MP?'

'That's the one; ex-Chancellor of the Exchequer, who
ruined thousands of lives by his stupidity in government.
I'm going to kill him after I kill Robert.'

'Robert? Robert who?'

Gheeta knew of course, but feigned ignorance.

'Robert Damon, my ex-son-in-law. He's next.'

Gheeta was quickly realising that although giving an outside impression of rational stability, Mrs Raynes was mad, quite mad. It was a sobering thought, and Gheeta knew she had to tread very carefully from now on.

'Why kill your son-in-law?'

'He could see Angela was cracking up, I told him many times. But he left her in the front line, to handle things with the creditors and take all the flack while he basically stayed out of sight. He should have made her pack up work when the trouble happened, and then she'd be alright now. But he didn't. He knew the writing was on the wall, and so did I; I was their bookkeeper. It was futile to keep going, futile; I told him many times he was heading for the cliffs, but he left things too late to do anything, the arrogant little shit! He lost the lot, and then walked out on Angela when she needed him most. They lived here for a while, you know; I could hear the arguments every night, him shouting at her, taking out his frustrations of failure on her instead of going round and punching the real bastards on the nose. When she needed his support and love, he gave her abuse. How do you think a mother feels to see that?'

'Awful, I should think.'

'Awful? No, not awful. Hatred is what you feel, pure hatred. And I still feel it.'

She paused and took a seat in the corner of the room away from the door; far enough away from Gheeta so that should the police officer make a move there was plenty of time to fire off both barrels before she reached her.

'I was on my way to Robert's flat to kill him yesterday, but you beat me to it. I watched you go in, two at the front, two at the back. Then you came out with him in handcuffs.'

Gheeta interrupted, as her memory bank clicked back to the elderly lady she'd seen walking towards them on the pavement outside Robert Damon's flat; the lady who had crossed onto the common and taken a seat.

'Of course! It was you outside the house when we arrested him, wasn't it? You went and sat on a bench on the Common.'

Mrs Raynes smiled.

'It was. I must admit, when I opened the door to you I wondered whether you'd recognise me. Funny isn't it? You actually saved Robert's life that day, you know. But I'll get him now. I was beginning to think that the bodies must have disappeared into thin air; four murders all with a link, and nothing on the news or in the papers. You must have found them? They couldn't still be lying where I left them. So I suppose you kept it quiet for some reason?'

'Copycats.'

'Oh?'

She was surprised by this.

'Oh, I see. I never thought of that. That could be interesting; lots of bodies turning up all over the place with PBT on their foreheads.'

She found the concept amusing, as she pre-empted Gheeta's next question.

'Pay Back Time, my dear. That's all it meant, pay-back time. The ultimate pay-back too, isn't it?'

Obvious, thought Gheeta, so obvious when you think about it; too damn obvious in fact. How did they miss that? She felt she was slowly building a relationship with Mrs. Raynes, who seemed to have calmed down after her rant about the bankers.

'Mrs Raynes, what are you going to do with me?'

Raynes thought for a moment.

'You mean am I going to kill you too? No, no I don't think so. You've done nothing to me or Angela have you, so that would be a pointless killing. But I can't let you go either, can I? Not yet in any case. And I can't keep you here, because this is the first place they'll come looking. No, I just need to get you out of the way for a couple of days so I can finish off my work. I have a safe place for you to stay for a day or two.'

She stood up, and her manner became threatening again.

'The bottom line, as they say in banking, is that I get the job finished. Nothing else matters to me now, so please believe me when I say that if you try anything silly I will shoot you. Do you understand that?'

Gheeta nodded.

'Good. Now we are going to walk slowly out and down the drive to your car. You will drive, and I will be in the back. Your car keys, please; throw them onto the floor in front of me.'

Gheeta obeyed.

'Mrs. Raynes, where on earth did a nice lady like you get a sawn-off shotgun?'

Mrs Raynes bent down and picked up the keys, giving a smug laugh.

'A keepsake from Hamilton Jarvis's office; there it was, complete with bullets or cartridges or whatever you call them in an opened box, with a till receipt for that very day. He must have just bought it, which meant that nobody else would know it was there, and nobody else would know it was missing, A pure stroke of luck.'

Gheeta was incredulous.

'Jarvis had a *sawn-off* shotgun?'

'No, no, I did the sawing off bit in the shed in the garden. I hired a metal grinder to do it. Tried with a hacksaw, but the metal is too hard. It makes it so much more portable, doesn't it? Damn heavy thing. And I understand having the barrels sawn off gives it a greater spread of destruction when you fire it.'

'*You understand*? What social circles do you move in, Mrs Raynes?'

'No, no,' she laughed. 'Gangster movies, my dear; one of my passions. *Goodfellas*, *The Sopranos*, I love them. Don't worry, I'll make sure Ledbury is on his own when I pull the triggers. I don't want to injure anybody else.'

'You used an iron bar on the others?'

'Yes, but they were always on their own. A man like Ledbury will probably have security people with him most of the time and waving an iron bar at them won't really frighten them into moving away. But this beauty will…'

She eyed the gun with pride.

'Just me and him, and then… bang!'

She said it very casually.

'Right then, shall we go? Nice and easy now, no silly games. Remember, I've nothing to lose.'

They left the house and walked to the patrol car, Mrs Raynes hiding the gun under a coat held in front of her.

'Get into the driver's seat,' she said, through a large smile for the benefit of anybody watching from behind their curtains. As Gheeta did so she slid into the back seat, her coat-covered cargo held firmly at an angle towards the back of Gheeta's head. She passed the keys over the headrest.

'Drive to the end of the street and turn right.'

Gheeta started the car, slipped it into gear and moved off.

'One thing I don't understand, Mrs Raynes; why did you kill Ian McDougal?'

'Who?'

'Ian McDougal.'

'Never heard of him.'

'He was found dead in Worcester, with PBT on his forehead.'

'Not guilty. Don't think I've ever been to Worcester.'

Now that, if true, changed things quite a lot.

Sergeant Singh let Mrs Raynes give her directions to the Peckham Warehouse, although she'd been there herself the day before; she strained her memory to recall the layout, in case she was blindfolded. They entered through a side door off a small car park at the back of the building, the entrance to which was from a quiet side street, not through the main gate where Gheeta had entered yesterday. Their footsteps echoed in the empty building.

'I come here once in a while to remember the good times.'

Mrs Raynes sounded quite sad.

'A hundred and thirty-nine people made a living here, you know. The place was a hive of activity twenty-four hours a day, keeping up with the orders; machines whirring and clanging all day and night. Now look at it – dead.'

She moved Gheeta on with a wave of the gun.

'Come on, that way,' she said, indicating the portacabin in the corner of the factory floor.

Once inside she had Gheeta kneel down against a wall, and using the Sergeant's own Met issue handcuffs, secured her to an old-fashioned iron radiator pipe.

'I shall let them know you are here just as soon as I finish my work. I hope you won't be too uncomfortable.'

The piercing scream of police sirens in the distance split the air.

'I think somebody has worked out where I am already, Mrs Raynes. Why not unlock me, and we can quietly sort this whole mess out without any more deaths?'

Raynes was having none of it.

'Don't be silly, dear. I've still got work to do.'

And then she was gone, pulling the cabin door shut behind her; Gheeta heard the key turn in the lock. It was now pitch black. She thought that Mrs Raynes would leave the warehouse by the side entrance, the same way they had come in, while the police would come in through the main gate, unaware of that side entrance. The sirens were very close, and spluttered into silence. She could hear the dogs barking as their handlers sent them in first. She wondered if Palmer was there; of course he was. The sound of wood splintering signalled that an entrance had been made through the main door, and almost immediately she could hear the dogs sniffing and whining outside the cabin door. They'd found her.

'Sergeant Singh, are you in there?'

It was Palmer's voice, shouting from a distance.

'Yes, sir,' she shouted back. 'I'm on my own. She's gone out the back door.'

Ten seconds later, the cabin door flew open as the ram smashed into its lock, and two marksmen were inside, handguns at the ready behind bright power lights. A quick glance, and the 'all clear' was shouted and the lights shut off.

Palmer entered as one of the marksmen knelt to release Gheeta. His concern gave way to relief as he saw she was okay.

'Side door, sir; there's a side door where we came in.'

She scrambled to her feet, brushed past Palmer and led them running across the warehouse floor to the side door, their footsteps echoing off the walls. Outside, Gheeta's car was where they had left it; Mrs Raynes was nowhere to be seen.

'Well she can't be far away.'

Palmer turned to the rest of the team.

'Split into pairs and fan out.'

'She's got a shot gun, sir.'

Gheeta had forgotten all about that in the excitement.

'What? Jesus… Okay lads, you heard that; no silly heroics, and each pair with a marksman.'

'Five foot six to eight!' Gheeta shouted after them as they moved out. 'Grey perm, fawn overcoat!'

Palmer permitted himself a fatherly smile at Gheeta.

'Good to see you're okay, Sergeant. We'll get you back to the Yard and input all the info you can remember. Well, at least we know who the killer is now.'

'We know who *one* of the killers is, guv.'

'She's got an accomplice?'

'No, but she didn't kill Ian McDougal, guv.'

They walked outside and got into the back of a squad car. Gheeta tightened her seat belt.

'She said she didn't, and she has no reason to lie because she admitted to the other murders. She's never even been to Worcester.'

Palmer nodded as the car moved off.

'He wasn't on the bedroom wall either.'

'On the what, guv?'

'Never mind, I'll bring you up to speed on the journey. So, if she didn't kill McDougal, then who the Hell did?'

Gheeta shrugged.

'Don't know, guv. But whoever it was, they knew the PBT mark.'

'Then she *must* have an accomplice.'

'No, guv, definitely not; and the penny wasn't in McDougal's mouth, was it?'

'Okay, so the only people who knew about the PBT mark and the penny were our team and the officers from the local forces of the victims; we can cross them off the suspects list, can't we.'

Palmer steadied himself against the arm rest as they swerved round the Vauxhall Bridge roundabout at speed.

'Who's driving this, The Stig?'

'Who, guv?'

'Never mind.'

Gheeta was trying to puzzle things out.

'So the only other people who would have seen the mark would be the morgue attendants.'

Palmer laughed.

'Don't be daft; a morgue attendant doing a copy-cat murder? Sounds more like a John Grisham novel.'

Gheeta ignored him and carried on.

'Or whoever *identified* the bodies in the morgue? That theory works, guv, because whoever identified the bodies in the morgues would have seen the PBT mark, because they were still on the bodies prior to the post-mortems; but, they *wouldn't* know about the coin in the mouth.'

Palmer was impressed.

'You know, you could be right, Sergeant. Yes, you could be right. Get Claire to run programmes and see if we can find a connection to Worcester with any of the relatives who identified the bodies. It's a long shot, but you never know. Well done.'

He smiled at her.

'How are you feeling?'

'I'm okay, guv. It was strange really; Mrs Raynes is really just a concerned mum, whose concern for her daughter got out of control and changed into hatred. It was like talking to your gran, you know?'

'I don't think my gran was a psychopathic serial killer who carried a sawn-off shot gun!'

Gheeta laughed.

'No, but you know what I mean, guv.'

'Yes, yes I do. Takes all sorts doesn't it, eh? I suppose we all have a breaking point somewhere…'

He chuckled.

'I just hope Mrs P isn't near her's yet!'

Chapter 18

'The forensics report says it was a flat bar. The others were killed by a round bar,' Claire read from her screen. Palmer and Singh were seated with her in the Team room going through the McDougal forensics.

'You see, guv? Gheeta said. 'Same murder method and same PBT mark, but the bits the McDougal killer left out were the bits he couldn't possibly have known about; namely the coin in the mouth, and the type of bar.'

Palmer stood and paced the room.

'So, we *have* got two killers now. It's got to be somebody who saw one of the bodies and set up a copycat murder of McDougal. But why?'

A thought struck Claire.

'Maybe they had their own 'pay-back' to do, and used this as a cover.'

'But if you're a grieving relative, the reason for using the same MO on your own personal revenge must be pretty heavy, eh? I mean blimey, there you are with a murdered relative on the slab in front of you, and the only thing on your mind is how to use the situation to clobber somebody else who you've got personal a grudge against. McDougal must have done something pretty nasty for his killer to work all that out. Keep looking Claire, and well done; but in the meantime we have a mad granny on the loose with a shotgun, determined to nail her ex-son-in-law and an ex-Government Minister.'

He shook his head in disbelief.

'You know, this is either the most bizarre case I've ever known, or some talentless minor celebrity is about to burst through the door and yell 'you've been framed!' at me.'

To everybody's surprise, the door opened and Assistant Commissioner Bateman looked in.

'Everything under control, Palmer?'

His well-practised expression of false interest changed to one of genuine inquisitiveness, as he noticed all and sundry were suddenly fighting back laughter.

Chapter 19

'This is boring the pants off me.'

Palmer was sat in the back of a surveillance car outside MP Neil Ledbury's Westminster flat.

'She won't come here if she's told you he's on her list; she'll know his security will have been beefed up.'

Gheeta was intent on using her laptop, and merely grunted back. Palmer gave her a cursory glance, and shifted his position painfully.

'Left hand side of my arse has gone to sleep. What are you doing, playing Candy Crush?'

'Candy Crush? Guv, don't tell me you actually know what Candy Crush is?'

'No idea, but one of the grandkids is barmy on it.'

'I'm texting Claire on the internet. Look at this lot.'

The laptop screen was a mass of information.

'I think we have our copycat.'

She turned the screen towards Palmer, who pulled his reading glasses from an inner pocket and put them on as Gheeta continued.

'Remember we sent two of the team to do some digging into the McDougal case in Worcester?'

'Yes?' Palmer said, adjusting his specs.

'Well, I think they've come up trumps, guv. Have a read of that lot of info they've sent in; it seems our Archie Jarvis isn't the fresh-faced cherub he first appears to be.'

'Archie Jarvis? Surely not...'

Palmer read the screen for a couple of minutes.

'Well, well, well... Mummy wouldn't be very pleased with the company Archie is keeping, would she? Time for us to have another chat with Mr.. Archie Jarvis. Got your mobile handy, Sergeant?'

'Yes, guv.'

'Give Superintendent Dickie Hart a bell at West Mercia, and download all this to him. I think it's time he had a serious chat to the grieving Mrs McDougal. Then get a marked car and a couple of uniforms to meet us outside the Jarvis house; make sure one is a WPC, in case Mrs

Jarvis has a breakdown, and then get another team to take over from us here. Oh, and run me off a printout of that information Claire dug up.'

He sat back in his seat.

'Well, well, well; who'd have thought it, eh?'

Chapter 20

Archie Jarvis knotted his dressing gown cord and rubbed the sleep from his eyes as he opened the door to find Palmer, Sergeant Singh, a uniformed PC and a WPC filling his porch.

'Superintendent Palmer? It's two thirty in the morning and – '

'*Chief* Superintendent Palmer, actually. May we come in Sir?' Palmer asked as he pushed past Archie, taking him by the arm and propelling him down the hall into the sitting room. Gheeta and the WPC made their way up the stairs to find Mrs Jarvis and wake her up. The light switch in the sitting room was in the usual place just inside the door, so Palmer found it easily and flicked it on. The wall lights in their light pink art deco shell-shaped glass shades threw a soft hue over the room. He motioned towards the sofa.

'Sit down, sir, if you wouldn't mind.'

Archie obeyed slowly, his mind gradually taking in the realisation of the impending bad situation. He sat in silence until Mrs Jarvis came into the room in her night clothes, accompanied by Sergeant Singh and the WPC. She looked confused.

'What is it, Archie? What's going on?'

'Nothing for you to worry about, Mrs Jarvis,' Palmer said, offering her a kindly smile. 'Just that a bit of new evidence has come to light that Archie is going to help us with. Now, why not toddle off to the kitchen with my officer and make us a nice cup of tea; I'll pop in and explain it all to you just as soon as I can. Off you go.'

And he ushered her out, nodding to the WPC who went with her.

'No sugar in mine.'

He turned, and giving Archie a withering glance went and stood by the French door, turning his back on Archie; he could see Archie quite clearly mirrored in the door glass against the darkness of the outside night, and noticed, as had Gheeta, that his hands were shaking quite badly. She pressed her audio recorder to on.

'Anything you want to tell me, Mr. Jarvis?'

Palmer swung round like an aggressive predator with its prey cornered.

'Anything you think I should know that might have somehow slipped your mind before?'

'I think I'd like to call my solicitor,' stammered a shaking Archie Jarvis.

'Oh really? Call your solicitor, eh? And why would you want to call your solicitor, sir? You haven't been arrested, you haven't even been cautioned; I don't think I have even accused you of anything, have I? So why would you feel the need to call your solicitor, I wonder? Why would you want to get him out of bed at this time of the night? Perhaps you think I might be going to caution you, or arrest you. Do you think that, Archie? Do you have a guilty secret, Archie; one that I may have found out about?'

Archie kept quiet, as Palmer paced the room slowly.

'No? Nothing come to mind, Archie? Well then, let's try and jog your memory, shall we?'

He paused to admire a wall painting, continuing to speak as he looked at it.

'It's been brought to our attention by the local force in West Mercia that you've a bit of a taste for the ladies, Archie. A certain type of lady, too; the type that likes to entertain gentlemen for money.'

The colour had drained from Archie Jarvis's face. Palmer pulled the printout from Gheeta's laptop out of his pocket.

'You see, the local vice squad like to keep tabs on these ladies and who their regular clients are, just in case something goes wrong. And it seems you are quite a regular client, aren't you Archie? Your little pecker must be fairly worn out with all the activity it's been getting in Birminham recently.'

Gheeta's eyes widened at this; Palmer was not the sort to make that type of remark. She managed to stop herself laughing, but noticed the uniformed officer stood at the door was visibly shaking with held-in laughter. Palmer, however, remained very serious.

'When did you last go to Birmingham, Archie?'

'I'd like my solicitor.'

Palmer ignored him.

'When was the last time you visited a lady there by the name of Jenny McDougal, a very pretty lady, very attractive. She works her 'trade' around the Birmingham hotels usually, especially the Excelsior. But then you know the Excelsior, don't you Archie? You stayed there every time you went to Worcester for your monthly meetings with Hanniger Tools, didn't you? And on those visits you became acquainted with Jenny McDougal; very well acquainted I would say, looking at the hotel's phone records from your room to her mobile. Now then, let me propose a little scenario, and stop me if I get it wrong.'

'I want my solicitor, Superintendent.'

'*Chief* Superintendent, and all in good time, sir. I'll take a guess that on the third or fourth meeting with the lady, after you'd got to know her a bit and felt relaxed in her company, you probably told her a bit about yourself in a boastful sort of way, because you were probably spending quite a bit of money on her in return for sexual favours. Then on the next visit you give her a call, and surprise, surprise, she invites you to come to her own place for the evening, or perhaps the whole night. Sounds like a good idea, doesn't it sir? Especially since the hotel security staff have warned you about taking ladies up to your room.'

Archie's head jerked up at this.

'It's all in the hotel security log, sir. Anyway, off you toddle to her address; but surprise, surprise again, Jenny doesn't answer the door, does she? Her husband, Ian McDougal does; complete with a little present to show you. What was it, Archie; photos of you and Jenny, a CVD?'

No answer.

'I shouldn't think it was a very pleasant experience seeing yourself performing, was it? But you may not be surprised to learn that you were not alone in being a target for this little McDougal caper; my colleagues in the West Mercia force have seized quite a little treasure trove of similar stuff from the McDougal house, involving other men too. We've sent them a photo of you, Archie; we got it from The Accountant magazine's online archive, amazing what's on the internet these days. So now they'll be able to pull out all the photos and any other material that you are starring in, for use as evidence later. That should go down well amongst your colleagues, and no doubt mummy will be very proud of you when she sees the snaps.'

Archie raised both hands to stem the onslaught. The game was up.

'I only wanted – '

Palmer cut him off.

'Not interested, Archie; I haven't finished yet. So far you've done nothing wrong in law; prostitution is not a crime. No, I've got some sympathy for you, Archie. No doubt you thought you landed in heaven when such an attractive lady as Jenny McDougal took to you; trouble was, Archie, she'd taken to you like a spider takes to a fly. She spun the web and reeled you in, just as she'd done with the others. Tell me, was it photos or a CVD?'

Archie gave in. He was clearly a beaten man, with tears streaming from his eyes; he started sobbing, putting his head in his hands.

'A CDV, it was playing on the television when McDougal invited me in. I didn't know who he was when he opened the door; he said Jenny was upstairs and would be down in a minute, and we went through to the lounge. And it was playing. He said they wanted ten thousand pounds, or copies would be sent to my father and mother.'

'You paid?'

'A thousand a month, cash. He would come to the hotel each time I was up for the Hanniger meetings, and I paid him.'

'So you could afford it, a thousand pounds a month?'

'Yes, I could afford it; but I could see it was going to go on and on.'

'And then your father's death gave you a way out, eh? Or so you thought.'

Archie nodded slowly.

'It seemed ideal. When I identified father's body in the morgue, the attendant apologised for the PBT scrawled on his forehead, and told me that it had to remain there until after the post mortem as it tied in with other victims. I thought that if I acted quickly and got to McDougal, killed him and put the mark on him, then whoever you caught for father's murder would get accused of that as well. So stupid of me.'

'A little knowledge is a very dangerous thing, Archie, and you only had a little knowledge of the case. You didn't know that the murderer of your father and the other two left other signs with the bodies as well as the PBT message; signs that you didn't leave on McDougal, which set his murder apart from the others, and narrowed the field of suspects down; eventually down to you.'

Palmer felt a twinge of pain in his thigh. It had been a long couple of days, and his sciatica had had enough of keeping quiet as he sat uncomfortably in squad cars, ran across concrete warehouse floors, or paced around sitting rooms. It let him know it was still there.

'Just one more thing before we go to the Yard and take a full statement, Archie. Why did you take his trousers and pants off?'

'I don't know. I suppose I was so ashamed of the pictures of me with... in... well, I felt dirty and... It was so awful; private things put out for all the world to see....I just suppose in a mad moment I thought: right matey, let's see how you like it.'

'But he was dead. You'd already killed him.'

'I know, I know – oh, I don't know, I was just so angry at the time! I'm not a violent man, Superintendent – sorry, *Chief* Superintendent, not a violent man in any way. But when I caught up with him in that alley, he said to me:

'Hello, come to make an early payment?' with a sneer on his face, and I just… it was like a release valve had opened.'

Palmer had got the full confession, and Gheeta had it on tape so no wide-boy, expensive lawyer could dispute it. There was a hint of a satisfied smile on Palmer's lips.

'Right then, you'd better go and get dressed. The Constable and my Sergeant will accompany you.'

He turned to Gheeta.

'When he's all ready to go to the Yard, read him his rights and let him phone his solicitor; I think he might need him now. Oh, and find out who the family doctor is and get him round here now. I think Mr.s Jarvis is going to need more than a cup of tea after I tell her the joyous news about her beloved only son and his questionable social activities.'

Chapter 21

'You should have gone to bed ages ago, precious… no, I'm going to be a while yet….yes, I do know what the time is…'

Palmer stood beside the police car outside the Jarvis home, watching the second car drive off to the Yard with Archie. He was talking to Mrs. P. on Gheeta's mobile.

'Of course I'm hungry, but go to bed and I'll get something quick when I get in. God only knows what time that will be… I'll shove something in the microwave… no, don't make anything special, dear… okay, do an Irish Stew… and dumplings… no, I won't make a mess, just leave it on the side in the kitchen – and then go to bed, okay? Yes… love you lots.'

He gave the mobile back to Gheeta, who ended the call.

'That woman deserves to be married to a saint, not a copper. The boss upstairs broke the mould after he made her. Three in the morning, and she's defrosting an Irish Stew she made from the freezer, and doing dumplings to go with it!'

He leant on the car, raising his right leg which was giving him jip.

'Right then, let's just recap and make sure we haven't missed anything. Archie is on his way to the cells for the night, and his solicitor is due in the Yard at nine; Mrs Raynes is out and about with a shotgun looking for Neil Ledbury, who has been taken from his home by a protection squad to a safe house, so we know he's okay. Anything else, Sergeant? Or can we go and snatch a couple of hours' overdue sleep?'

'Mrs Raynes is also after Robert Damon, guv.'

'Who is firmly ensconced in a remand cell at the Yard, or if they're full then a cell at the Scrubs or Brixton. Either way, he's safe from her attentions.'

'He's probably not, guv.'

'He's probably not what?'

'He's probably not in a cell anywhere, guv. We never brought any charges against him, so the duty officer couldn't keep him even if he wanted to; I would think that Ernie Fredericks would have told him that, and he'd have walked. Hang on, and I'll check.'

She rang the Yard and spoke to the front desk, waited while they got her an answer and then relayed it to Palmer.

'He's out. Fredericks signed him out at four this afternoon.'

'Oh my giddy aunt! He's out on the street, not knowing that his mother-in-law is after him and intending to blow him to kingdom come with a shotgun at the first opportunity. Come on!'

He jumped into the back of the police car as Gheeta ran round and jumped in through the other side.

'Tooting Bec Common,' Palmer barked at the driver. 'As quick as you like, and make as much noise with the siren as possible.'

He took the mobile from Gheeta's hand.

'Which is the redial button? I'd better cancel those dumplings.'

Chapter 22

Robert Damon was fast asleep. It had been a long day, not one he'd liked at all; especially the time spent at New Scotland Yard. Gradually, the soft sound of tapping at his front door broke into his sleep and woke him. His watch showed two forty-five in the morning. It was cold, and as his feet touched the old lino it felt like ice under his toes. He put on his slippers and dressing gown, and silently parted the bedroom curtains a fraction, peering down to the road below and half expecting to see a police car sitting there, with Palmer gazing up at him. It was very foggy outside, and as far as he could see there was no car or Palmer outside; just the usual residents' cars parked for the night. The tapping continued. He broke out into a cold sweat as he slowly opened his bedroom door and looked down the hall to the front door. He was relieved to see the security chains still in place. A voice whispered his name urgently through the letter box.

'Robert? Robert! It's me, Angela. Open the door. I know you are in there.'

His brain raced. Angela? She was the last person he'd expected. He edged towards the door, keeping tight against the hall wall trying to avoid being seen through the spy hole or letter box. He reached the door.

'What do you want?' he said, his heart thumping like a mad piston in his chest. 'What are you doing here, Angela?'

'Open the door, Robert, we can't talk like this. It's about my mother. Do you know she's gone mad and killed people?'

'Yes I know, the police have been here already about that. They didn't know it was your mother though.'

He took a look through the spy hole and couldn't see anybody else with Angela, but he was still wary.

'I'm not opening this door Angela, so you might as well go home and we'll talk tomorrow.'

'Robert, don't be stupid. Listen to me.'

Her voice was very serious now.

'The police have found a list of targets in mother's rooms, and *you* are on that list.'

Damon gave an audible smirk.

'That's not exactly a surprise, Angela.'

'She apparently thinks she is doing these murders for me, as payback for the business troubles and you leaving. She's killed Johnson, Jarvis and Mouse already.'

'I know, the police thought I was the killer; I've been with them all day. I'm tired out Angela, so go away.'

'She's got a shotgun, Robert.'

'Jesus!'

'If she comes here now she'll just blast her way in and kill you; she's got nothing to lose. It's too late to leave now, she might already be outside somewhere. It's very foggy out there, you can't see a hand in front of your face.'

'I'll call the police.'

'Don't be stupid, Robert; if she hears them coming she'll just hurry up and finish the job before they get here. The only way to stop her is to let me in, then I can talk her out of it if she comes here. She thinks she's doing it for me, Robert, so she won't harm me; and we'll have a better chance than you on your own.'

It made sense. Damon slid off the door chains and opened the door a fraction to check that she really was alone, just as Angela Damon threw her body against it, smashing it into Robert's face and knocking him half-unconscious to the hallway floor. In an instant she was in; she shut the door and knelt on his chest, as his winded lungs gasped for air. She pressed her face close to his.

'It was my plan,' she hissed venomously into his groggy face. 'My plan, not mother's. She must have found out what I was doing from the plan on the wall in my bedroom. Oh yes, Robert, I had it all planned out on a wall chart, all very business-like. I didn't know mother had a key to my rooms, so she's known all along that I was killing them. And I did so enjoy it! I took a shotgun from Jarvis's office too; I even cut the barrels down so I could carry it easily in a shopping bag. But I haven't used it, Robert; I prefer to get up close and personal for my revenge, with an iron bar; it gives me a feeling of personal revenge as I smash their greedy skulls. So when the police came for me, her mothering instincts must have taken over, and she's set about finishing the job herself with the shotgun. The police found the wall chart too, and I fooled them into thinking they were mother's rooms, not mine; they believed me, the idiots. I killed the other three, Robert; and that just leaves you, Robert, you bastard. I want to savour this; this will be the best bit. You used me, you used my family; you used our money, then lost the lot and walked away. Bastard! Bastard!'

The four-inch blade of the kitchen knife entered Robert Damon's chest and heart five times with the ferocious force of hatred. When she had finished, the eerie silence in the hallway was only punctuated by her panting as she stood up from the body, leaving the knife standing proud. She felt good, very good; like a great weight had been lifted from her. She was actually smiling. The smile was turning into laughter, which she had to stifle in case the neighbours heard. She took the felt-tip from her pocket and wrote PBT on Richard's forehead, slipped a coin into his open mouth and left the flat, closing the door quietly behind her. Police sirens could be heard approaching, which shook her mind back to the present. She couldn't use the front entrance now as they would be there, or near enough to see her leave. She went to the rear end of the communal landing and tried the old sash window that led to the rickety iron fire escape, but the window was stuck fast by layers of paint put on over the years. She could see the flashing blue lights of the police cars lighting up the hallway below, could hear voices approaching. She had to get out. A broken child's tricycle abandoned in the landing provided the answer, as she swung it through the glass and followed it out onto the fire escape.

Chapter 23

Sergeant Singh was making her way with a uniformed
officer through the overgrown shrubs along the side of the
house when they heard the sound of breaking glass. On
reaching the rear of the house they saw the child's tricycle
bouncing noisily down the iron slats of the fire escape,
coming to a halt in the bushes nearby; two storeys above in
the fog, they could just make out a figure scrambling out
of the window before making its own way down. She
motioned the officer to back into the shadows, and they
waited. If this was Mrs Raynes coming down with a
loaded shotgun, she had no intention of presenting herself
as a target; she hoped Palmer was aware of what was
going on at the back, as he'd gone in the front. She could
hear more police cars arriving at the front, and the muffled
barking of orders.

The figure on the fire escape had descended to be
near enough in the fog for Gheeta to get a good look. It
wasn't Mrs Raynes; that was a relief. She stepped out of
the shadows with the officer and called out: 'Police. This
is the Police. Stop right where you are and put your hands
on your head.'

The figure obeyed.

'Come down slowly to the ground.'

The figure did as it was told, and on reaching the
ground finally spoke.

'Oh, thank God you're here.'

The voice was urgent and fearful.

'There's been a murder up there,' she said, pointing
up to the broken window. 'A man has been killed.'

Gheeta's torch lit up Angela Damon's face.

'And who are you ?'

Angela's heart had been fluttering, not knowing
whether either of these officers had been at the Harrow
house and would be able to recognise her. But neither of
them had.

'I live in the flat next door to Mr Damon. I could hear
it all; a terrible row, and then a loud shot...'

She put her hands to her face.

'It was terrible, terrible!'

Gheeta's torch beam showed the blood on her hands, which Gheeta naturally assumed had come from breaking the window to get out.

'Okay, you're safe now. But you need a medic to bandage your hands. How many people are up there?'

'One, I think it's a lady; and Robert is lying in his hallway.'

'Right, this officer will take you through to the front and see that a medic gets your hands seen to. We will want a statement once you're patched up and calmed down, so don't leave. You feel okay now?'

'Much better than I did up there!'

The officer and Angela Damon disappeared along the side of the house towards the front. Gheeta looked up towards the broken window; if Mrs Raynes was up there she probably had a second barrel loaded; or both, if she was carrying spare cartridges. Palmer could be walking right into it, if he hadn't waited for a marksman to arrive; and knowing him, he hadn't. Taking a deep breath, she started to climb the fire escape, making sure her CS gas canister was in one hand. *Not much protection from a double-barrelled shotgun, in the hands of a lady who was already a triple killer*. She felt herself shaking slightly at the thought. *Deep breaths, take deep breaths, it gets the oxygen into the blood stream and works wonders*. As she got to the broken window, she could see that four uniform officers were outside the open flat. She clambered over the sill carefully and they acknowledged her as she past them and went into the flat, where Palmer was already standing over Damon's body.

'She beat us to him.'

'Then she must still be here somewhere, sir. She hasn't come out the back.'

'There's nobody here, Sergeant; we've been through the whole place, even the empty flat next door. We've officers on the first floor and the ground floor, so if she hasn't come past you she's either on the roof, or she'd left by the time we arrived."

'The flat next door, sir, did you say it was empty?'

'Yes, been empty for years by the look of it.'

'But I had the lady who lives there come down the fire escape a few minutes ago. It can't be empty.'

She looked down at Damon's body.

'He wasn't shot!'

'No, Raynes must have run out of bullets; multiple stab wounds.'

'Oh shit, sir! This lady who said she was the neighbour said she'd heard a gunshot.'

The alarm bells rang in both their heads.

'I sent her to the front with an officer 'cause her hands were covered in blood, which I thought was from smashing the window to escape! She wasn't Mrs Raynes, sir; no way.'

They ran along the landing to the front window. Palmer wiped the grime away with his sleeve and they looked down to the street below, which was full of activity. The fog was lifting as the early morning sun took it on; a Police Crime Scene tape had secured the front of the house, as a sizeable crowd started gathering behind it, and SOCO vans were now pulling up, as was the pathologist.

Angela Damon had assured the medics that she was alright by wiping the blood off her hands with an antiseptic wipe, and been sat in the back of a patrol car to await being taken to a local station to give her statement. She waited until the attention had gone away from her, then deftly opened the offside car door and slowly slipped out of the car unobserved, mixing with the crowds behind the police line.

From the second floor window, Gheeta spotted her.

'There, guv!'

She pointed a finger, which Palmer tried vainly to follow.

'Second car from the left, offside door, about ten yards along the back of the crowd; brown trouser-suit, fawn headscarf.'

Palmer rocked back on his heels with surprise.

'Angela Damon! That's Angela Damon! What the hell? She's in it with her mother! Come on.'

He raced along the landing and took the stairs two at a time, with Gheeta forging ahead as his sciatica once again forced him to revert to one at a time, the rest of the uniforms overtaking him too. He made a mental note to spend a couple of days flat on his back on a hard bed, as soon as he could spare the time.

Gheeta got to her first. She circled round the outside of the crowd, keeping the fawn headscarf in view; coming at her from the side with the force of an All Black Hooker, Gheeta took no chances and soon had Angela Damon face down, winded and handcuffed on the soggy common, with a knee firmly placed in her back. The others arrived moments later.

Palmer looked down at her.

'You had us fooled didn't you, eh? Get her searched for a knife, lads; then in a car and down to the local station.'

The now large crowd had done an about turn, and were swarming quietly all around like kids at a school playground fight. He turned to them and waved them back.

'Nothing to see folks, clear the area please. It's all over!'

'Not quite, Chief Superintendent. Not quite all over just yet.

They all turned to where the voice had come from, as Dorothy Raynes, shotgun pointing towards them, emerged from the fog on the common. She must have been visible for fifty yards as she approached them, but all eyes had been on the business in hand with daughter Angela, and she'd made her way to just ten yards from them unnoticed.

'Release the handcuffs from my daughter's wrists and then back away please, or I will shoot into the crowd. You have ten seconds… nine….eight…'

Palmer had to do something.

'Mrs Raynes, this is stupid; you have nothing to gain by this. They're all dead, and Robert's dead now too. The job's done.'

He spread his hands and took a step towards her.

'So I've nothing to lose by shooting you, Chief Superintendent; or shooting into the crowd if you take one more step towards me, have I? Release the handcuffs. Now!'

She swung the barrels towards the now silent throng. Panic ensued, and the crowd ran in all directions away from her, women and children screaming.

Palmer hoped the marksman had arrived and was taking aim. He nodded to Gheeta, who was still pinning Angela Damon to the ground.

'Unlock 'em. Do as she says.'

She did so, and Angela Damon struggled to her knees, unsure what was happening.

'You spoilt it Angela, didn't you?' Mrs Raynes said. 'It was all going to plan, *your* plan. You must have realised what I was doing? I was following your plan to the letter! So why did you come here? Why get involved? You were in the clear, you would have been set up for life. All you had to do was let me finish it, and then the police would have thought I'd killed them all; and then you'd be in the clear to write the book and take the money. You fool, Angela!'

'I didn't think you'd get to him, mother,' Angela sobbed. 'I just had to make sure. My whole plan was aimed at him; it would have failed if he'd lived. He broke us all mother. I didn't think you'd get near him with the police after you. I just had to do it.'

Palmer spoke softly.

'It's over, Mrs Raynes, the job's finished. You won't get away, you know you won't. So just lower the gun and we – '

She interrupted him forcibly.

'Superintendent, please don't patronise me! I know what I've done, I know what I am. I'm a sixty-six year old serial killer, and I'll go to prison for the rest of my days; or maybe some clever lawyer will get me put into a secure mental institution for life. Do I look the type to relish that prospect, Superintendent? Do I?"

Palmer remained silent. Just which of them *was* the serial killer? Angela had murdered her husband, he knew that; but which of them had killed Jarvis, Mouse and Johnson? And whose room was it at the house that had the plan across the wall? And where the hell was that marksman? He needed time.

'I don't believe you killed the other three,' he said, taking a gamble. 'I think you found your daughter's plan and realised she'd killed them, and so you decided to make it look like it was you by killing Robert. That's why you're here; if you had managed to kill him, and then hand yourself in and falsely confess to the others, Angela would get off. You're a mother trying to protect her daughter, that's all. You're not the killer, Mrs Raynes; Angela is. Your plan hasn't worked. Put down the gun now, and you'll get a light sentence for wasting police time.'

'Oh you *are* good aren't you, Superintendent. And Angela, what will she get?'

'It's *Chief* Superintendent, and she'll get the help she needs, that's what she'll get. Look at her.'

He pointed to the sobbing wreck kneeling in the mud.

'She'll get the help she needs.'

'You mean she'll spend the rest of her life in an institution, don't you *Chief* Inspector? She's a serial killer, so they'll never let her out; she'll be locked away for life. She'd be better off with me.'

'With you?'

What was she talking about? Come on marksman, where are you? Get her in the legs. He glanced sideways at Gheeta, who was coiled ready to spring towards Raynes. She raised her eyebrows inquisitively, as if to say '*do we rush her?*' Palmer gave a slight shake of his head; Raynes was too far away to get to before she'd be able to fire both barrels. Pointless.

'Yes, with me. Come here, Angela, come over here with me; we are going to get away. Let her go, Sergeant.'

Gheeta looked at Palmer, who nodded yes; they wouldn't get far. Gheeta released Angela's arm from her grip, and helped her to her feet.

Mrs Raynes smiled as her daughter stumbled over to her.

'We have one more thing to do, Chief Superintendent, to finish the job.'

Palmer's thoughts raced; it had to be Neil Ledbury. Mrs Raynes was slowly walking backwards into the fog with her daughter. He shouted after her.

'You won't get Neil Ledbury, Mrs Raynes; we've taken him away to a safe house. You won't find him.'

The pair were just dim outlines in the fog now as she shouted back.

'Ledbury? Oh, I'm not after a worthless MP; no, you were right earlier when you said I was a mother protecting her daughter. You see, after all she's done to avenge the family, I can't let Angela be put away to rot in a secure institution for the rest of her days, can I?'

'You'll have access,' Palmer shouted.

'And when I'm gone? No, I can't allow that. This is a much better ending, for her and for me.'

Palmer, Gheeta and the gathered officers watched in horror, as she raised the shotgun towards her daughter's head. A single shot rang out, and it was Mrs. Raynes who slumped to the ground at Angela Damon's feet, the shotgun falling beside her.

It took a brief second for Palmer to comprehend what had happened. He swung round, and twenty yards to his rear the marksman lowered his HK417 and looked bewildered at Palmer.

'Well done, son. Better late than never,' Palmer shouted to him.

'That wasn't me, sir, I didn't fire,' came back the shouted reply.

Palmer turned back towards Mrs Raynes and Angela, as the loud crack of another single shot rang out. Angela

Damon's head jerked forward, her knees folded, and she slowly slumped to the ground beside her mother.

An indistinguishable figure was moving towards them out of the fog behind the two bodies, holding a rifle above its head in a surrendering manner. As it came nearer in the gloom, Palmer and Singh recognised who it was.

'Hamilton wasn't the only shooter in the family Chief Superintendent,' shouted Mrs Jarvis, as she dropped the rifle on the ground and held her hands above her head. 'My husband is dead, and my only son will be in prison for a long, long time because of her.'

She looked down at Angela Damon's dead body.

'I wasn't about to let the murdering bitch spend the rest of her days in the comfort of an institution. And now she won't.'

Palmer walked towards her.

'How did you know about Damon?'

Mrs Hamilton laughed.

'Oh, that was easy. Archie told me about Mouse and Johnson being killed, so I looked through my late husband's papers and the only Company that all three worked for was Damon's; the papers even had their address and phone number in Harrow. I phoned on the pretext of collecting a debt, and dear Mrs Raynes denied her daughter lived there anymore and gave me his address here. So here I am, ready for revenge, but his wife beat me to him; and from what I overheard in the fog just now, I would have shot the wrong person had your intervention not flushed them out. Now, if you don't mind I'm rather cold, Chief Superintendent, and a ride to a police station in a warm car would be very much appreciated.'

Chapter 24

Palmer sat at his kitchen table, looking at the plate of Irish stew and dumplings. There was something quite relaxing and comforting in looking at it. Five hours ago he'd been right in the middle of the nasty underbelly of human life, as a mother who was about to shoot her daughter, who had already murdered four people, was shot by a widow set on revenge. And now, what a difference; he was relaxed, his dog Daisy lay under the table ready to pounce on any left-overs, Mrs P was watching a romantic film, or on the phone to one of their children or grandchildren in the lounge, and he was about to enjoy one of his favourite homemade meals. He tucked in as he thought about the case.

Yes, what a difference indeed; the two sides of human life in just one day. Same the world over, he supposed. He had often wondered whether the normal public and their normal everyday families really understood the fine blue line that protected their happy, safe lives from the dark side of humanity that they rarely saw. What a shock they would get if that fine line ever broke. Oh well, on the positive side at least the team had got the case done and dusted in time for his cruise to go ahead. Sergeant Singh could handle the paperwork at the office over the next few days, and he no doubt would be chauffeur and porter to Mrs. P. as she hit the shops and bought lots of stuff she would insist was needed for the cruise that would never even come out of the suitcases once on board.

He finished his meal deep in thought, then lowered his plate to the floor so Daisy could have the last few bits of meat and gravy-soaked dumpling he'd purposely left for her; Mrs P would not be happy if she saw that. He gave the dog a pat, then smiled to himself as he sat back in the chair and let his belt out a notch. *Peace and quiet. lovely*.

Then the phone rang.

THE END

The Author

B.L.Faulkner was born into a family of petty villains in Herne Hill, South London. He attended the first ever comprehensive school in the UK, William Penn in Peckham and East Dulwich, where he attained no academic qualifications other than GCE 'A' level in Art and English and a Prefect's badge (though some say he stole all three!)

His mother had been a fashion model and had great theatrical aspirations for young Faulkner and pushed him into auditioning for the Morley Academy of Dramatic Art at the Elephant and Castle, where he was accepted but only lasted three months before being asked to leave, as no visible talent had surfaced. Mind you, during his time at the Academy he was called to audition for the National Youth Theatre by Trevor Nunn – fifty years later, he's still waiting for the call back!

His early writing career was as a copywriter with the advertising agency Erwin Wasey Ruthrauff & Ryan in Paddington, during which time he got lucky with some light entertainment scripts sent to the BBC and Independent Television Companies and became a script editor and writer on a freelance basis, working on most of the LE shows of the 1980-90s. During that period, while living out of a suitcase in UK hotels for a lot of the time, he filled many notebooks with Palmer case plots; and in 2015 he finally found time to start putting them in order and into book form. Six are finished and published so far, with more to come. He hopes you enjoy reading them as much as he enjoyed writing them.

These days besides formulating more cases for DCI Palmer he has an interest in the world of antiques and owns an auction house.

You can find out more about B.L.Faulkner and the *real* UK major heists and robberies, including the Brinks Mat robbery and the Hatton Garden Heist; plus the gangs and criminals that carried them out, including the Krays and the Richardsons, (B.L. used to clean their Rollers as a

child) on his crime blog at
www.geezers2016.wordpress.com
    Take care, and thank you for buying this book.

B.L.

PS...BL did not follow the family career path into petty crime, honest!

PPS...wanna buy a cheap Rolex?

Printed in Great Britain
by Amazon